# RAVEN

## REAWAKENING

# Raven

## Reawakening

BOOK ONE IN THE DEMONIC DESIGNS SERIES

# MITCHELL HOGAN

RAVEN
REAWAKENING

WIRAYA
Scale in Miles
0
500
1000
Ruruc
THE
WASTES
SIMORGA SEA
Atya
PLAINS OF
KHISIG-UGTALL
NIYAS
Ivrian
Kroe
Sohrah
JARGALAN
PLASSE
2017

YMALTIAN MOUNTAINS
THOUSAND LAKES
Caronath
Nantin
Crystal River
OCEAN
STATES
Kyuth
Nagorn City
Sansor
KAILE
TRACKLESS
Valborg
GREAT MOUNTAINS OF THE SOUTHERN OF EALYSIA
RISTART
COMBINE
Mazin
AK-SETTUR
SEA
OF
MINGOL
Manela
Gessa
JARGALAN MOUNTAINS

# ONE

*Some women are knives.*
- Jargalan saying

CRYSTAL-CLEAR WATER LAPPED AT THE green sand on the north side of the island town of Sharrow, while farther out to sea, crashing waves broke over the reef. Three wharves projected into the turquoise ocean, and close by groups of men and women repaired nets and prepared boats in the fading light for the morrow's fishing. In the town center, drums were already beating and giant pits filled with timber and stones blazed merrily. Tonight was the Festival of the Full-dark, held once a year on one of the few nights when the moons, white Chandra and red Jagonath, both stayed below the horizon, and various deities' blessings were plentiful to ward against the darkness. Barrels of beer were broached and sampled as revelers from far and wide packed the streets, excited about what was to come during the untamed night.

Shadowy figures moved along the edge of the town. Some carried crossbows slung across their backs, while others held no discernible weapon. They moved furtively, unlike the island's inhabitants, keeping to lengthening shadows and avoiding contact where possible. Three split from the group, and someone familiar with the town would see their path led them to a row of run-down shops, entirely different to the prosperous businesses closer to the town center.

Inside her antiquities shop, Saskia prodded an artifact with a finger and grunted. The object was the size of an orange and shaped like a clenched fist. Faint Skanuric runes could be seen through the verdigris.

"What's that one?" asked Keld.

She knew he was only feigning interest. He was only here because she'd not visited him for a while. Saskia had befriended the old fisherman soon after arriving on the island. Keld had been grouchy initially, but had still helped her to find temporary lodging, and then put her in touch with local workers to build her hut in the hills and fit out her shop. He visited her occasionally, when, she figured, his loneliness became too much for him.

"I'm not sure," she said. "The majority of these are worthless, but there's always a chance I'll find a gem among the dross." Saskia used her fingernail to scrape at the verdigris covering the tiny statue. A green particle flaked off, revealing orange metal beneath. Odd. She moved the statue to one side.

"You found something, Dania?" asked Keld, using the name Saskia had been known by on the islands for the last three years.

"Maybe. Could be orichalcum. I'll have to do more testing to know for sure."

"The rest don't look like much. Hope you didn't pay too much for the lot." Keld glanced out a window. "It's getting dark. You gonna close up? Feel like a few hands?"

Saskia nodded, then covered the artifacts with a cloth. Keld moved to a table next to a wall where there were two chairs. He took out a pack of cards from his pocket and expertly shuffled them while she grabbed a bottle and two glasses from the back room, along with a jar of mismatched buttons.

"No unorthodox methods this time," Saskia said with a grin. She placed the jar of buttons on the lacquered table then poured a healthy measure of rum into both glasses.

"Don't need to cheat, you know that. Maybe soon, though. You're getting better."

Saskia downed her drink and poured herself another one. "I'm learning from the best." She suspected he'd done something less scrupulous than fishing when he was young.

"Go easy on the drink, girl. I want to win fair and square. You know, if we practice more, we could travel to the mainland and fleece some nobles."

"My guess is you've done that before."

Keld downed his drink in one go and she refilled his glass. He shuffled again and dealt five cards each, his movements nimble, despite a couple of missing fingers. Saskia poured buttons from the jar and portioned out a few dozen each.

"Five Card Malice?" Saskia asked, as she picked up her cards.

"What else?" Keld tapped the edge of his cards on the table, then peered at her. "Your nose twitches when you have a good hand."

"It does not!" Saskia sipped her rum, then covered her mouth with the back of a hand to conceal a burp. She knew Keld was joking. She'd been trained to keep her thoughts and emotions from her face. "Two buttons." She slid the wager into the center of the table. "And if I win tonight, you'll ask the widow Reena out to dinner."

"Seen you running sometimes, early morning," said Keld, changing the subject. "Don't know how you keep it up. I've been meaning to join you again, but…"

"Save your strength for the widow Reena, Keld. She'll give you a workout like—"

"Hush, Dania!" Keld grumbled something under his breath and sipped his rum.

Later, after a dozen hands, Keld swept up his winnings, leaving her with only three remaining buttons.

A muted sound outside the shop caught Saskia's attention. She listened for a long moment, but it didn't repeat, and the crickets began to chirp again.

"Probably one of those damn lizards," said Keld. "Or a jungle spider."

Saskia corked the bottle, of which they'd only drunk half despite their quick start. Out on the now-dark water, a trading ship's bell rang in the distance, signaling the eighth hour.

"I'll tidy up a bit and then lock up." Saskia rose from the able and scooped the buttons back into the jar.

"I'll help."

"Thank you, but I've some book entries to make as well."

"You actually earn money?"

"Very funny. Enough to get by."

"You thought more about going farther south, past the Jargalan mountains? Plenty of artifacts to be found down there, or so I've heard."

Saskia smiled ruefully. "I've abandoned the idea. I'm happy here. Besides, I don't speak the language. And the thought of falling foul of the part-blood Orgol nomads there gives me the shivers."

She had chosen the islands south-east of Gessa for her home because they were far away from any place where she'd been active and there was no chance anyone would recognize her. On the islands they spoke a bastardized version of the northern common tongue, which she'd picked up quickly. Saskia spoke seven languages, but it irked her that she couldn't remember learning most of them. Her few memories from before her transformation were fragmented and unclear.

"Ask the widow Reena out, Keld. She'll be good for you."

"I ain't got time for a woman. I suspect all that drink has addled your wits."

"You'll regret it, later."

"I'll add it to my list."

Saskia laughed and immediately Keld followed suit, clasping her in a hug that Saskia returned after a moment's hesitation. When he released her, he ruffled her hair, which she always hated.

"I still marvel at your hair, girl. It's like mercury."

Saskia smoothed down the mess he'd made and tried to ignore the pit that had opened in her stomach. Her hair was a constant reminder of what she'd gone through, a mark of her unnaturalness. But she'd kept it as an act of defiance. "Thanks for checking up on me."

"I was just passing by."

"You'd better get going or you'll be caught up in the festival."

Keld nodded, then left by the front entrance, pushing aside the beaded curtain.

Saskia listened to his booted footsteps as they faded, then she gathered up her new haul of artifacts and secured them in a lockbox in the back room of her shop. The only one of interest, the potential orichalcum fist statue, she examined further by the light of a lamp, scraping off more of the green patina, which shouldn't have been possible if it was the natural corrosion of copper. It just might be that she'd found something worth reselling, perhaps on the mainland. But her find could wait until tomorrow. Visiting sorcerers often came to check out her wares in the hope of stumbling upon something of value, but Saskia made sure anything arcane found its way into a rival's shop. She didn't want to draw attention to herself.

The beaded curtain of her shop rattled, jolting her attention from the statue.

Saskia brushed her long, platinum hair from her face and glanced at the mechanical clock hanging on the wall. It was dented and tarnished, but easily the most valuable thing in her shop. Which wasn't saying much. It was getting late, and she wanted to be off before the night-time revelries ramp up. The town would become raucous before long, and she preferred to cozy herself away in her hut in the hills during the annual celebration.

"Keld? Is that you?"

As Saskia stepped through the curtain separating the back room from the front, something looped over her head and around her neck. She jerked her hand up and under the garrote just in time to stop it tightening around her throat. The wire bit into her hand, drawing blood. She clenched her jaw against the pain and rammed an elbow into the assailant behind her, then stamped on his foot, drawing from him a grunt and a momentary relaxing of the deadly pressure. Blood ran down her wrist and arm as she threw herself backward. The timber wall rattled as she drove her attacker against it, hooked a foot behind his leg and twisted, heedless of the wire biting deeper. She jerked her whole body, forcing her would-be assassin off his feet, and they slammed to the floor, Saskia on top.

She groped for the knife hidden in her boot and stabbed the blade behind her head without looking. It hit something pliant and the man screamed, so she stabbed again, and again. A muted howl sounded in her ear as a hot gush sprayed across the back of her neck and hair. The garrote loosened and she pushed her hand against it, ignoring the pain, swung around and hammered her knee into the man's crotch. Somehow the assassin twisted his leg and her blow slammed into his inner thigh.

He was lean and middle-aged, and brown-skinned to blend in with the townsfolk. Scarlet streamed from a gash on his cheek and a larger one in his neck. One of his hands pressed against his neck wound to stem the blood, and he swung at her with the other, still clutching the now-useless garrote wire. She dodged the blow and returned one of her own, a palm thrust to his face. The man's head rocked back, then his eyes went wide and he thrashed violently, throwing her against the wall.

She scrambled to her feet and kicked him in the stomach as hard as she could just as he rose. His legs buckled and he dropped the wire, reaching instead for a dagger at his belt. Saskia tried to kick the blade from his hand but only landed a glancing blow. He held his grip on the hilt and lunged at her. She danced back but hit the wall, rattling the shelves that held useless curios.

Saskia knew she was in trouble. He shouldn't have lasted as long as he had with the neck wound and everything else she'd done to him. Either he was extremely well trained, or drugged to the eyeballs, or he'd been augmented like she had.

She threw the knife at his eyes and rushed in behind it as he threw up a hand to protect his face.

She leaped forward, slamming her heel into the side of his knee. Bone and cartilage cracked, and he shrieked and stumbled.

Saskia scooped up the wire and leaped again, past the man, twisting in the air. She looped the garotte around his neck and clamped both her legs around his waist. Her muscles bulged as she pulled against the wooden handles attached to the wire. Blood streamed from the slice in her hand, but in the heat of combat she didn't yet feel any pain. He tried to twist his hand to cut her leg with his dagger, but his futile slashes became feebler, his consciousness fading as the wire bit deeper.

He attempted one last gambit, staggering a few steps backward to slam her against the wall, which only caused the garrote to bite deeper. Saskia tightened her grip, chest heaving from exertion, sweat stinging her eyes. He finally slumped to the floor, twitched a few times, then was still.

Saskia released her grip on the garrote, then staggered away and fell into a chair, hands trembling. It had been years since she'd had to kill someone, but the stench of sweat and blood felt like home to her.

Her hand was messy, and now ached like damnation, but she could still flex her fingers so there was no lasting damage. Most of the blood that soaked the front of her shirt was from the dead man. The cloth stuck to her skin, cold and clammy. She shuddered and realized she hadn't reached for her dark-tide powers during the desperate struggle. She was rusty and making poor decisions.

Clearly this was no ordinary thief, but she'd made a lot of enemies before she came to the island. Except no one knew where she was…or what she looked like. Well, it had been a good few years here. Better than she'd expected for someone who was supposed to be dead.

Now, something had changed and she was no longer safe. Nor were those—like Keld—who knew her.

Once Saskia caught her breath, she moved to the back room and found a dust rag to wrap around her hand; then she grabbed her small lockbox full of marks. It held mostly coppers, with a scattering of silver coins—but she'd need all she could get her hands on. Except the coppers would weigh heavily and jingle. She settled for just the silvers.

Returning to the assassin's corpse, she rifled through his clothes but found nothing of use except three more silver coins. She hesitated, not wanting to take what wasn't hers; but she'd need the coins if she couldn't access her emergency stash. Other than the silvers, he'd carried only the garrote and the dagger, both of which were cheap. There was nothing to tell her who he was or who had sent him to kill her.

The latch on the back door rattled slightly. If her blood hadn't been up she would have missed it. Someone was trying to pick the lock, and if they knew what they were doing, they'd be inside before long. Saskia doused the lamp and crept inside her closet, peering through a hair-fine crack between its doors.

A pale hand pushed the back door open. With no windows, the room was dim. The assassin might think he was hard to see, but with her augmented sight he wasn't. She watched as the intruder moved cautiously forward. One of his hands came to rest against the edge of her cluttered desk, his long fingers touching a couple of the artifacts laid out there before seeming to dismiss them. Leading with his loaded crossbow, he moved toward the doorway. The clock on the wall chimed. He pivoted smoothly toward it but didn't shoot. Saskia heard him sigh faintly.

She exploded from the closet, hammering her knife between his ribs once, then again. It was over before he'd even registered her appearance. He dropped the crossbow and it discharged, the bolt slamming into the desk. The assassin slid to the floor, his lifeblood staining the boards she'd been meaning to re-polish for over a year. Now there would be no reason to. Soon she would be gone.

She wiped her knife on the intruder's pants before returning it to her boot, then stepped over him to retrieve the crossbow. Sea-ray-skin grip, ivory and mother-of-pearl inlays, a split-limbed compound set-up, and a clever catch to hold the bolt in place. A showy weapon, not suited to night work, but expensive and a fine crossbow. Not good news, especially combined with the first assassin.

Saskia squatted next to the dead man and retrieved half a dozen quarrels, then rearmed the crossbow. The tip of the bolt was covered with a tacky ocher substance—no doubt fatal.

A faint scrape sounded from behind the curtain to the shopfront. It parted just as she threw herself to the floor and fired close-quarters at a hefty silhouette. A grunt sounded, and a crossbow bolt tore through the air and thumped into the wall by Saskia's head, before her attacker dropped to the floor, the bolt sticking from her chest. A woman, this time.

Saskia hunkered into a corner and hastily rearmed. She waited. Ten heartbeats. Twenty. Nothing else moved. If there were more assassins, they would be waiting to see what she did. She would have to go outside sometime.

Saskia jumped to her feet and ran to the front of her shop. The room was dim, but not dark. She crouched low and scurried to the side of the beaded doorway, where she stilled her breathing, ears straining to catch any sound. Drums and music from the other side of town were all she heard. Nothing from the back of her shop, and nothing close by out front.

She carefully placed the crossbow on the floor and removed her bloody shirt, then rubbed the unstained side through her hair to soak up as much blood as possible. She wore scanty underclothes, but in this climate many people went about in even less, so she shouldn't stand out too much. Still, she should find a shirt, and at least her pants weren't ruined. And her blood had stopped spreading across her makeshift bandage, which meant the wound on her hand was clotting. She'd suffered worse and lived through it. She had always healed unnaturally quickly.

Well, perhaps not always…

Glancing through her dirty window, she saw a dozen or so people carrying torches wandering around outside. Not enough of a crowd to disappear into. But if there was one thing she'd learned in her old life, it was to trust her instincts. And her instincts said run.

She drew a breath and took one more look at the bloodbath her little shop had hosted. Saskia considered taking the potentially valuable fist statue, but immediately discarded the idea. The curios trade on the islands had given her a meager living for the past three years, but she'd learned never to value something so much you couldn't leave it behind. Nothing good would come from delaying, and she was worried about Keld.

She hastened to a chest of drawers and from the space behind took out two shreds wrapped in an old shirt. The shreds were an amalgam of sorcery and metal and looked like two harmless black rocks. But they were deadly when splintered with a burst of dark-tide sorcery. She shoved them into a pocket and tugged on the shirt. It smelled musty and was speckled with a black mildew, but it would have to do. She then held the crossbow against her leg so it was less noticeable, the catch ensuring the bolt didn't fall out.

Saskia pushed through the beads covering her door and walked down the street, keeping her eyes open for anything out of the ordinary. She'd have preferred to have a cloak to completely cover her head and body, but wishes wouldn't keep you alive.

A few of the townsfolk were already drunk, mostly the younger men. Four acolytes of the goddess Sylva Kalisia moved along the street carrying spherical white paper lanterns hooked atop long bamboo poles. The goddess had dominion over the moons, supposedly, and her worshipers came out in force every year during the festival.

A man yelled and Saskia darted to the side, raising her crossbow before lowering the weapon just as quickly. "Idiot!" she told herself. She forced herself to breathe slowly, to calm her rushing blood. Her pulse had other ideas. Her instincts were rusty, but it wouldn't take long for everything to come back.

She strolled across the road and ignored the lecherous smirk a drunken reveler gave her and her underclothes. A woman, no less. On another night she might have seen where that would lead. But tonight…tonight death had touched her with its familiar caress, and nothing would be the same again.

She checked the windows of the shops she passed to see if anyone was following her, but the poor quality of the glass warped the reflections, and light shone from within, making it difficult to tell. With her charcoal skin from her pure San-Kharr heritage and subsequent darkening, she didn't stand out too much among the bronzed natives, and there were other dark-skinned travelers on the island. But she wanted to get her hands on her rapier. Made from an ensorcelled orichalcum alloy by the Order of Eternal Vigilance, the blade was worth a small fortune. It remained sharp without needing a whetstone, and could even penetrate an arcane ward if the sorcerer wasn't strong enough. It wasn't a weapon you left behind if you could help it, even though she knew going back to her house on the outskirts of town was a bad idea.

She kept to the shadows and stopped fifty yards from her place, wary of any watchers. One of ten built along a cleared area of forest, her house was second from the east end.

Along the road in front of the houses, a number of people entered the town—presumably for the festivities. Some were on horseback or mules, and a few rode in carts and wagons, but most were walking. Saskia hunkered down and waited. She was good at that.

When nothing moved near her house, she stepped cautiously across the road and along a dirt path shrouded by bushes. Circling the houses, she couldn't see anything that triggered her anxiety into alarm.

On her second circuit, she approached her house from behind, moving through her neighbor's vegetable patch. She took her time to search her surroundings again. No watchers, no one up any trees, no people loitering around or along the road, no lights visible through any of her windows.

A twig snapped behind her, and she raised the crossbow. A large lizard regarded her, its forked tongue flicking as it tasted the air. It went back to eating the melon it had already half devoured, and Saskia took several deep breaths to slow the pounding of her heart in her chest. It could be that she was more than a little out of practice. It had been hard to keep her skills sharp without drawing attention to herself.

She took another few silent steps toward her house, then caught movement and a glimpse of something shining in her peripheral vision. Maybe a blade, maybe armor, outside a house a few doors down from hers. She peered into the shadows but couldn't see anyone. That didn't matter. Someone was there.

The crossbow bolt came with no warning and whizzed past her face. She threw herself backward and scrambled behind a row of dense bushes that separated the vegetable patch from the jungle.

She heard a mechanism cranking, then another string twanged about fifty yards away, the bolt flying harmlessly through the bushes to the right of where she'd pressed herself into the dirt. The darkness had helped her. Now the only question was whether to run, or to take her attacker down. She wanted to fight—to feel their blood on her hands, see the life leave their eyes. But she had no idea how many there were or anything else about them, which left her at a disadvantage. If Saskia had been running the operation, there would be others under strict orders to be patient and not give their positions away.

She crouched low and loosed a bolt at what she guessed was the crossbowman's position, then sprinted for the back of the houses, dodging and weaving through the vegetable patch. Her attacker was probably waiting for her to enter her house; or there was another inside, hoping she'd make a mistake and they could finish her off.

Saskia leaped a low timber fence and snaked around the corner of another house. Her attacker was probably wasting precious time deciding what action to take. Those moments could be the difference between life and death. She ran effortlessly through the dark at a pace she could keep up for a long time.

A bolt slammed into the wall beside her, and she swallowed a quiet yelp. She ducked between two houses and stopped, keeping her breathing low and steady. As she reloaded her own crossbow and listened, she heard two horses trotting up the road below. The clop of hooves ceased and booted feet hit the ground. Saskia broke into a sprint, vaulted over a fence, then cut back the way she'd come. A second bolt struck the wall beside her, while a second shattered a ceramic pot on the veranda. She ducked and loosed a bolt in the direction they'd come from, then scrambled for cover.

A third bolt whistled by her head, so close it buzzed in her ear.

Saskia threw herself to the ground and rolled into the crawlspace under a house. She scrambled across the damp, musty dirt. Pausing to catch her breath and reload, she saw two pairs of boots hurrying along the back of the house, then heard a soft chittering.

A shadow moved along the floor beams. A hairy, brown jungle spider with a body as big as a dinner plate. Saskia suppressed a groan and mentally cursed herself for her stupidity.

She tried to ignore the spider as the creature edged closer, its mandibles waving and the chittering getting louder. Saskia focused on the darkness toward where she'd heard the horses. She'd been hoping to save her dark-tide energy in case it was needed, but now was a good time. She blinked and poured her awareness into the shadows around her; felt her body and mind melt and drain away, then re-form. When she opened her eyes, she was no longer under the house, but a few dozen yards away in a dark pool of shadows. A wave of weariness and nausea swept through her—apart from a trickle now and again, she hadn't used her dark-tide power for years, and she was no longer used to the toll it took on her body. The nausea and pain were unwelcome reminders of her old life. Saskia dashed tears from her eyes and clenched her jaw in anger at her weakness.

A man stood on the road, clutching the reins of both horses in one hand. In the other he held a crossbow trained on the house she'd just left. Saskia took aim with hers and loosed the bolt. It burst through his head, and he dropped to the ground. She discarded her crossbow and drew a knife and one of her shreds.

A shout came from the second house on her left, and she heard a crossbow twang. Saskia blinked and felt herself melt again, then she re-formed in the darkness three houses down. This time she staggered as exhaustion hammered her.

Two men were crouched low and peering around the corner of a house toward the horses and their dead companion. Saskia lobbed the shred toward them. It hit the ground close by, the thud muffled by the soft earth. But even that was enough to alert them. They both turned, aiming crossbows at her. She smiled at them and sent a pulse of dark-tide power into the amalgam of sorcery and metal. The shred fractured with an almighty crack, and shards of solid darkness ripped through the two men, sending sheets of blood across the wall and ground.

Saskia's knees gave way, and she doubled over and retched. Three uses of her dark-tide abilities in such a short span of time meant she needed a dose of her strong medicine. She wiped her mouth with the back of her hand and stumbled to her feet. She wasn't particularly enamored of the thought of using the cravv lozenges again as it had taken her months to rid herself of the resultant addiction. But she'd do what she had to do to survive.

A light came on in one of the houses. Probably not one of the assassins; they wouldn't be so careless. Saskia ran as fast as she could to her own house and slipped beneath the back veranda. Feeling around, she located the oilcloth-wrapped bundle on a ledge and scrambled out again. She unwrapped the package to reveal her sheathed rapier and belt. It only took a moment to buckle the swept-hilted weapon around her waist. Feeling a great deal better with her favorite blade on her hip, she ran to the horses. Unfortunately, both had been pierced by the shadowy spikes from her shred and lay unmoving in the street. She grabbed her crossbow from where it lay near the assassin's body and kept running along the road, but soon slowed to a walk. Weariness had sapped her muscles of strength.

At the junction she saw a man on a horse trotting toward her.

She recognized him as the son of a noble who lived close by, but she didn't know his name. He was probably on his way to the festival to tumble as many of the local girls as he could. Saskia waved at him, and he stopped and looked her up and down in the faint light.

She gave him her best radiant smile and affected the accent of a local. "Are you heading to the festival? I need a ride. And in the spirit of the festivities who knows what the night will bring?"

He returned the smile. "I am. You could ride with me, if you—"

"Thank you," Saskia said, stepping on his boot and hauling herself up behind him. She put one arm around his waist and squeezed tight.

"That's a nice crossbow. Where did you get it?"

"I'm Alika." A good local name.

"Bernard." He twisted around to smile at her, and his eyes flicked down to her sword. "And a nice rapier."

A weapon a local woman wouldn't carry. She had to get rid of Bernard as soon as possible before he started asking questions. Still, it was a lucky break. She needed to rest from the effects of the dark-tide power she'd used; and her attackers and the Watch would be looking for a lone woman, not a couple on horseback.

"A gift from an uncle. I barely know how to use it, but it looks dashing on me, doesn't it?"

"It certainly does. And might I say I didn't expect to find a young lady as lovely as you tonight."

"The gods and goddesses can be kind," Saskia said. "But I'm hardly young. I have a little experience."

Bernard coughed. "I dare say you do. Your hair is delightfully exotic, and we don't get many San-Kharr on the islands. Where are you from, originally?"

Saskia laughed and tightened her grip around his waist to

distract him. "Here and there. But tonight is the Festival of the Full-dark, and these questions are best left for the morning. Ask me then."

The crowd grew thicker, and close to the beach Bernard reined in his horse to avoid a group of drunken revelers. Saskia slid to the ground, said, "Thank you, Bernard. Have a good night," and vanished into the crowd. She heard him cry "Wait! Alika!" but anything else was lost in the noise of the revelers.

Her hand throbbed with pain as she considered her options. With any luck it would be morning before the corpses of the assassins were found in her shop. The weaver next door, Selene, popped in every morning for a chat before opening up her own place. The local Watch would go on full alert, and Saskia would be wanted for questioning at the very least. Here, in this backwater town, a bunch of dead bodies would create an uproar, and probably ruin the festival.

It was fully dark now, the only illumination coming from torches and lanterns hung around the streets for the festival. It was too late to find anyone willing to ferry her across the water to the main island, but that didn't mean she couldn't find a boat herself. Except the Watch were likely staking out the wharves if they had already found the corpses of the assassins she'd left behind. She didn't like her chances if she tried to hide, even with the festival in full swing.

Apart from the main wharves where the bigger fishing boats docked, there were numerous smaller wharves spread out along the beach. She should be able to find something small to take her across the strait.

Saskia glided into the mass of festival goers, just another person enjoying herself. Among the sun-browned natives were dusky-skinned Inkan-Andil, some Illapa with the greenish tinge, and a very few almost coal-black San-Kharr, with various shades in between from the mixings. Many a marriage was known to result from the night's simmering possibilities, and not a few children.

Music surged around her—drums beating, lutes strumming, and fiddles yowling—its intensity matching the growing atmosphere of lascivious mayhem spilling onto the streets. A woman wearing a skimpy beaded dress that left little to the imagination danced past Saskia, hips swaying in time to a drummer behind her. A group of young girls drank from a bottle they passed between them and eyed a trio of muscular-looking men watching them from the other side of the street. A vendor holding a tray of grilled meats wrapped in flatbread looked to be doing a brisk trade. With the festival in full swing, no one would be guarding the fishing boats. There might be a patrol of the Watch hanging around, but Saskia should be able to avoid them easily enough.

A hand touched one of her pouches and she grabbed it, while at the same time drawing a knife. A young islander girl of around twelve years old found herself with Saskia's blade at her throat. She gave Saskia an apologetic smile and backed up. Saskia sheathed her weapon and shooed the girl away. She'd been so caught up with her plans and watching for potential assassins that she'd forgotten about the local petty thieves who would be out in force tonight. She'd have to be more careful. Beggars, and pickpockets disguised as beggars, wove through the crowds. Saskia took a moment to hand a few coins to the youngest she saw. Even if they were thieves, they were in a desperate situation and she didn't begrudge them some of her coin. She might need it later, but they would need it to survive.

As she ducked down an alley, boots squelching in the mud, she spotted clothes drying on a line. She quickly took a shirt.

Slipped out of her musty, mildewed one and shrugged on the clean shirt. Then she placed a silver coin in the pocket of a pair of trousers. She wasn't a thief. The shirt was too big, but it was the best she had to work with.

As she moved back onto the main avenue, she dodged a group of loud young men and women, but they were too interested in their conversation and the bottles of rum they were drinking to notice her crossbow.

Soon she was moving along the shoreline, the relative isolation affording her time to think. Whoever had tracked her down was deadly serious. The crossbows were specialized, and their wielders were obviously trained professionals—even though they hadn't been up to this particular task. Saskia's carefully constructed existence in the carefree beachside town had been torn apart, but why now? And by whom? It didn't make any sense. Especially as she'd been "dead" for the last five years.

Someone caught her attention up on the street. A spiky-haired man dressed in a faded blue coat, despite the humidity and heat. Obviously not a local. He was keeping pace with her and it didn't look like he was here for the festival. One hand remained underneath his coat, presumably on a weapon of some sort. Saskia's mind raced through possible plans. She needed to ditch the man following her, and she also needed to gain access to her emergency stash, which included a good deal of coin. And get her wounded hand taken care of.

A group exited an alley up ahead, laughing and joking with each other. Using them for cover, Saskia took the opportunity to leave the shoreline and raced down the alley they'd just left. Farther along the alley was a tavern she knew, which had numerous exits as well as a busy main bar area. During the festival it would be crowded, and presented an opportunity to lose her follower—assuming he wanted to remain unnoticed and wouldn't shoot at her in a crowded street or tavern. Judging from the earlier attempts on her life, they wanted to take her out with minimum fuss. Although, that hadn't worked out well for them, so she'd have to assume all options were now on the table.

Music and shouting came in waves from the Mermaid's Pearl tavern, twenty yards to her right. She slipped past a group of men and women drinking just inside the door. As she'd thought, the tavern was packed. Raucous laughter rang out, along with cheers whenever a drink was spilled or finished. The air stank with the scent of too many sweaty bodies and smoke. Locals mixed with out-of-towners, all of them holding either mugs of beer or glasses of rum and a local spirit that was made by infusing orange peel and the dried leaves of a certain plant with pure alcohol. Waitresses bustled among the throng, carrying trays of drinks or returning to the bar with empty glasses and mugs.

She kept her crossbow below waist level and pushed her way through the mass of revelers toward one of the waitresses she recognized. She edged her crossbow behind her back, out of sight, and turned so her rapier was hidden then grabbed Halina by the elbow and shoved a silver coin into her free hand.

"Dania!" said Halina. "I didn't think to see you here. I know you don't enjoy the festivities. What's the silver for? Buying a round for friends?"

"I need to piss," Saskia said over the din. "But a friend is meeting me here and should arrive at any moment. He has spiky hair and is wearing a blue coat. Get him a mug of the good stuff, and make sure he doesn't say no. I'll be back as quick as I can."

She didn't like involving people she knew in deception, but it wasn't as if she had much choice. With a smile at Halina, Saskia shouldered her way through the crowd toward the door leading to the jakes. A few jostled patrons frowned at her, but any bad feeling quickly dissipated under the influence of the alcohol and the festival cheer. She resisted the temptation to look over her shoulder to see if the man tailing her had entered. Outside, she made a quick detour to the tavern's kitchen and grabbed a brown cotton apron hanging from a hook. She wrapped it around her hair like a headscarf and tied the strings to keep it secure. At least now her platinum hair wouldn't give her away. She'd dyed it brown when she first arrived on the island, but good dye was almost impossible to procure and she'd soon given up.

There were a few people outside, going to and from the jakes. Saskia wandered casually over to the back wall, and, when she thought no one was looking, jumped up and grabbed the top. Her injured hand ached in protest, but she bit her lip and hauled herself up and over, dropping silently to the other side. With a quick glance toward each end of the alley she was now in, she took off at a jog. The time for furtiveness was over; she needed to put some distance between her and her attackers. Their initial plan to kill her had fallen apart, and whatever their backup plan was, she knew their only goal would be to kill her as quickly as possible. But they were already four men short.

A shout of alarm came from behind as someone—likely the spiky-haired assassin—spotted her. She sent a burst of dark-tide to swirl the air around her to deflect any missiles and kept running. A crossbow bolt streaked past and tore a chunk out of the bricks to her left, and she heard a clunk as a second bolt ricocheted off the same wall. *Too close.* If she hadn't churned the air the bolt would have skewered her head.

Saskia put on a burst of speed. A third bolt whizzed past, missing her by a wide margin. She risked a glance behind. Two men were firing through the narrow-slatted windows of the jakes. Someone inside the Mermaid's Pearl started shouting at them. She had no chance of hitting either man from here, so she raced on to the end of the alley. Their crossbows would lose accuracy for every yard she put between her and them.

She turned the corner into a narrow street, and a woman ran toward her. The assassin hesitated, not quite recognizing Saskia but evidently suspicious. Saskia shot first, her poisoned bolt striking the woman in her hip. The assassin went down, but triggered her crossbow. Saskia dodged, and felt a tug at the bottom of her newly acquired shirt. The bolt had torn a hole through the loose material at her waist, missing her by no more than a finger's width.

The assassin dropped her crossbow and delved into a pouch at her waist. Saskia didn't hesitate—she ran straight at her. The woman took out a vial and fumbled with the stopper. Antidote, realized Saskia. Unable to remove the stopper, the assassin lifted it to use her teeth. Saskia's heel hammered into her temple and she fell to the ground, motionless. The vial dropped from her fingers and rolled away across the ground, unbroken. At least she'd be unconscious when the poison hit.

Saskia grabbed the vial and quickly removed the woman's belt with its pouch of poisoned bolts and buckled it around her own waist. Her injured hand made hard work of the relatively easy task, her fingers fumbling. The crossbow was almost identical to the one Saskia already had, and there was no point burdening herself with two of the weapons.

A shadow moved in her peripheral vision. She threw herself down and to the side. Her hand struck the ground hard and went numb for an instant. She managed to bring the crossbow up to shoot before remembering it wasn't loaded—just as a booted foot collided with the weapon and sent it skidding sideways.

Saskia rolled as the boot kicked at her, startling her attacker by twisting and palming the blow aside. She aimed an up-kick at the man's crotch, but only managed a glancing blow on his inner thigh. He danced backward, and she took the opportunity to leap to her feet. He was short and stocky, with a scraggly beard and yellow teeth. He brandished a dagger in his left hand, his right rubbing his thigh where she'd kicked him.

"You're dead, bitch, and they'll pay well for your head," he snarled, showing Saskia he wasn't a professional. Talk was for after you survived.

There was no time to draw her rapier. She came at him, hands extended, and he slashed at her with the dagger, further confirming he was probably local hired help. *Thrust with a knife,* her instructors had drilled into her. *Never slice.*

He must have read her mind because now he jabbed the knife at her. She side-stepped, grabbing his wrist to force the blade down, and elbowing him in the face at the same time. He dropped like a stone. As the knife skittered away into the shadows, Saskia threw herself on top of him and hammered another brutal elbow into his nose. It shattered with a crunch, and blood spurted across his mouth and chin.

His fist smashed into her face and her head snapped back. Blinding pain shot through her jaw, before strong arms wrapped around her arms and back as he attempted to trap her. She wrenched one arm free and rammed the heel of her hand against his already ruined nose. He screamed and his grip on her loosened.

She aimed another blow at his nose from a different angle, but he turned his head aside, deflecting the potentially lethal strike. Saskia immediately drove her thumb into his eyeball, digging in with her nail. He howled in anguish, and his hands scrabbled at her to push her away.

She slammed her elbow into his temple, cutting off his scream. And again. His hands fell away from hers. She grabbed his hair and smashed the back of his skull into the road. A sickening crack echoed around the street. He went still, and blood dribbled out from under his head. Somewhere close by a woman screamed.

Saskia rolled off him onto her knees, sucking in lungfuls of air. She staggered to her feet and wobbled over to her crossbow. It wasn't damaged, luckily. She loaded another bolt.

A figure peered around the corner of the building to her left, the curve of a crossbow's limb coming to bear on her. She reacted instinctively, whipping hers up and loosing the bolt. Summoning a long-neglected talent, she pushed at the projectile, guiding it home with a burst of dark-tide energy. If the assassins had a competent sorcerer among their number, Saskia would have known by now.

The side of the man's face erupted in red as the bolt smashed through his eye and into his brain. His dead body collapsed back behind the building. Saskia darted toward it and hid herself around the corner, frantically reloading. She had around ten of the poisoned bolts remaining. She crouched over the corpse as she considered her options. She could either keep running, or stay and take out anyone left to pursue her. Neither of the two men she'd just killed was the spiky-haired man who'd been following her, so there was at least one assassin remaining.

She peered cautiously around the corner, back in the direction she'd come from, but the street was empty. Whoever had screamed earlier was long gone, probably to alert the Watch. *Bloody darkness*—things were going to get a lot more complicated soon. The spiky-haired man would likely exit from the front of the tavern and loop around. Maybe she could anticipate his approach. Or perhaps he'd scaled the wall like she had and would come from the alley.

Keeping an eye on both the alley and the street, she pawed through the dead man's clothes. A few coins and another six crossbow bolts. That gave her sixteen remaining. Stowing the bolts into her pockets and belt pouches, she melted into the darkness of a nearby doorway, reloaded and waited for the next attacker.

No one came, except a small child running past on some errand, a basket clutched in his hands.

She waited some more, and heard a commotion in the street as people gathered around the dead bodies. A couple of them rifled through the corpses' clothes, talking excitedly to each other.

The Watch would be here soon, and it would be best if Saskia made herself scarce. She eased out of her cover and edged away through the shadows, as silent as a ghoul. Her thoughts turned to her assassins. How had they found out where she was? And why had they tried to kill her? There was only one person who could possibly know she was still alive. She'd covered her tracks with the skill and expertise that had taken her to the top of her profession.

She was dead. Her past life was dead.

But maybe not quite as dead as she'd thought.

# TWO

FIVE STREETS ALONG, SASKIA TURNED and headed toward the beach to Keld's. The section of beach below where the old fisherman had made his home was quiet. Most of the locals would be in the center of town for the festivities. Keld would be home though; he wasn't much for celebrating these days. He had been widowed twice—both wives had perished in unfortunate accidents—and had given up fishing after he lost two fingers in a mishap. Now he made a decent living scrimshawing whale bones to sell to merchants in nearby cities.

She ascended the rocky steps to Keld's shack, slipped her rapier, the crossbow and all of the bolts underneath his wooden porch, then knocked and entered without waiting for a reply. The workshop was organized, clean, and illuminated by two oil lamps. Keld was carving fine lines into a bone with a sharp knife made for scrimshaw. He glanced up at her in surprise.

"What's this, then? Nothing to do with old Keld for weeks,

and now I get to see my favorite girl twice in one evening. If you've come to harass me about the widow… Here, now, what's happened?" He placed the bone on a soft cloth, along with the knife, then stood.

"I'm afraid this couldn't wait, Keld."

"If it was those boys again, I'll—"

"It was my fault," Saskia said, cutting him off. She knew she looked terrible. Her face must be starting to swell, and her hand was a bloody mess of cloth. "I was so stupid. That artifact, the statue shaped like a fist, turned out not to be a fake. It made a strange noise and began to glow, and I tripped over myself trying to get away. Banged my face pretty hard on my desk and fell onto a knife, which cut my hand. I'm going to see a healer when I'm done here."

"A healer? Does it need sewing up? Bloody ashes, girl, you must have hit your head hard. Are you seeing two of me?"

Keld stood and moved to a side table, where he poured a generous measure of rum into a tin cup and handed it to her. Saskia downed the drink in one, and wiped her lips with the back of her hand. The sweet liquor burned her throat and brought a welcome heat to her stomach.

"Thank you," she said. "I needed that. Now, I need to get my things."

"Never mind that. You need to see a healer, but we'll have a hard time finding one with the festival on."

He dragged a chair closer to his own, and gently pushed Saskia until she sat down. A grateful sigh escaped her lips before she could stop it. Keld rummaged around in a chest with six small drawers a side, opening and closing a few until he found what he wanted. He placed two vials on the table next to her, along with a small leather case and some clean cloth, then unbound and examined the wound in her hand.

First, he rinsed it with an antiseptic solution Saskia recognized as made from a local plant that grew high in the hills.

"Are you a healer now?" she asked him.

Keld peered at her wound. "I know a thing or two. Sometimes you can't rely on anyone else to fix you up. I expect you know what I mean."

The old man saw more than he let on and was too smart for his own good. Then again, that was probably one of the traits that had led her to trust him. She'd still given him her false name when they first met, though. She regretted lying to him now, but it had been a wise move at the time.

"Nothing major damaged," he continued. "'Course, I'm no expert, but you should be able to go back to work soon. Though I'd forget about doing too much with that hand for a while. I'll give you some poppy oil for the pain, then I'll stitch the cut closed."

"No poppy oil, thank you. Just get it over with." She needed a clear head.

Keld's eyes narrowed. "Listen, young lady, this isn't the time to—"

"Please, just sew me up and I can get out of your hair."

Saskia healed quickly, and as long as the wound was stitched up properly, in a few weeks no one would know her hand had been sliced open. Her bruises would disappear quicker than normal too. The hellish ordeal she'd been forced through had some benefits, but on the whole she wouldn't wish it on her worst enemy. Well, maybe a few people.

Keld stitched the wound closed then wrapped it with a clean bandage. Saskia flexed her fingers, clenched her hand into a fist, and nodded. Loss of movement was minimal, and the short-term discomfort she could handle.

"I appreciate you doing this," she said.

"Are you going to tell me what this is really about?"

"No. I'm sorry."

An awkward silence grew between them. It seemed to Saskia that Keld spent an inordinate amount of time fussing around as he cleaned up his vials and leather case full of needles and thread. Her heart ached—for the lies she'd told him, for the way she had treated him. He deserved better.

He shuffled over to stand in front of her. "You said you need your stash?"

Saskia bobbed her head. "The artifact I stumbled upon might be dangerous, and there are some things I need in case the situation gets worse."

The lies tumbled easily from her lips. But wasn't most of her existence on this island a lie?

Keld sighed. "You're too bull-headed, girl. You know the rules about artifacts. You might be in a lot of trouble. If you need your box, I can get it, but promise me you'll go straight to the Watch after this. They need to know what you've found."

"It was an accident, and I'm sure I can handle it. But I promise to notify the Watch." She wouldn't, of course.

"I'm worried for you, Dania," Keld said.

"I can take care of myself."

"I'm sure you can. You're definitely not soft." He chuckled. "I didn't mean that the way it sounded."

"I know. Could you let me access my stash and give me some time alone, please? I hate to ask."

"It's fine. I'll uncover the hole then go out for a bit."

Keld shifted a chair and a table, and rolled up the rug underneath them to reveal a trapdoor. He pulled a brass ring set flat into the timber, and the door swung open on oiled hinges. Inside was a shallow storage area filled with boxes and pouches that belonged to Keld, and a one-foot-by-two-feet rectangular blackwood case that was Saskia's.

"Thank you," she said.

Keld nodded then left, closing the door softly behind him. That he'd left her alone with all his valuables said a lot about how much he trusted her. And she was breaking that trust by lying to him. It couldn't be helped; the less he knew, the better. It would keep him alive. Although those words, *it couldn't be helped*, had never yet prevented people she knew getting killed.

Saskia barred the door in case she was disturbed, then went straight for the blackwood case. The wood was rare, and known to dampen sorcerous abilities and emanations. A box this size was worth its weight in gold. She lifted it out and placed it flat on the floor. It was still locked, and a fine hair she'd glued to the side was undisturbed—a sign that no one had opened it.

Using a silver key from a chain around her neck, she clicked the lock open and lifted the lid. Her trembling hands reached immediately for a waxed-paper package with smaller waxed parcels inside. Saskia ripped the paper off one inked with an "X" and shoved the lozenge into her mouth. She chewed quickly, wrinkling her nose at the old sweaty boots taste that wasn't disguised by the honey coating. The alchemical and herbal compound would take effect soon, causing her nausea and pain to fade. Unfortunately, the narcotic cravv included in the compound would make her want more, especially after so long without it. She'd have to worry about that later, along with the crippling pain and exhaustion that would hit her like a runaway wagon when the delayed effects of tide-use kicked in.

Saskia glanced at the door then began her inventory of the

rest of the contents of the blackwood case. First came another blackwood box, this one only the size of a hand. Even with the exotic wood's ability to dampen sorcerous emanations, she could feel a faint vibration from the Orgols' artifact inside. This was another reason she might be hunted. She wasn't meant to have this artifact—she'd kept it when she should have turned it over to the Grim Hand. Even thinking the name of her old team brought back memories she'd rather forget: of her transformation, of the others like her, of too much blood and death.

Next came a black leather belt that held numerous small pouches, each containing a shred. She checked each one to make sure they hadn't degraded. Luckily, all seven still looked like black rocks, without any signs of the whitening that would indicate the alchemical-smithing process used to create them had broken down.

Another belt held two razor-sharp knives in black sheaths. There was a set of lock-picks in a calfskin case—sometimes a mechanical solution was preferable to using the dark-tide; and a set of miniaturized tools: a saw, a file, an awl, a hammer, and a pry bar.

The remaining items were a small leather backpack containing bandages, packets of herbs, and bottles of alchemical compounds with various effects—sleep, purification, disorientation. Finally, she withdrew a heavy purse. Inside were gold coins and six gemstones.

Saskia buckled her knives around her waist, along with the two other knives she'd taken from the dead assassins. She wore the belt containing the shreds as a baldric across her chest. Everything else she crammed into the backpack; then she relocked the case and returned it to the compartment.

She felt better with her familiar weapons back in her hands.

Unfortunately, she'd left her greatest weapon in Gessa, the closest city to Sharrow—if weapon was the right word for the orichalcum sphere and its smaller twin that amplified and extended her abilities. Once she had those artifacts back in her possession, there wouldn't be much that could stop her. It had seemed like a good idea at the time to distance herself from the spheres, and also to store them under arcane wards so strong they couldn't be traced. Now, she wished she'd kept them with her. But perhaps then she'd have been found years ago.

She returned the rug, table and chair to their original positions and unbarred the door. Shortly after, Keld returned.

"I'll come with you," he said before Saskia could speak.

She shook her head and placed a hand on his shoulder. "Thank you again. But I think you should stay here."

The old ex-fisherman eyed her newly donned belts and knives. "Anything I should be aware of?"

"You barely knew me. Ran into me once or twice. Thought I was crazy for opening a shop selling artifacts and curios."

Keld sniffed. "I ain't much of a liar."

"If I don't return in a few months, you can have the blackwood case I've left here."

"You trying to buy me off?"

"No, it's a gift." She felt bad for the way she was leaving things with Keld, but it couldn't be helped. There it was again, her excuse for everything. "It'd be worth a trip to Gessa to find an agent who deals in that type of thing," she added.

"That type…?"

"Rare materials such as blackwood, orichalcum, that sort of stuff. Find someone you can trust."

"Trust doesn't come easily these days."

"I know. I'm sorry." She wrapped the old man in a hug. He

responded stiffly, but softened after a moment.

"You stay safe, girl, you hear me?"

She kissed his cheek. "Goodbye."

"Call on me, if you need anything else," Keld said as she left.

Saskia didn't answer. Her aches and pains and nausea had finally disappeared, and she felt energized, as if anything were possible.

Soon, Saskia was jogging along the road that ran parallel to the beach, heading away from the main wharves to the smaller ones spread out along the shore. A warm breeze drifted over her from the hills surrounding the town; it smelled of the jungle—musty and wet. She wasn't the most competent sailor, but that breeze should help her get across to the main island, from where she'd find her way to Gessa.

She kept running until she came to where the most dilapidated boats were, some of them almost falling apart. Out on the water, sounder boats rocked gently at their moorings, their ropes gently creaking. The area was dark and unlit. Perfect.

The water and wharves were quiet, other than the music of the festival drifting down the beach. She could make out some lights moving in the jungle behind her, but they were probably young kids looking for frogs to eat. Out to sea, three large ships were anchored, with lamps shining on deck and through windows. Merchants and traders probably, with most of their crews on shore for the festival. They'd anchored a little way out to deter would-be thieves.

A Watch patrol had just finished a circuit and were heading back toward the main wharves. Saskia crouched behind a stack of barrels in the darkest spot she could find. A displeased cat shot her a wary look and hissed. The two men and one woman of the Watch wore the white leather masks that indicated their allegiance to Zihanna, the goddess of justice and mercy. Rumor had it the masks bestowed powers upon the wearer, but Saskia didn't believe it. Gods and goddesses made their own decisions about who they chose to wield their power. Nevertheless, she waited until the three figures were another hundred yards up the beach before making her move.

There were two well-maintained boats lashed together at the wharf—a sign they were owned by the same person. There were crab pots stacked at the back of each boat, so Saskia placed a gold talent on the floor of one and placed a pot on top of it. The locals weren't wealthy, and she didn't want to steal a boat without leaving some recompense.

She slithered over to the second boat, which was filled with fishing nets and long lines festooned with hooks wound around large wooden disks. She untied its mooring lines, slid two oars into the rowlock and sculled away from the wharf as quietly as she could. Within moments she had left the island and her life there.

A dozen boat lengths out, she shipped the oars and unfurled the small sail attached to the mast. A shout echoed across the water behind her. She glanced around to see a man of the Watch in his white mask standing on the wharf and pointing at her. He grabbed something from around his neck, and a sharp whistle broke the quiet. Answering whistles came from the direction of the main wharves, where the earlier trio had disappeared to. They were bound to send a boat after her, which meant she'd need to put on enough sail to outpace it. Her shoulders slumped as she studied her vessel's one sail. It was old and tattered. Still, the boat sliced through the gentle waves eagerly, if not quite as fast as she'd like. And it would take time for the Watch to organize themselves to come after her.

In the distance she could just make out the shore of the main island of the archipelago. All she needed to do was point the boat, sail, and hope for the best. She left the oil lamp attached to the mast unlit, preferring to sail by the light of the stars—which would also make her difficult to see.

The strait between the islands was narrow, and she'd made it halfway across before she spotted a sleek boat knifing through the water toward her.

"Bloody darkness!" Saskia cursed.

The boat wasn't much larger than hers, but its sail was, and it was bellied by the breeze. Lamps illuminated a few figures on board: one at the tiller, and two more at the bow, probably ready to pepper her with bolts as soon as they were within range. None of them wore masks, so they weren't the Watch—which meant they had to be part of the team sent to eliminate her. No doubt they'd had the boat ready to sail, and when they'd heard the uproar from the Watch, they knew she'd fled by sea.

She tied a line around the tiller to keep her bearing straight, and made sure her gear was secure. She debated shooting a few bolts at the ship approaching her, but they might return fire, and that she didn't want. The crossbow had served its purpose on the island, though she had one last use for it.

She crammed another cravv lozenge into her mouth and chewed hurriedly. She'd need it to hold the nausea and pain of using too much dark-tide at bay, but she dreaded the after-effects when they finally hit her. She was already running at the edge of her endurance. She took a shred from her pouch and dropped it to the bottom of the boat; hesitated, then added another. Then she held up the crossbow and waved it in the air, before heaving it over the side where it disappeared with a splash. With any luck, that would give them pause and she wouldn't have to dodge bolts flying around.

Saskia sat on the starboard gunwale and affected the shoulder slump and bowed head of a defeated opponent. While she waited for her pursuers to close the remaining gap, her little boat continued toward the main island. She estimated that by the time they caught up with her, she'd have crossed three-quarters of the strait. Good enough. She took off her boots and double-checked her gear. The bottom of the boat was cool and rough underfoot, and she grimaced as she stepped in something slimy.

The other boat was forty yards away now, and Saskia breathed a sigh of relief as no bolts came hissing over the water toward her. Perhaps her assassins wanted to be much closer to get a clean shot and a verified kill.

When they were thirty yards away, she gripped the gunwale tighter, ready to throw herself down in case they decided to chance a few shots.

At twenty-five, she mentally checked her repository of dark-tide power: enough for a few more surges, and maybe a shadow-step or two. But she was already weak, and even though her medicine staved off the worst effects, there was still a risk she could push herself over the edge into exhaustion. Shadow-stepping over water was highly dangerous too, as the shadows constantly twisted, coalesced, and dispersed. She'd heard of one person who had tried it in desperation and ended up splintered into a hundred pieces. That wasn't the way she wanted to go out.

At twenty yards she stood, confident they were waiting to get close enough to make sure they finished the job. At fifteen, she raised her hands above her head. She could see her pursuers clearly now: rough, scarred men with mismatched clothes. Men accustomed to spilling blood for coin. Certainly not trained assassins.

At ten yards, Saskia waved at them, then pitched herself backward and overboard. Before the water enclosed her, she heard a bolt hiss through the air where she'd just been standing. She twisted around and kicked hard, pushing herself deeper. She was safe from crossbow bolts this far under the water, but that wasn't what she was worried about.

When she heard the thump of timber on timber as her pursuers' boat bumped into hers, she sent a pulse of dark-tide power into each shred. Both cracked so close together she heard them as one sound. A spike of darkness grazed her shoulder, searing a trench across her skin. She clapped a hand over the wound and pressed tight. There were sharp-tooths in these waters and she didn't want to make it this far only to be torn to pieces by fish.

She surfaced cautiously, only letting her eyes peek above the water, even though her lungs burned with the need for air. Black smoke roiled from her boat as it continued on its way toward the main island, too far away for her to catch it. Besides, it was peppered full of holes and leaking like a sieve. The second boat floated aimlessly nearby, similarly damaged, with three figures slumped inside it, dark trails of their blood leaking from holes in the hull. By the time anyone found either boat, she would be miles away.

Saskia took a few moments to gulp in air. The shore was only a few hundred yards away now, and she began a smooth, measured stroke, gritting her teeth each time her injured shoulder pained her. The thought of sharp-tooths beneath her filled her with dread. The less time spent in the water, the less chance of being eaten.

A short time later she pulled herself up onto a deserted green sand beach. An alchemist had once told her the color was the result of a mixture of minerals that reacted with saltwater, but he'd been a bit erratic and, Saskia suspected, a little too into his own concoctions. The band of stars crossing the sky seemed brighter as she stood panting on the sand, dripping seawater and blood.

She judged she was around a mile from the fishing village of Chork, which lay to the west. After making her way there tonight, she'd wait until morning to hire transport to the main port of Rillar across another narrow strait, where she could lose herself in the crowds.

She gathered a pile of small driftwood branches to make a fire, using her last tiny spark of dark-tide power to set it alight. She unbuckled her pack and belts, stripped out of her damp clothes then wrung the water from them. She draped them over a driftwood log near the fire, then tilted her head back and gazed at the moonless, star-banded sky. She knew she was keeping busy to distract herself from the inevitable consequences of using too much dark-tide power and medicine.

Soon enough, her stomach twisted in agony and her muscles cramped with savage spasms. She whimpered, curling into a ball, as wave after wave swept through her, blazing spikes of pain along her nerves and into her brain. A massive pressure enveloped her eyeballs, squeezing them until she felt they would pop out of her head or be crushed to goo. A scream tore from her throat, pulled out of her by white-hot hooks. Mind awash with agony, thoughts tumbling, Saskia held onto only one thing, a memory so precious she feared losing it more than anything: her daughter Amelia. She clamped on tight to that burning warmth of love she'd never found again, and lay there whimpering and crying, her nails digging into the flesh of her legs.

Finally, the racking torment lessened and she gathered herself enough to dress in her dried clothes. She wanted another of her potent lozenges but stayed her hand, knowing it was the narcotic cravv calling to her.

She inhaled deeply. The salty air held the syrupy sweetness of the dark-tide. Sorcerers replenished their power from the dawn- and dusk-tides at sunrise and sunset, but Saskia's demon-given abilities drew on the dark-tide, which she could only feel during the full-dark when both moons remained below the horizon.

She closed her eyes and opened her arms. The dark-tide enveloped her—a soft caress at first, then it grew in intensity, stinging her skin, getting hotter, burning her. She clenched her teeth against the pain and opened herself to the power. Dark. Sweet. Blistering. It washed around her and coursed through her.

She fixed herself firmly in her mind, as she'd been taught, and weathered the waves of power surging over her, drawing in enough to replenish her repository. As meager as it was, she was finished in a few dozen heartbeats and closed herself to the dark-tide. It lingered around her, as if reluctant to leave.

The relief she felt at having survived her assassins now turned to wrath. She recognized the swift rhythm of her heart as the flame of rage took hold of her. Whoever wanted her dead was still out there, and unlikely to give up. As much as Saskia had tried to leave Raven behind, and as much as she hated what the Grim Hand had forced her to become, the only way to ensure her survival was to return to the assassin self she'd thought buried forever.

Saskia closed her eyes against the starlit sky...and Raven opened them.

She looked around, as if seeing the beach for the first time, then got to her feet and began the trek into the fishing village. Dawn would arrive soon enough, and she would start on her journey to find out who wanted her dead.

# THREE

SUNLIGHT BLINDS ME. ON INSTINCT *I pivot, and my opponent's blade slides past my shoulder. I blink as I step right, and now the sun is behind me and it's his turn to shield his eyes. I thrust for his sternum. Somehow, he parries. I slip my leg behind his calf and shove, and he hits the ground with a thud.*

*Someone cheers. My opponent curses. He can't accept being beaten by a woman. All around us, the clash and clang of steel as the rest of our unit spars.*

*"Ma'am!"*

*A man in uniform runs over from the barracks and gives a sloppy salute.*

*"You're wanted in Captain Dunn's office."*

*He looks too young to be a soldier. "Now? Can I at least clean up?"*

*"Now."*

*I make my way to the office, wiping sweat from my face.*

*Inside wait Captain Dunn and two men I don't recognize. All three seem nervous: fidgeting hands, darting eyes. The strangers are sorcerers—that much I can tell from their robes and the talismans hanging from their belts. One has a patchy beard that looks as though it has been scorched to the skin in places; the other has a lazy left eye.*

*Captain Dunn hands me a red-glazed cup filled with acrid-smelling tea.*

*"Saskia," he says, "I have been told your performance is exemplary. The City States need dedicated soldiers like you."*

*"Those with your talents will be looked after," says the sorcerer with the patchy beard.*

*Captain Dunn waves him to silence.*

*I have no idea what they are talking about.*

*"Our enemies would see us dead in a heartbeat, if they could," continues Dunn. "And their ambition knows no bounds. And while our armies might seem strong to you, we have weaknesses. It is these weaknesses that our sorcerers aim to address. You are being given a chance to become something greater than the norm. To develop powers that, up to now, were thought unavailable to ordinary humans." He gestures toward my cup. It is an order.*

*I gulp some of the tea and grimace at its bitter taste. "Sir," I say, "what is it you're asking of me?"*

*"Only that you prove your loyalty."*

*I frown. My loyalty is beyond question, surely? I try to speak but my lips won't move.*

*"And I'm sure you understand that time is short," Dunn says. His voice sounds echoey and far off. "Both mine and the City States'. Hence we have to hasten things along."*

*The room swims around me, and my tongue grows numb. My limbs shiver as they grew cold and an icy chill sweeps through me. The cup clatters to the floor.*

*I gasp as I wake. Try to sit up. Can't move my arms or legs. I am strapped to a table, naked. There are markings painted over what I can see of my body: arcane runes.*

*The two sorcerers are there with another stranger. Two more men bustle about a bench cluttered with alchemical equipment and flasks filled with colored liquids.*

*"We're going to make you better," the sorcerer with the patchy beard says.*

*"Stronger. Faster," says Lazy-eye. "Unfortunately, you're not a sorcerer, able to manipulate the dawn- and dusk-tides, but if all goes well, you'll be able to harness shadow-powers used only by creatures of the abyssal realms. That will be something, eh, won't it?"*

*On an adjacent table lies a creature I have never seen before. Scaly yellow skin covers its muscular frame, and finger-length horns protrude from its shoulders. Orange eyes peer out from under its jutting brow. A tube of some kind extends from its forearm. I can't move my head, but I follow the tube with my eyes and find the other end sticking out of my own arm. A scream wells up within me, but no sound escapes my lips. I try to wrench my arm away, but it won't obey me.*

*I whimper, and the sound of my own fear sets my heart racing.*

*"There, there," says the patchy-bearded sorcerer. "You'll thank us when we're done—if you're alive, that is, and your mind isn't too far gone. The process isn't perfect yet. We've lost a great many subjects, but luckily there's a steady supply. It's the demons that are hard to procure."*

*He nods to someone else, and one of the men standing by the bench comes over to the creature's table. He pours some oil from a flask into his palm and rubs his hands together.*

*A woman with a pockmarked face and bad breath grabs my hair and yanks my head to the side, away from the demon on the other bed. I want to curse the woman, but my throat remains tight and my lips numb. Panic rushes through me. I have to fight! Next to me, the demon's breath grows heavier, faster.*

*The woman holds up an alchemical globe that glows with white light and peers into my eyes. She places two fingers on my neck to check my pulse and grunts as if satisfied.*

*The demon utters a gurgling moan and the woman looks over at the creature. Her nose wrinkles and her mouth twists in disgust. "I suppose it's necessary," she mutters under her breath.*

*She pushes my head to face the ceiling. In my peripheral vision, I see Lazy-eye holding a flask filled with a viscous black fluid and what looks like dark-green threadworms writhing inside. Patchy-beard takes the container from him and adds a clear yellow liquid, swirling it until both fluids combine.*

*He approaches me, but the woman beside me holds up her hand. "Use it only on the men. We've lost too many women to the ravages of the change; we can't risk losing any more. Our employer demands better results, and dead experimental subjects are of no value."*

*"The other mixture isn't as potent," Patchy-beard says.*

*"Do not argue with me."*

*She turns back to me, grabs my hair and pries my jaw open. A tube scrapes my throat as the woman shoves it inside. There is a funnel attached to the other end. My heart pounds in my chest and sweat trickles down the side of my face.*

*"Stop! Please stop!" The sounds come out of my mouth no more than whispers of breath.*

*The bearded sorcerer returns holding another flask, this one containing a violet fluid. He pours it into the funnel. The liquid hits my stomach like liquid fire. Agonizing pain batters me. My insides shift as if someone has reached in and twisted. My flesh burns all the way down to my marrow. I taste bile and my muscles spasm. Unvoiced screams echo around my skull as blackness closes in.*

The fishing village of Chork was named after a sizable species of delicious blue-shelled crab that lived in the mangroves surrounding many of the islands. Raven strolled along the beach toward the village, enjoying the sand under her feet and the warmth of the morning sun on her face. She knew she looked like she'd just survived a shipwreck, but there wasn't much she could do about that. She ran her fingers through her tangled hair, smoothed it down and managed to work it into a decent braid. As soon as she reached somewhere more civilized, she'd procure new clothes and endeavor to make herself look respectable.

As Raven moved past boats brought up onto the beach for the night, a flock of island-gulls erupted in raucous cries from a grove of trees. No doubt feasting on the yellow-green beezle fruits dangling from their branches. Her feet left green sand for hard-packed earth, and she scattered chickens blocking the road.

She made her way along a shabby wharf where fishermen were coiling lines and folding nets in preparation for the day, and approached an old man who was scorched brown by the sun and sinewy from hard work. The silver band on his upper arm denoted he had wealth to spare and probably owned his own boat.

She stood close by him until she caught his eye. He acknowledged her with a nod, then went back to mending a net. Raven couldn't help but smile.

"Looks like it'll be a good day for fishing," Raven said, "but perhaps I might persuade you to take me to the mainland instead, to the port of Rillar? Given it's a day's sail from here, I'll also compensate you for the time it takes to return."

The fisherman didn't cease his mending, but his eyes flicked to her again. "The weather will be good for a few days yet. That's a lot of fishing to miss out on."

"I'm a traveler," Raven replied with a tinge of amusement, "without many worldly possessions. But I'm sure we can reach an agreement."

"You carry a lot of knives for someone so poor," the man said.

"That is true. A woman can never be too careful."

"That is also true." He straightened, knuckling the small of his back. His eyes were narrowed in a permanent squint, the result of years spent on the water. "This is my boat here. She's not the fastest, nor the prettiest, but she won't sink."

The boat was, in fact, the most seaworthy-looking of the lot, and Raven could see the trim and seats had recently been sanded and varnished.

"I'm not interested in how she looks, but where she can take me. Three silvers, one for each day of the journey there and back."

The old man nodded slowly. The offer was more than fair, and far more than he'd make fishing. "And if someone asks after you once I return?"

He was no fool. "Tell them what you know," she said. "You might make a few more silvers." Once she was in Rillar, she'd disappear and no one would be able to trace her.

He nodded, and they shook on the bargain.

The old man smiled as she handed him a silver coin. "The name's Azzaras," he said.

"Alika," replied Raven, using the same name she'd given to the nobleman on the horse.

Raven boarded immediately, and they pushed off from the wharf. She grabbed the tiller as Azzaras ran up a sail, the morning breeze filling it nicely. If the wind kept up, the trip would be quicker than she anticipated, depending on the currents.

When Azzaras came to take over from her, she moved to one side and trailed a hand in the water. Her stomach grumbled, but she'd worry about that later. Her priority was to put as much distance as she could between herself and the corpses she'd left behind. She checked behind them in case they were followed. Only a few island-gulls flew in their wake, in the hope of devouring fish scraps, until they lost interest and headed back to the shore. There would be easier pickings when the village's fishermen returned with the day's catch.

Relaxing, Raven watched the mangroves pass by, and the jungle farther inland. There were relatively few beaches on the islands; mostly the mangroves continued into the sea, and the seabed dropped quickly a few yards from shore.

As the boat sailed on through the azure water, Azzaras handed her an oatcake. She thanked him and nibbled on it, her thoughts circling back to her situation. Hunted by unknown assassins, chased from her home of three years, and no real idea what to do next, apart from try to stay alive.

The boat hit a wave and jolted Raven from her reverie. She saw Azzaras had rigged up a sunshade at the front of the craft using bamboo and sheets of thin canvas. He gestured to it and smiled, and Raven nodded her thanks. She wriggled into the coils of rope beneath the shade until she was comfortable, closed her eyes and tried to sleep. But the thoughts roiling inside her head kept rest at bay.

There were two possible ways someone could have found her, and both rested on Scorpion betraying her—the only difference between them was whether he'd done it knowingly, or unknowingly. If it was her fault, from having messed up years ago, then that would have caused problems earlier than now. And this scenario was virtually impossible. Considering her abilities and skill level, there was no chance she had been followed or traced.

Raven found it hard to believe Scorpion would knowingly betray her. He had nothing to gain by doing so, and much to lose. And she believed in her heart that he had loved her, in his own way. But the reality was that Scorpion still lived in her old world, where nothing was certain, morals were fluid, and deception constant.

She needed to figure out who was after her and why. It had to be someone from her past.

Assassins working for a noble she'd crossed paths with on one of her missions. A criminal organization. One of the merchant cartels. Even a cabal of sorcerers, if they knew of her acquired talents and wanted to unravel the secrets of her power for themselves. She'd been sent by the Grim Hand all over Wiraya, from Caronath in the north to Sohrah in the south, from the islands of Ak-Settur to the Plains of Khisig-Ugtall across the Simorga Sea to the west. Possibly the Orgols had tracked her down, if they believed she still had their sacred artifact. Her list of likely enemies was long and included her own City States.

Trying to figure out who wanted her dead was going to be impossible without figuring out how they knew she was alive, and then how they'd found her.

Which brought her back to finding Scorpion, the only person who knew she was still alive. Which was a problem, because like Raven, like all the Grim Hand's assassins, Scorpion was paranoid and took the utmost precautions to remain untraceable. As the leader of the Grim Hand he tended to stay close to the City States, but moved around constantly, never staying in one place for more than a month.

A nudge woke her. Azzaras. Raven scrambled out from under the sunshade and stretched, noting the sun was on the opposite side to when she'd fallen asleep. The boat could be turned the other way, but the red moon Jagonath was already appearing over the horizon, which meant it was late afternoon.

She drank her fill from a waterskin Azzaras offered, and devoured another oatcake. After a few minutes, he pointed over the prow to where the jungle broke and buildings emerged.

"Rillar," he said. "Didn't take as long as expected. Good winds and good currents."

Raven shielded her eyes against the descending sun. Soon she'd lose herself in the bustling port town and then be on her way north to Gessa. She drew four silvers from her purse and handed them to Azzaras. He eyed the unexpected bonus coin, then tried to hand it back. She refused, and they frowned at each other for a long moment before both burst out laughing.

Raven was pleasantly surprised by the port town of Rillar. The last time she was here, years ago, the place had been a mess, its buildings going to ruin with peeling paint and dilapidated roofs. Many of the ships moored to the rickety piers had been rotted and rusted, and were crewed by disreputable sailors who would have looked more at home as brothel guards. It seemed like the town's fortunes had changed since then, though. New warehouses and merchants' buildings stood on the waterfront, and the old putrid stench had been replaced by a fresh sea breeze. As Raven walked along the docks, she noticed many of the merchants were purveyors of copper, gold, and silver. She guessed that new mines had been founded in the mountains to the west, and Rillar had benefited greatly.

She headed inland, passing elderly locals sitting by the side of the road, chatting and laughing as they watched people walk by, and stopped at the first market she came to. A young girl leaned against a wall, her dress too thin and revealing. She stared at Raven with dull eyes before looking away to scan for potential customers. Raven handed her a silver, and the girl's eyes widened at the unexpected generosity. She nodded a startled thanks before scurrying away. Raven watched her go and wondered what her own life would have been like had Amelia lived. Perhaps they would have made their home in one of the major cities. A child needed good schooling, after all.

Raven silently wished the girl luck, then entered a shop and bought provisions along with two canteens filled with water. She also bought a voluminous robe with a rope belt. The robe had many patches and repaired holes, and she wouldn't be surprised if some of them were knife punctures.

She asked directions to an inn that catered to the not-quite-poor of the town. It offered a view of the square in front, and took up an entire block, which was perfect. You could never have too many escape routes. Raven circled the building before entering and was pleased to note long wooden planks joining it to two adjacent buildings. A thieves' road most likely, and another way to escape if things went downhill.

The timbers of the inn's floor were worn smooth and shallow-grooved by decades of traffic. A rail-thin man with a face like a ferret's glanced up from polishing a counter with wax. He looked Raven up and down and plastered a smile on his face.

"What's the rate for a room for the night?" Raven asked.

"We have a lovely top-floor apartment for a silver," the man wheezed. "Or single rooms for two coppers. That's the best I can do, I'm afraid. No haggling. Unless you can cook? The kitchen's short-handed—"

"The top floor will do," Raven said, passing over a silver mark. That would give her easier access to the roof and the thieves' highway if it was needed.

The man handed her an iron key. "Use all the water you want from the well in the courtyard. There's a public bathhouse down the street. And I'd usually recommend you have dinner here but…"

Raven smiled. "But the kitchen's short-handed. Thank you."

The apartment was as good as could be expected. It comprised a large room with a bed, and a smaller room with a desk and a chair and a window that took a few tugs to open. The bedroom smelled like someone with a fondness for perfume had stayed here last, and the staff hadn't changed the bedding.

Raven left her provisions and all but one set of clothes there, and made her way to the bathhouse. A copper mark bought her a bowl of liquid soap, a coarse brush, a clean towel, and a blissful bucket of hot water. After scrubbing herself clean, she rinsed off with fresh water, then enjoyed a too-short soak in a hot tub. When she dressed and re-geared, she felt almost normal again.

Before finding a place to eat, she made her way to the square where the merchant wagon trains left from. At this time of day there would be no departures, but better to survey it now than in the gray light of dawn tomorrow. There were three wagon trains in the square, all fully laden and with guards on watch. Unemployed hopefuls loitered nearby, and Raven knew they would likely be hired tomorrow morning for the cheapest price. If dead-eyes attacked, these desperate hopefuls would be the first to fall, and with any luck the dead-eyes would defile and devour them while the real guards protected the goods and merchants from harm.

A short time later, Raven was seated inside a small restaurant with tables and chairs spilling into a side alley. Surprisingly, the alley was well lit by lanterns and seemed a favorite of couples holding hands. She'd chosen a table against a wall and scanned the patrons for anyone suspicious. A fidgety man with darting eyes caught her attention, but she breathed a sigh of relief when he tried to keep the comely waitress talking.

Raven ordered grilled billfish in a lemon sauce, along with a wheat beer. As she ate and drank, she considered her options. She couldn't stay here long. If she'd been hunting a lone subject, she would have positioned watchers at all major towns along the coast. Every town and city had people who traded in information, with networks of spies. A few coins, and the promise of more if the information held up to scrutiny, would be sufficient. Based on the number of men sent to kill her, Raven couldn't discount the possibility that whoever wanted her dead had done the same.

Back in the street, she found a tailor and procured a free-flowing skirt and a shirt of good quality, along with practical boots and a couple of headscarves. Once in Gessa she'd need to look the part, so might as well prepare now. Then she hurried back to the inn, moved the bed so the dawn light would fall upon her face and wake her, and fell into a deep sleep.

# FOUR

I WAKE, YET AGAIN SURPRISED *I haven't died in the night. The sorcerers are surprised, too. But today I feel stronger, my focus sharper.*

*The sorcerers prod and probe me, use bright lights to look into my eyes, my throat, other orifices. They draw my blood using a thin tube.*

*"You'll be released today," says one. The woman with the pockmarked face and bad breath.*

*I nod numbly. The skin of my hand is darker than I remember. Where I sit with my back against the wall it is impossible to get comfortable. I reach around to touch my back and feel hard growths beneath my skin.*

*Someone hands me a mirror. I gasp. My midnight hair has been transformed into a shocking platinum.*

*"What happened?" My voice is slightly lower and grating to my ears.*

*"The process affects everyone differently," a sorcerer says, taking*

back the mirror. "The growths might be the beginnings of horny spikes. Most of the lower order demons have them in some shape or form. And your skin and hair, well, you should count yourself lucky you're alive. Only one in twenty make it through. And of those, only one in ten show signs of success. We'll test you soon."

Whatever they've done to me, whatever I have become, I am no longer human.

"What do you remember," asks the sorcerer. "From before?"

"Before? There was something…" I shake my head when nothing comes to me. I remember Captain Dunn, and before that…nothing. "Who am I? My parents…my life? I can't—"

"Shh. Rest. You're still not fully recovered. Here, drink this."

A cup presses to my lips. I drink automatically. Funnily enough, I remember the searing pain and torture of my transformation as if it had happened yesterday.

"We're calling you Raven," the sorcerer says. "On account of your charcoal skin. A new name for a new beginning. A new future both for you and the City States. The memory loss is normal. The alchemical and sorcerous process isn't exact."

I nod. "It was demon blood, wasn't it?"

"Among other fluids. Do you remember your old name?"

"No," I say. But I do. Saskia. I cling to the memory, and somehow, in the desolation of my soul, it gives me strength. The memories of my name, my old hair and skin color, are all that remain of my previous life.

"Who are you?" asks the woman.

"I don't understand…"

"Who are you?" she says more firmly.

I swallow, my hands trembling. "Raven. I am Raven."

Raven woke well before dawn. Her body ached as though she'd fallen off a horse and then been trampled by another dozen. Would she ever be free of the painful effects of her transformation? She thought not, as the pain in her muscles hadn't diminished. Though she didn't know what was possible and what wasn't, she was too scared to confess what had happened to her to a healer.

She unwrapped a lozenge and grimaced as she chewed. She carried two types of painkillers: one for easing her everyday aches, and one more powerful for when she used too much dark-tide. Under instruction from the Grim Hand's alchemists, she'd learned to manufacture both from ingredients found at regular apothecaries and herbalists. The lozenges were easy to carry, and easy to swallow, but both tasted like the inside of someone's boot, despite the addition of honey.

She strapped on her gear and pulled the patched robe over her head. She tied the rope belt loose, so she looked heavier than she was, then wrapped a headscarf around her platinum hair until it was completely covered. Lighting a foul-smelling lamp, she used the reflection in the window to rub some dirt from the floor under her eyes and across her cheeks so her skin appeared dull and rough. She now looked a dozen years older. The discoloration from her wounds would soon fade, and no one paid much attention to a woman with bruises.

She stored her remaining belongings in her backpack and tugged it on, then dropped the room key behind the downstairs counter on her way out. It was too early for any of the staff to be awake yet.

The sky was the texture of tarnished silver, and lightening with the dawn. She found an early morning market stall catering to shift workers and devoured two sweet buns filled with fruit and nuts, washing them down with hot tea. She bought a few more buns for the trip and loitered around nursing another cup of tea until it was time to leave. Just before the square with the wagon trains, she stopped to adjust her scarf, then leaned against a wall to survey the area. Something wasn't right. She hadn't developed a full-blown sense for danger like her ex-team member Smoke had, but something had manifested along with her other innate talents, and occasionally she had a feeling when things were awry.

On the opposite side of the square, a man lounged on a wooden bench in front of a jewelry shop that hadn't yet opened. Smoke trailed from a pipe clutched in yellow-stained fingers, and his pants had seen better days. He brushed a greasy lock of hair from his face as he glanced at a couple approaching one of the merchant trains, then returned to puffing on his pipe. If he'd seen Raven, he didn't appear to view her as anything other than the lowly farm laborer she'd dressed as. She considered finding another way to get to Gessa, but it would look suspicious if she left now. So, she kept her face lowered and walked slowly across the square.

Of the three merchant trains, one looked to be better maintained. Its wagons were well built with sturdy axles and wheels, and pulled by dray horses that were specially bred for the job—considerably bigger and stronger than normal horses. The wilderness was a harsh place, and the less time spent on its roads the better.

Raven approached one of the guards at her chosen wagon train. "Are...are you traveling to Gessa?" she asked, pitching her voice high and wringing her hands. Anyone watching would think her inexperienced and nervous. At least, that was the plan.

The guard, a heavy man turning to fat, rolled his eyes. "Take a ship from the docks. It'll be more expensive but less dangerous."

He was correct, of course. But a ship was the obvious route, and obvious got you killed.

"I can't afford passage on a ship," Raven said querulously. "And I get terribly sea-sick. Is there someone I could speak to?"

"You're speaking to me."

"What about the merchant who owns this train. Can I speak to him?"

The guard sighed through his flat nose. "Can you pay?"

"I have enough for the trip…I think."

"Wait here." He gestured to another guard to take his position and disappeared behind a wagon, one finger rooting around in his ear.

The new guard, a young boy with a few wisps of hair sprouting from his chin, frowned at her in an attempt to look menacing. His arms were so thin, Raven wondered if he could even lift the heavy, iron-bound cudgel hanging from his belt. She hunched her shoulders and did her best to look intimidated. As she did, she turned slightly so she could see the pipe-smoking man. He was on his feet and looking in her direction. Raven's hand slipped through a slit in her robe to grip the hilt of a knife. She didn't want to kill him if she could avoid it, as it would cause a scene and put the Watch onto her, confirming to her assassins that she'd been in Rillar.

The first guard returned with a middle-aged woman with long golden hair. She was dressed in travel leathers, with rings adorning her fingers and a workmanlike sword hanging from her belt.

"Seeking a place on my wagon train, are you?" she said, studying Raven.

Raven bobbed her head. "As I told this warrior here, I can't afford a ship. And I get sea-sick something terrible."

The younger man sniggered at her description of the heavy-set guard, who glared at him.

"How much do you have?" the merchant asked.

"How much is a spot?"

"What do you think is a fair price?"

"Five chickens."

The merchant raised her eyebrows. "And what's that in silver marks?"

"Two. Maybe three, if they're meaty birds."

"Three, then."

"Including meals, of course," Raven said, and smiled. "I can help with the cooking."

"All right, then. Three silver talents, meals included. You sleep under a wagon with the rest of us. And if we come across any dead-eyes, you're on your own."

Raven stuck her hand out, and they sealed the bargain. She handed over the silvers, then asked where she should sit.

"Second wagon. Up front with the driver. And keep out of the way, if you can. We're traveling fast."

Raven nodded her thanks and tossed her backpack behind the seat of the second wagon. She climbed up and sat, hands clutched in her lap. The wagons were almost full, and if they wanted to reach the first safe way station before dark, they would have to leave soon. The guards ignored her, except for a tall, dusky-skinned man who stopped to stare at her for a few moments. He had long black hair and wore a short sword at his waist and a long sword across his back. His leather armor was good quality, worked with flat metal rings. He grinned and winked, then went to sit in the first wagon beside the merchant woman. He'd seen straight through her disguise. Raven marked him as deadly, and someone to watch, but the trip wouldn't take too long, and if she kept to herself maybe she could avoid him.

Her other watcher had returned to his seat and his pipe, but she couldn't discern whether he'd marked her or written her off. Hopefully she'd make it to Gessa without any trouble.

They set a punishing pace, the sturdy horses pulling the spring-wagons with relative ease, and there had been no encounters with dead-eyes, which was almost unheard of. Nevertheless, each day the guards eyed the passing forests and grasslands warily, their hands always on their crossbows. If they needed to piss, they did so over the side while the wagons were still moving. Each night they set a double watch, and kept fires blazing and lanterns lit.

One night they heard a banshee keening nearby—a creature that even dead-eyes and ghouls avoided—and remembering her terrifying encounter many years ago with one, Raven couldn't get back to sleep. She rose from her thin blanket and moved to one of the cookfires that someone had recently added wood to, and the flames sent shadows flickering around the camp.

The dangerous dusky-skinned man sat cross-legged a few yards away, his scabbarded long sword across his thighs. He still wore his ringed mail. As she approached, he watched without a word.

She checked the kettle in the side coals and found it half full of tea. Pouring herself a mug, she looked around to make sure the guards were still alert, then squatted in front of the fire. The tea was bitter and strong.

"Banshee keeping you awake?" the man said.

She nodded slowly and sipped her tea. Her hand trembled and she willed it to stop.

"Do you play cards?"

Raven hesitated. "No."

"Shame. I find myself with a lot of spare time and playing helps. Well, if we can't play, then we'll talk."

"Not much to talk about. I'm only a farmer—"

"I'd ask you your name, but I don't think I'd get an honest answer."

Raven reached for the dark-tide and moved a hand to rest it by her collarbone. If the man tried anything, he'd be in for a surprise. And then dead. But for some reason, she had the feeling that whatever happened wouldn't be over so quickly. She'd learned to assess people by the way they moved and spoke, and something about this man was off.

He was more than dangerous. If she'd been on a mission, she'd have aborted the kill and returned with backup. She pretended to be busy drinking her tea. She'd finish up and then return to her blanket.

"Encountered a banshee before?" he asked.

"No." *Yes.*

"I think you have. There's a fear survivors have. It stains their bones. Not that many survive."

"I get lucky sometimes."

"I don't doubt that. At first I thought you were Tainted Cabal, but even though you stink of demon, I think I was mistaken."

Raven tensed and reached for the dark-tide, but stopped when she saw the man's sword already half out of its sheath. On the blade there was an engraved image of a woman with wings.

"Don't," he said. The words were devoid of emotion. "No one else can smell it. I doubt even most tainted of the Cabal could. I would ask more questions, but these days my curiosity has given way to melancholy. So I'll leave you to yours, and you leave me to mine." He slowly slid the blade back into the sheath.

Raven tossed the dregs of her tea into the fire. She stood and gave the man a nod, then huddled in her blanket until the sun rose.

The rest of the trip Raven kept to herself as much as she could and said hardly a word without prompting. She wore her robe and scarf the whole journey, and kept her face smudged with dirt. The dusky-skinned swordsman winked whenever he passed her, but nothing more. She wasn't sure what his game was and didn't care to know. The guards all trod warily around him, as if he were a venomous snake of uncertain temperament.

By the time the wagon train approached Gessa, ten days later, Raven's hand and shoulder had almost healed. The bruises on her face had faded a few days into the trip.

Gessa, as usual, was a seething mass of humanity crammed into not enough space. The poor quarters were best avoided as they were rife with cutthroats and thieves. The wealthy quarters were much the same, only they didn't stink as much, and the people were better clothed. Raven found herself an inn somewhere between the two areas—a serviceable place named the Cat and Mouse, which looked less likely to collapse than the buildings around it.

It also wasn't too far from her reason for coming to Gessa: the safehouse of Sheelahn the Ethereal Sorceress. The sorceress had used her formidable powers to establish the preeminent business in all Wiraya where people could store their treasures safely, or buy or sell ancient artifacts through her auction business—and she had branches in all major cities.

Raven's room at the inn was tiny but clean, which was all that mattered. The press of the streets grated on her nerves after so long on the island, and she needed somewhere to sit and think without people crowding her.

But first, she had a few other tasks to attend to. She found a shop that sold products for women and purchased some hair dye, paying extra for the better-quality kind as she didn't want it to wash away in the first rainstorm. In another shop close by, she had her hair cut to just below her shoulder blades, and even made a few coins selling the long platinum offcuts to be incorporated into a wig. The tressdresser lathered the dye into her hair for her, and rubbed a powdered tint over her face to lighten her skin color. A short while later Raven emerged with dark-brown hair. When it was dry she'd braid it tightly and perhaps weave in some Soreshi clan colors to throw off any observers. Though her coloring wasn't anywhere near pale enough, the Soreshi grasslands clan did take in outsiders.

She wandered along the streets, making random turns and even doubling back a few times to check for anyone who might be following her. She didn't notice anyone, but that wasn't to say she wasn't being observed. They might be exceptionally skilled, or even using sorcerous means. If a sorcerer had something of hers—especially skin or blood—they could scry her location without any trouble. Her mind flashed back to the samples of both the sorcerers had taken from her in their laboratory. But if someone was using those samples to seek her out, they would have come after her years ago. So whoever was after her now had located her using another method.

But right now, she needed to find something to eat. Ten days of waggoneer fare hadn't sat well with her, and it would be a long time before she ate another bowl of barley stew.

She went in search of a clothing shop, and traded the robe and scarf for a small discount on a pair of well-made pants and a shirt, and a lightweight coat to conceal her knives—all woven from quality material in different shades of gray. She also purchased a broad-brimmed hat that went some way to concealing her hair, which she braided tightly and tucked down the back of her shirt.

Food came next, and she stopped at a street filled with food vendors set up for the night. A few skewers of meat grilled over hot coals, and some charred okra fingers washed down with water, and she almost felt herself again. She entered an inn that seemed to cater to genteel clients and ordered a hot tea. When it came, she sipped slowly, going over options in her mind. Since running from her home on Sharrow, she'd been driven by the necessity of putting as much distance between her and her pursuers as possible. But after that, what was her plan? She wouldn't get anywhere by simply reacting. When you reacted, you gave others power over you. But when you acted, you became the aggressor; you took the power back.

To find out who'd located her and how, she needed to go back to her old life, which she'd thought was gone forever. But how could she find Scorpion? Like Raven, none of the Grim Hand's team members had homes to go to. They lived like ghosts, with no memory of their past or their previous identities, using only the names they'd been given by their masters.

Raven paid for her tea, then took a stroll along the cobbled streets as she headed back to her room. She was buying peaches from a street vendor, delighted to have found them as she hadn't eaten any in years, when an idea hit her. There was a place where she might be able to find one of the Grim Hand. Crooked had been working undercover in Kroe when Raven had staged her death, and rumor had it he'd be there for years. The metamorphosis they had all undergone had left him with bent limbs, which caused him continual pain and restricted his mobility, so the Grim Hand used him for different tasks than the others. Crooked was a long-term asset, and it may be that he was still in the same place in Kroe where Raven had last had contact with him. It wasn't much, but it was somewhere to start. And knowing more about Crooked than an enemy searching for him would work in her favor. His deformities required ways to deal with sometimes debilitating pain, along with rare herbs and alchemical concoctions. Raven had sometimes wondered if many of those that had survived the transformation had been too deformed or uncontrollable and were simply killed. She was almost certain it was the case. Crooked must have found himself just on the right side of that line. A few months before her disappearance, she'd been tasked with delivering him a package of powerful chronic pain remedies on her way through Kroe.

And if Crooked was still there, she might be able to use him to contact Scorpion. What would happen then, she didn't know. Perhaps Crooked would receive orders to kill her. Or perhaps the City States would welcome her back with open arms.

Somehow, she doubted it. Who knew how much they had advanced their techniques during the past five years? Perhaps her old team was now a hundred strong. Still, for the first time since she was attacked, she felt like she had a decent plan. She was acting, not reacting.

Kroe was a wealthy city, and home of the famous Thaumaturgy School, which brought together students from every country to study and be recognized for their sorcerous and scientific achievements. But underneath the surface, the city was a seething bed of corruption and vice. It was also on the other side of the continent. A journey that could take months. Even if she shadow-stepped as much and as far as possible, she was limited by line of sight and how much dark-tide power she had. All too soon it would run out, and her orichalcum sphere would be useless until she absorbed more at the next full-dark.

Unless… The beginnings of an idea took hold.

Sheelahn somehow managed to transport artifacts from city to city without ever losing a single one. It was also rumored that Sheelahn was able to be in multiple places at once, or at least in different cities on the same day. Which should have been impossible. There was also the instruction given to Grim Hand trainees as a get-out-of-trouble option if all else failed: find one of Sheelahn the Eternal Sorceress's establishments and tell her the Grim Hand required her assistance. Sheelahn could transport you swiftly back to the City States, who would pay the high price of the service. Which, Raven concluded, meant Sheelahn must have some secret way of moving between her establishments all across Wiraya.

If Raven could persuade the sorceress to transport her to Kroe, those pursuing her would be fumbling around in the dark, while their quarry was almost two thousand miles away.

As she turned into the street that led to the Cat and Mouse, she registered three scruffy youths behind her. She drew two of her knives and held them up, and the miscreants scattered, leaving a sour, sweaty reek in their wake. Raven made a note to stick to the well-lit main streets in future. At least she'd realized she was being followed. Her instincts were coming back to her. Though the old Raven would have killed all three and not broken a sweat.

# FIVE

I STUMBLE, FALL TO ONE *knee, a hand touching the ground to steady myself. My lungs burn as if on fire, and my chest aches. Sweat drips down my face, stinging my eyes and cracked lips.*

*"Get up!" my trainer yells.*

*She's a heartless bitch and I feel like strangling her, but she is also backed up by armed soldiers. I suck air in and get back to my feet. The finish line is only a hundred yards up the steep incline, but right now it might as well be miles. A line of fire erupts along my back as the trainer strikes me with a bamboo switch. Where it hits one of my lumps the pain is intense, and a warm trickle down my back tells me that my skin has been split.*

*"Move your sorry ass, you worthless piece of shit! Are you going to quit this close to the finish?"*

*I move one foot forward, then the next, my shoulders hunched all the while, expecting another blow. I focus on the ground in front of me: sandy, rocky, my boots covered with dirt, the path narrow where it leads up the cliffs. Far below, waves crash into rocks. Above, seagulls screech.*

*Another step, then another, until I manage a slow run. My thighs and buttocks ache, and I can't seem to breathe enough air.*

*When the path flattens out, I throw myself down on a patch of tough coastal grass and will myself to recover. I know I don't have much time.*

*"Up! You're rested enough. You know the drill. Two hundred pushups, then we'll see if you can handle a sword when you're exhausted. Not started yet? Add another fifty."*

*I groan and roll over, palms on the coarse grass. A column of ants snakes between them. I lower myself until my nose touches the ground.*

Raven stirred the next morning to the sounds of the city of Gessa waking. People shouted and children wailed, roosters crowed and street vendors hawked their wares. She quickly dressed and strapped on her gear, taking all her belongings with her. Outside, she found a stall selling boiled eggs, along with small, freshly steamed buns filled with a spicy bean mixture. She ate one, then went back for another to eat while she made her way uphill. As she crossed an intersection, a small girl ran in front of her. Raven's breath caught in her throat. A woman chasing the girl grabbed her and waved a finger in front of her face, scolding her. Raven couldn't help staring at them for a few moments before moving along. Amelia would have been three years old by now—able to walk, to talk, to understand when her mother told her she loved her. The dust from the dirty streets made Raven's eyes water.

She hailed a carriage and gave the driver a few copper talents.

"To the Ethereal Sorceress, please."

It wasn't long before the driver announced they'd reached their destination. An imposing building reared up from the cobbled street. Doors of blackwood bound with iron were set into a granite slab wall with barely visible seams. There were no windows, and the cube-shaped structure looked as if it were one giant block of stone. Rumor was it had been constructed in one night by summoned spirits. There had only ever been one attempt to breach its walls to steal the arcane valuables stored inside—which had ended with the thieves' charred and dismembered corpses scattered in the street outside.

Raven ascended the wide steps to the huge doors. Before she had a chance to knock, one of them swung open to reveal a glossy checkered floor of white and green marble, and a doorman wearing a face mask of polished blackwood. The mask had no features, except for two eyeholes. He wore a thick coat the color of dark rainclouds and had long black hair twisted into multiple braids. On the far side of the chamber behind him, Raven could see a dozen more blackwood doors.

"Enter," the man said, voice muffled. "You are expected."

Raven nodded. She bet they greeted everyone like that. She peered at the eyeholes in the man's mask but couldn't see anything. It was just black.

"I'd like to access my safe box," she said.

"Sheelahn will see you."

Raven paused. This was almost unheard of. The last time she was here, she'd dealt only with functionaries similar to this one. Whatever the Ethereal Sorceress wanted, it meant Raven had caught her attention, and that was always bad.

"I'm honored," she replied, one hand surreptitiously checking her knives. Not that they'd be of any use against a sorcerer of such power. The shreds might be more effective, but she didn't really want to find out.

The functionary led her to one of the inner doors and opened it with a brass key. There was an iron cage inside. Raven hesitated, then realized it was some sort of lifting device to reach the upper floors. She entered, and the functionary closed the door on her. The floor lurched, and Raven's stomach rose as the cage began to lower. Interesting. She'd expected to be taken higher, but perhaps this was part of Sheelahn's defenses. Sorcerers couldn't replenish their dawn- and dusk-tides deep underground.

There was a metallic groan and a clunk far above, and the cage stopped. Another door faced Raven. She pushed it open and saw a corridor with a deep green carpet that looked almost like grass. Alchemical globes in wall sconces lit the space.

Sheelahn sat behind a blackwood desk carved with miniature monkeys scrambling over fruit-bearing vines. Raven saw one was picking its nose, while another seemed to be shitting into its hand. Whoever had carved the wood had a strange sense of humor. An orichalcum mask covered Sheelahn's face, with a cross-shaped opening behind which Raven saw only an impenetrable blackness. The sorceress wore robes so thick they hid any sense of what lay underneath, and each fold of the fabric stood out precisely, as if pressed and starched. Black silk gloves covered her hands.

Sheelahn stopped writing in a thick ledger, and placed a metal implement down beside four inkwells. Raven noted the inks were different colors: black, red, green, and purple. The sorcerer stood and moved in front of the desk. The orichalcum mask tilted up. Raven imagined if the sorceress had eyes, they would be regarding her.

Raven swallowed and stepped forward, stopping at least ten

paces short of the figure.

When Sheelahn spoke, her voice was strangely musical and reminded Raven of birdsong. "You have come for your artifact."

"Yes. I paid for storage. It is mine."

The mask tilted forward slightly. A nod. "Our agreement will be honored."

Raven removed the blackwood box containing the Orgols' artifact from her pocket. It vibrated slightly in her hand. "I have something else I'd like to deposit."

"I will take it, with reluctance," Sheelahn replied. "Its sorcerous emanations are…interesting. Standard rates will apply."

Raven dug out five gold talents but didn't hand them over. "Where's the artifact I left here last time?"

"First, a few questions."

Raven tensed. "Is this part of our agreement?"

"No."

"Then if I answer your questions, you will owe me. That's the way I see it."

For a long moment Sheelahn remained completely still. Raven couldn't determine if she was even breathing. The blackness behind the face mask was unnerving.

"Agreed," the sorceress said. "First, where did you come by the orichalcum sphere?"

So, she wasn't interested in the Orgols' artifact, but the one from the Grim Hand. "It was given to me."

"More information."

"I was…trained to use it," Raven said.

Another long pause. Raven shrugged to rid her shoulders of an uneasy tingle. The sooner she was gone from here the better.

"You are no demon," Sheelahn said. "If you were, you would not leave here alive."

A chill swept up Raven's spine. The Ethereal Sorceress knew what had been done to her—or had shrewdly guessed at it. "Sometimes I think I am."

"Who did this to you?"

"I don't really know," she said. "Some sorcerers. After they… well, I was taught in secret. My teachers did not have precise knowledge, and sometimes it was difficult."

"What will you do with the artifact you are here to collect? And why return for it now, after so long?"

"Someone tried to kill me. I need to find and kill them. The sphere amplifies my abilities." Her reasoning sounded hollow. Kill or be killed. Was that to be her life from now on?

"Is that what you want from life? To kill?" Sheelahn said, echoing Raven's thoughts.

"I…no."

"You were treated like a weapon, but you are more than that."

"Am I? Once I would have agreed. Not now."

Sheelahn advanced, and Raven took a step back, her grip tightening around the blackwood box. The sorceress stopped and opened a gloved hand. Raven's artifact lay in her palm: a rune-covered orichalcum sphere the size of a duck egg, attached to a silver chain.

Raven swapped it for the blackwood box and five golds, and opened the clasp on the sphere to check its companion was inside. It was identical, except the size of a blueberry, and nestled inside the larger sphere like a pit in a peach. Where the Grim Hand had gotten such an artifact Raven didn't know, but to her it was as valuable as a shipload of gold and gems. To anyone without her talents, it was useless. She slipped the chain over her head. Immediately, she was aware of the dark-tide assailing her senses. Her ears ached and the sound of her heartbeat grew until it hammered through her skull.

The sensation died down as quickly as it had arisen, and Raven took stock. Her dark-tide repository had grown. This morning only a few pulses had remained; now she felt as if she could use her talents a score of times without fail.

She opened her eyes and saw Sheelahn still standing in front of her, motionless. Raven's blackwood box and coins had disappeared.

"If you survive, return here," the sorceress said. "My patronage will offer you some protection, and I have need for one such as you."

She wanted to make use of Raven. The sorceress knew what she was and hadn't flinched.

"You will owe me twice over, then," Raven said.

"Agreed. Our bargain is struck."

Under Sheelahn's protection, Raven would be safe. But at what cost to herself? She'd had enough of killing, but it seemed death hadn't had enough of her.

"As payment for your good sense," continued Sheelahn, "I'll provide you some information, no strings attached. That's how it's said, isn't it?"

"Yes," replied Raven slowly.

"The people you seek are still in Kroe."

Raven's eyes narrowed. How did Sheelahn know who she was looking for or where they were?

"I make it my business to know," the sorcerer said, as if she could hear Raven's thoughts.

"What people? I'm only looking for one person in Kroe."

The Ethereal Sorceress remained mute. Well, either Sheelahn was right, or she was wrong. There was only one way to find out. "I'll use one of those favors right now," Raven said.

"I can tell you more about your spherical artifact, if you like."

A shiver ran up Raven's spine. That there might be more the sphere could do was no surprise, but it was information that could wait. She smiled and shook her head. "Perhaps another time. I do have two favors owed to me."

"I am well aware."

"I want to travel to Kroe."

"Done. I will arrange a ship—"

"No. You misunderstand." Was it her imagination, or had she seen a brief flash of emerald light across the impenetrable blackness behind the mask at the interruption? "I need to arrive there today," she added.

Sheelahn didn't move. Raven began to have misgivings. What if there was more than one Ethereal Sorceress, and her idea of traveling to Kroe was crazy? Would she use up the favors the sorceress owed her only to find out she was wrong?

A section of wall beside the sorceress hinged open silently. Her black-gloved hands adjusted her robes around her thighs. "And so the debt will be repaid," she said. "Follow me."

She glided across the carpet to the opening, and Raven followed cautiously. When she reached the doorway, she saw the sorceress was already twenty yards ahead. She hurried after her, boots scuffing along more green carpet, the passage lit by a radiance that had no discernible source. The sorceress turned a corner and was lost to sight. Raven broke into a sprint, and almost crashed into Sheelahn as she rounded the corner. She skidded to a halt, eyes darting around for any tricks.

Ahead was a room with a polished granite floor and a circle of runed orichalcum set into the stone. The sorceress stepped into the circle and indicated Raven should follow. When she did, Sheelahn chanted words in Skanuric and the light flickered.

Sorcery scooped Raven up and shattered her into a million pieces, scattering them across the void. Eldritch lights lanced out of nowhere, punctuated by cracking thunder and the scent of burned wood. Reality rippled and lurched as Raven was pulled and twisted, then sucked into a sensory-free nothingness for a dozen heartbeats. Finally, darkness became light and Raven fell to the granite floor, convulsing. Her eyes ached and her ears rang with discordance. Her mouth filled with bile, and she heaved.

When she had recovered enough to sit up, she found herself in exactly the same place: in the center of the orichalcum ring set into the granite floor.

"Come," said Sheelahn, standing straight and tall, as if the sorcery had no effect on her.

A blackwood door opened to reveal the corridor where Raven had met the Ethereal Sorceress. Sheelahn stepped to the side to allow Raven through, and pointed to another door at the end of the corridor.

"My debt is repaid," she said.

*Bloody darkness!* The sorceress had played a trick on her.

"Not yet it isn't," Raven told her. "We haven't gone anywhere. And you owe me two favors. Is this supposed to be funny?"

Sheelahn remained silent.

With a furious wrench of self-control, Raven managed to still her tongue. She walked along the corridor to the other door, which opened onto the mechanical conveyance. It wasn't until Raven had entered the cage and felt it jerk upward that Sheelahn spoke. "Good luck."

When the device stopped, Raven opened another door and emerged into a massive room with a checkered floor of white and green marble, lit by chandeliers of alchemical globes.

A functionary stood waiting for her. He wore a black mask, a dark-gray coat, and his long black hair was woven into multiple braids. He appeared identical to the man who had let Raven into the building.

He bowed from the waist. "It has been a long time since another has been allowed to use the izindel."

The word wasn't from any language Raven knew, and certainly not Skanuric, the language of sorcerers.

"Hopefully it'll be the last time," she said. "Is this Kroe?"

"Indeed it is."

Raven strode to the large double doors and pulled on one of the cast-iron handles. The door opened onto a paved path that led through a grove of trees. The sun was high in the sky, and the air was a good deal cooler than in Gessa. She breathed a sigh of relief.

She turned to the functionary. "How much time has passed?"

"Approximately seven glasses," he said.

An old measurement of time, now that far more precise mechanical clocks were in circulation. One hourglass was a twentieth of a full day. Raven knew from her studies that the sun reached different parts of the land at different times.

Raven grunted and descended the wide steps to the path. She turned back to ask which way she should go, but the functionary had already closed the door.

# SIX

*Kaile, Great Southern Mountains of Ealysia*

THE FIVE MEMBERS OF THE exploratory expedition had set up their folding tables on top of a promontory jutting out from a sheer cliff that gave them a view over the entire valley. Each referred to the maps and books laid out on their tables, making sketches and penning further notes in the margins of the bundles of loose pages that made up their reports. Occasionally a glance or a word would be exchanged, but not much else. Three months out here in the remote mountain area had left them weary of one another's company. But soon they would be heading home to report on their significant discoveries to Blasius Matheo, the wealthy merchant who had funded the expedition.

Caius Jaklin, a master of the Thaumaturgy School in Kroe, pointed to a cluster of darker trees in the distance. "That's ruin…

designation, er, seven, I think."

The others followed his finger and stared at the trees. Ruin seven had almost been…ruinous for them.

"I don't care if I never see this place again," said Valtin Omer, a sorcerer famed for the prodigious capacity of his dusk-tide repository. "Those bloody dead-eyes almost did for us more than a few times."

Caius couldn't help but give him a condescending grin. "We'll be back, all of us. To find so many ruins in one place is unheard of, plus the orichalcum vein. Blasius will want to take advantage of it—and through him we'll earn more coin than you've ever imagined."

"Well, next time we'll bring more warriors, then," Valtin said, glancing at the two mercenaries engaged to escort them. "And it's not just the dead-eyes we need protection from, but the bugs that chew on you at night, and spiders the size of dinner plates—"

A thunderous crack reverberated through the air. All five of the surveyors staggered as the ground lurched under them. Valtin threw up a spherical ward around himself. His face was as white as a ghoul's.

"What the bloody hells is going on?" shouted Caius, his voice higher than normal.

There was an immense grinding sound, and they staggered again, then the ground dropped away.

Valtin glanced at Caius, eyes wild. "Run!" he shouted.

But it was too late. Screams of terror filled Caius's ears as the entire promontory plummeted several hundred yards to the valley floor. He flailed his arms, tried to think of a thaumaturgical cant to save himself, failed. The ground rushed toward him— and somehow turned to a pool of molten rock in an instant. All he could think before he hit was that someone wanted to make completely sure they all died.

An icy wind blew from the east, down the slopes of the Great Southern Mountains of Ealysia and through the streets of the city of Sansor in the country of Kaile. It sent flurries of snow at the struggling inhabitants as they fought their way home from work. A stench soured the air over the city—too many peat fires belching smoke from houses and manufactories burning coal. Lacquered wood carriages trundled along, drawn by shaggy horses resistant to the cold. On the edges of the roads trudged men and women wearing stained and patched clothes, with rags shoved into too-big boots in an effort to keep their feet from freezing. The people plodding through the snow occasionally glanced up at the wealthy driving past them, warm and carefree in their carriages, but did little more than sniff and sigh. In Sansor, where there was a great deal of wealth to be made, many thought they were merely temporarily poor, and any day their luck would change.

Blasius Matheo stared out the massive stained-glass window he'd commissioned, which featured a tree in autumn bathed in orange that never ceased to calm him. Through its panes he regarded the city that was, for all intents and purposes, his.

On the top floor of his mansion in the Merchants' District, the highest area in Sansor, his private study was perhaps the most secure place in all of Kaile, and perhaps all of Wiraya. Excluding some of the ancient ruins, of course, but only fools and sorcerers trod there. He owned every house surrounding his, and they were occupied by his private security forces. Sorcerers and mercenaries equipped with the latest, most expensive gear and weapons protected him from his city's—and the world's—competitors, adversaries, and malcontents.

A groan escaped his lips as a hunger pain twisted in his belly. His muscles were also beginning to stiffen and ache after his lengthy exercise and sparring session. He turned to a table against a wall that was filled with delicacies. He sampled some of the delights his private chefs had prepared today: pickled butterflies dusted with crystalized honey; a sharp-scented cheese writhing with maggots; transparent slices of raw horse meat with ginger and red onions; crab eggs piled atop thin wafers of bread; and, wonder of wonders, was that a Nimbras caterpillar? He skewered the legged worm, which dripped with a sweet brown sauce, and popped the entire thing in his mouth. Ah, yes! The first of the season, and all the tastier for being the most expensive. Luckily, his rigid training routine kept his heavy frame from running to fat.

Munching noisily, he moved to another table in the corner, where a bottle of his favorite wine awaited: pearlescent alchemical brandy, retrieved a few years ago from a sunken wreck that had remained undiscovered for decades. Each bottle was worth a small fortune, and he'd bought the entire shipment. He poured four fingers into a glass and dropped a cube of pressed, crystalized honey into it. To his palate, the vintage wasn't quite sweet enough. He raised the glass to his lips and sipped, pausing to appreciate the taste of the green liquid filled with yellow sparkles. He drained the glass and poured himself another before retiring to his desk, a large blackwood item with a matching chair reinforced with steel.

People would forgive him such luxuries; after all, he was the most powerful man in Kaile, and one of the wealthiest in the world. His business spanned the continents, most in and around Kaile, but some were so far-flung as to exist in places the uneducated thought were myths.

Blasius Matheo strode along the hallway that led to the Oratory Balcony. Guards in full ceremonial armor hurried to match his pace, while his secretary, Remillo, stumbled along behind them. Through the thick stone walls and metal door, Blasius could hear the hum of the crowd that had gathered outside, eager to hear his speech promising them all a better future. Idiots.

"Is there a big crowd, Remillo?" Blasius asked.

Ordinarily he wouldn't have cared. His view was that commoners were good for cheap labor, and not much else. But this speech was important. He needed the commoners on his side. And nothing would achieve that more effectively than the promise of coin for all. The discovery of the ruins and orichalcum seam would both be very lucrative new income sources for him. The mercenary he'd hired, Hanno Dinnas, had done the job he'd been paid for and killed the expeditioners and delivered their research to Blasius. If anyone of consequence found out about the discoveries, he'd make a great deal less coin. And that was unacceptable.

"Indeed it is, sir. They come to hear you speak of bringing them great wealth and defending them from Kaile's enemies. Er…you and the Ruling Council of Kaile, of course."

"Of course." Blasius fixed his secretary with a stare and the weaselly man flushed and looked away. "Is it time?"

"Almost." Remillo took a brass case out of his pocket and flipped open the lid to reveal a mechanical clock.

"I'm ready now," Blasius said. "Let's get going."

Blasius followed Remillo toward the immense bronze doors.

His secretary pulled the doors open and a wave of sound washed over them as the buzz of the crowd rose to a roar. Chest swelling with confidence and pride, Blasius strode out onto the Oratory Balcony to give one of the most important speeches of his career. The Ruling Council of Kaile had made a terrible mistake. Today was the day Blasius would turn the populace to his will and consolidate his already considerable power.

Blasius stopped at the podium, raised his arms, and waited for the cheering and thunderous applause to diminish. He wrinkled his nose at the scent of humanity rising from below, then fixed a wide smile on his face.

*City of Lipa, South of the Orgols' Kingdom*

The morning shower reluctantly yielded to allow bright blue sky to peek through a patchwork of clouds. Rain barrels overflowed and moisture dripped from eaves and foliage onto dirt roads that had turned to mud. The city of Lipa was located far inland, where humidity and encroaching vegetation were a constant. Frequent incursions of dead-eyes and ghouls had rendered its original location on the coast uninhabitable. Sorcerers capable of protecting the civilized pockets amid the wilderness were few and far between, and too expensive to keep around, except in the wealthiest cities, of which Lipa definitely wasn't one.

At the edge of the city was a sad excuse of a main market, surrounded by ramshackle buildings seemingly held together by cracked paint and makeshift repairs. Stallholders half-heartedly called to the few customers wandering around, attempting to sell fruit and vegetables; meat that already looked a bit gray; and leather goods, pottery, and copper wares. In the distance, vine-covered barricades held back the jungle's creep and the now rare dead-eye incursions.

A wagon train creaked and groaned as it entered the market, before stopping to disgorge a few travelers who'd paid for a bumpy ride from Morgane, the closest town. Traders and their hired men—guards and laborers all in one—disembarked and began to unload their goods, merchants from the nearby trading houses ambling over to browse the new deliveries.

Two women and a man emerged from the largest trading house on the edge of the market and stood on the steps leading down to the rapidly drying mud. All three wore knee-length boots—a necessity because of the constant rain at this time of year that turned the dirt paths and roads to mush. They shielded their eyes from the sun's glare. After exchanging a few last words and shaking hands, the man bowed to the women as they departed, his pale skin shining with sweat. The women produced fans, which they vigorously waved as they strolled around the worst of the mud. The man took his time, glancing across the market, looking to the streets that entered it, before walking toward a stall set in the middle of the square. He slowed to examine the wares displayed: purportedly valuable artifacts retrieved from nearby ancient ruins, but in reality tawdry representations of what an ignorant person expected such objects to look like.

Two snake-like shadows emerged from the mud, wrapping around one of the man's feet before he knew what was happening. He jerked as if stung, unable to move his boots. He opened his mouth, and another snake shot up his torso to jam itself into his throat. Screams erupted from the stallholder and passersby. Then a sharp crack sounded as the man's skull exploded, splattering blood and gray matter across the fake artifacts. His body crumpled, before what was left of his head hit the ground with a wet splat.

On the balcony of an abandoned building a hundred yards away, Abasir smiled and recalled the demonic servants. Moments later, the snakes appeared in the center of his summoning circle, which had been marked out in sparkling sand and chalk runes. He murmured a release cant and the demons vanished; then Abasir used a broom to sweep away any trace of his circle. Satisfied, he descended the deserted stairs and joined his companion, Sigrid. She was already mounted and held the reins of Abasir's horse. She eyed him without comment, then scanned the area as he climbed onto his horse. Disarming the crossbow resting on her lap, she twisted to stow the weapon in a saddlebag, and they set off away from the market.

"Did everything go well?" she asked Abasir.

Abasir wiped sweat from his brow and gave her a savage grin. "He didn't know what hit him. Grim Hand bastard. Hanno will be pleased, and so will whoever's paying us."

# SEVEN

I AM KEPT ISOLATED. FOR *my own safety, they tell me.*

*My only contact is with harsh trainers who never tell me their names. Sometimes I see other people coming and going—mostly shadowed glimpses at the end of hallways. My schedule is heavily regimented, the same exercises and training spread over three days. Roiling fury powers me. Keeps me going. Keeps me sane.*

*Anger for what I've lost.*

*Already they have broken me.*

*They will not do so again.*

*The door to my cell opens unexpectedly. Outside stands the sorcerer with the pockmarked face.*

*"Raven, come," she says.*

*"Where?" I roll off my bed, tug on clean pants and a shirt.*

*"You have recovered enough. Now it's time for the real testing to begin."*

*I back away a few steps, my rapier held in front in a middle guard position. The trainer wipes blood from his cheek with his hand, glares hate at me. He spits onto the hard-packed earth. He bleeds from two other cuts: one on his thigh and another on his side. But he doesn't call a halt to the session; nor does Scorpion from the sidelines.*

*A few weeks ago, it would have been me bleeding, me glaring hate, me hoping for a halt to be called. Now, I wait. I know I won't see this trainer again. He will disappear, like many of the others before him. I am beyond him now. Better.*

*I grasp something—a force I cannot see. They say it is an abyssal talent, one conferred upon me by my transformation. I don't know what the truth is, only that I can sense it, take hold of it, and mold the force to do my bidding.*

*The trainer shouts and lunges, but I am ready. I fling my power out, causing the scattering of loose dirt around us to swirl, to rise and dash into his face. He coughs as I slip to the side and his blade slides past. I raise my rapier. A thrusting weapon, but it has an edge. And in the right hands, an edge is all you need.*

*"Halt!" Scorpion calls.*

*My blade stops an inch from the back of the trainer's neck.*

Raven liked the White Tree Inn due to the subdued interior in dark wood paneling and the quietness of the entry foyer. She still felt uneasy about traveling almost two thousand miles in seven hours, but perhaps it was not so much the distance as the lost time in the transfer. She'd felt neither passing, but somehow the time worried her more.

Kroe was the southernmost province of the Pristart Combine, and was frequently invaded by the barbarians from the Jargalan Desert across the strait. The barbarians were mixed bloods with mostly human features—though the farther south you traveled, the more they tended toward the muscled and black-skinned pure-bloods of the deep desert Orgols. Raven herself was almost as dark as an Orgol. Indeed, it was said the gray-skinned San-Kharr race was created when Orgols bred with humans, but that was likely just a story to undermine the San-Kharr. Because of the regular invasions, Kroe was permanently on a war footing. There were squads of leather-armored soldiers at intersections, with whole companies stationed at the main gates and the harbor. Ballistae and trebuchets protecting the docks were manned day and night. There was a constant edge in the air, as if violence could erupt at any moment.

Raven paid the owner of the White Tree Inn for her room. She was of San-Kharr descent as she must be, although her skin was lighter. She hoped the woman didn't ask any awkward questions she couldn't answer about her heritage.

"There's a curfew, just imposed," the innkeeper said. "From sundown to sunrise. A barbarian raiding fleet was sighted a few days south along the peninsula."

"Raiders? What kind?" For a moment Raven thought they might be Orgols, come to find and kill her for their artifact. She hoped not, given it was now stored with Sheelahn and should be undetectable.

"The usual Orgol part-bloods. Young ones mostly, and not good sailors. But if they make landfall they can cause havoc. Vicious killers the lot of them. And I hear the Orgols are worse."

"Thank you for the room," Raven said, and left the woman

to her job.

She debated going out to scout the apartment where Crooked had been living last time she'd been in Kroe, but decided to err on the side of caution. Being out after curfew, with jumpy soldiers patrolling the streets, would be an easy way to get herself injured or locked up. She slept instead, until woken by the dawn. Her body ached, and a particularly painful cramp sent her reaching for a painkilling lozenge. She lay back down and waited for the medicine to take effect.

Once she felt more human again, she dressed in her pants and shirt, then added her knives and pouches, with her short coat over the top. She wrapped a scarf around her face to keep the dust out; as an added bonus it helped with her disguise.

A long rectangular shaft of light speared through the window, painting the floor. It almost looked like a tower.

Raven winced as needles of pain lanced through her mind. Memories erupted in a forceful wave: a great stone tower a hundred yards high; three daisies in a red enameled vase; the warmth of a comforting hand enclosing hers.

As quickly as they'd appeared the impressions faded away and Raven tottered to her bed on wobbly legs. Her heart hammered in her chest and the room spun. She couldn't focus. She sat on the bed and grasped the sheets with both shaking hands.

Where were these images from? The hand around hers…were they deeply buried childhood memories? They had to be. She focused on the bar of light on the floor again, but try as she might, she couldn't force them to return to her.

She'd thought her memories gone, along with her childhood, but it seemed that they might only have been suppressed. Was there someone who could help her unlock them? Perhaps Sheelahn?

Raven shook her head to clear it, then, feeling her strength return, leaned her elbows on the windowsill and gazed at the towers of the Thaumaturgy School, which were lit orange by the rising sun. A number of men and women were on the school's roofs, some of them naked, all facing the sun, arms outspread. Sorcerers, partaking of the dawn-tide. She'd decided the only place in Kroe that would need years of covert subterfuge to infiltrate was the Thaumaturgy School. It was as good a place to start as any. Sorcerers needed many years of training before they could effectively use the dawn- and dusk-tides, and the schools were notoriously secretive, wary of outsiders and those without power. But first she needed to gather as much information as she could to nail down Crooked's whereabouts. She doubted he'd still be at the apartment he'd been in when she'd delivered his medications, but she could always hope.

The breakfast the inn served was quite delicious: flatcakes the size of a plate, smothered with a sweet syrup and fresh fruit, along with all the hot tea she could drink. She had to stop herself eating too much or she'd feel lethargic.

Afterwards, she took a single-horse trap to the busy marketplace. She spread a few coins around and soon had the name of a shady information dealer named Beetle. His office was at the top of a narrow staircase, which creaked as if it had been constructed for that specific purpose. Raven pushed the door open and entered. Shelves filled most of the room, crowded with books, statues and carvings, a large shell, wooden boxes and leather folders, jars of powders and herbs.

Behind a desk sat an imposing man. He was clad in a tight, dark-blue shirt that accentuated his muscular arms; his head and face were shaved clean. Beetle, she presumed. He was writing on a sheet of paper and didn't seem to notice her arrival.

Raven waited. She could be as patient as a stone if she decided to be, and in fact had once spent a night at the bottom of a pond clutching a stone and breathing through a reed in order to surprise a mark.

Eventually, he looked up. "Sit, please," he said in a quiet but firm tone.

She sat in the chair in front of the desk. "I need you to find a man for me."

"Straight to business. I like that. But a woman like you shouldn't have trouble finding a man."

Raven frowned, before realizing what he meant. "Not a lover. Or a husband. An associate I've lost track of."

"Name and description?"

"How about we talk price first?"

Beetle pursed his lips and gazed at the ceiling, moving his head from side to side as if calculating. "Twenty silver talents."

Raven scoffed. "No. Five now, five if you find him. And I need it done quickly."

"Speed will cost extra."

"It won't."

Beetle's eyes narrowed, but he nodded. "I should have known. You look like trouble."

"You should see me on a bad day," Raven said. "I'll be waiting in the market around the corner. Send someone to find me."

She gave him a description of Crooked, and places she thought he was likely to frequent. Apothecaries who dealt in cravv would be a good starting place.

"Miss?" said a young woman wearing tight woolen pants and

ineptly concealed daggers. Her hair was long and loose and would be a distraction in a fight.

Raven placed her half-drunk tea on the table and reached for the piece of folded paper the woman held out.

The woman pulled it back and smiled. "Five silvers is what Beetle said."

Raven handed over the coins in exchange for the note. "Why is he called Beetle?" she asked.

"His shiny head, of course."

Raven scanned the note's contents. A man matching Crooked's description frequented an apothecary close to the Thaumaturgy School, as well as a nearby brothel. That sounded like Crooked. At the bottom was an address of an apartment.

Raven walked to the area where the apartment was located and wandered around to acquaint herself with the surrounding streets. It was quite close to the Thaumaturgy School, but on the opposite side from the White Tree Inn, and it seemed less affluent—most likely because of the nearby tanneries and leatherworkers, dyers, alchemists and apothecaries. The stench of the manufactories filled the air. But for Crooked, with his need for frequent medication, it meant supplies easily available and close by.

She approached the apartment from a back alley, trying to look like she was hurrying to somewhere important in case anyone was watching. Her eyes drifted up to the top-floor window, and her heart skipped a beat. A lamp burned atop a pile of books on the windowsill. It was a signal she knew from her past. It meant danger. She doubted that an occupant other than Crooked just happened to mimic one of the Grim Hand's signals.

She kept moving into the next street, then stopped to peer through the window of a clothing store, using the reflection to check the streets behind her. Three men lounged against a carriage, as if waiting for their employer to return. Two other men, engaged in a heated discussion, walked along the street toward Raven. She placed a hand on the hilt of a knife and didn't relax even when they continued past without anything untoward happening.

She couldn't stand around in the street for too long without attracting unwanted attention. She circled around the back of the apartment again, this time with an eye to whether someone was surveilling it. A difficult task, given the multi-storied buildings all around that could hide a watcher behind a window, but perhaps she could question some of the locals. Every neighborhood had a few unemployed busybodies, some of whom would sell their mothers for a copper talent or two. She made another circuit, then, before returning to the main street, she unwrapped her headscarf and tucked it into a pocket. It wasn't much of a change, but it was the best she could do. Her coat had to stay on, or she'd reveal her weapons.

She crossed the road in front of the apartment building and entered a general store, where she busied herself browsing the goods on display—mostly victuals and household odds and ends. The proprietor, an old woman with thinning gray hair tied up in a bun, gave her the once-over before returning to hanging bunches of onions and garlic on hooks attached to the ceiling beams.

Raven examined a few wooden and copper spoons on a table in the front window, all the while glancing outside. This was her only lead, and she couldn't risk barging in until she knew the situation.

A tinkle of broken glass reached her ears, followed by a muted thump. The floor shook, rattling the glassware in the shop.

"Oh, my goodness, what was that?" gasped the proprietor.

Raven rushed outside to see smoke belching from the top floor of the building opposite—the floor where Crooked's apartment was. Flames licked the window from the inside.

A quick glance down both sides of the street, and she saw the three men leaning against the carriage had gone. She could just see the back of the carriage as it disappeared around a corner.

"Fire!" someone shouted, and more people crowded into the street, gazing up at the building, which was now billowing smoke.

A few dashed into other buildings and emerged with buckets, then ran down a side street. There must be a fountain or water pump close by, Raven realized, as people returned with full buckets and rushed into the building and up the main stairs.

She had to get out of here. The danger signal had been a warning for whoever Crooked was working with. But she couldn't leave without knowing if he was injured or dead. She raced to the side of the building and climbed the corner blocks of stone until she reached the roof. Onlookers would think she was attempting a rescue; and if someone else was watching, she was happy to blow her cover to find out what she needed to.

She grabbed the edge of the roof and wriggled along until she was beside Crooked's window. The glass had been blown out in the explosion, and smoke poured from the opening, but that meant the floor of the room should be clear. She stepped onto the sill and ducked inside, keeping low—and winced as heat washed over her. Flames licked the ceiling and two walls.

A charred and blistered body lay against a wall, facing away from her, clothes burned to blackened shreds. Raven scrambled over to it, hot air scalding her lungs, grabbed the shoulder and rolled the figure onto its back.

She gasped when its eyes opened.

"Ra…ven," breathed Crooked. "You…dead."

His face was cracked and red, but he'd managed to shield it from the worst of the explosion. The rest of his body hadn't fared well. He had to be in immense pain. She unwrapped one of her lozenges and shoved it into his mouth.

Crooked spluttered, and his tongue shoved the gummy mass out. "No…point." He was dying and he knew it. There was only so much damage a body could take, even a transformed one, before it gave out.

"Where's the meeting place?" Raven asked.

When an operation went sideways like this, the imperative was to disappear, make sure you weren't being followed, and return to a nearby base of operations.

"Herb—" Crooked broke off, wheezing, and his eyes closed.

When Raven had been here last time, she'd picked up a package of painkillers for Crooked from an herbalist in a village on the outskirts of Kroe. The woman was a go-between, unaware of the machinations of the people she was dealing with; but Raven remembered her incessant chatter, and her mention of another house close by that she owned and rented out to "warrior-looking types" who were hardly ever there. Raven had assumed it was one of the safe houses the Grim Hand used when they ran operations in the area. They usually had a few available and swapped between them.

Crooked's blackened hand twitched, and his eyes opened to slits. "We were…failures…even when…we thought we weren't."

"What do you mean? We survived. We passed their tests."

"Jealousy…betrayal…the Cabal." Crooked's face twisted in pain. "Kill…me."

"I can't, Crooked. Don't ask…"

But she couldn't leave him like this, wishing for the agony of his charred body to stop. Death would be a mercy, wouldn't it? Her own skin burned in the heat; her flesh felt as if it were cooking. She couldn't stay here much longer.

She clasped Crooked's hand, then thought better of squeezing it. "Go in peace," she said, and stood and drew her rapier.

Its ensorcelled steel shimmered in the flickering orange light of the fire as Raven thrust the blade into Crooked's heart. He convulsed, then his chest fell and didn't rise again.

She wiped her weapon clean, then left the same way she'd come. This time, she hung at full stretch from the sill and dropped to the ground before disappearing down a back street.

Her thoughts churned feverishly as she walked. It seemed Crooked's mission or his cover had been compromised. By whom? Maybe Beetle had sold him out. Maybe not. He'd mentioned a Cabal…who did he mean?

If he'd survived, Crooked would have headed to the safe house near the herbalist's. The team members would gather there to discuss what had gone wrong, and whether it was possible to continue the mission, or whether it was a failure and they should scatter. Raven had no idea how large the team would be, but it had to be more than just Crooked. The Grim Hand wouldn't keep someone like him in one location for such a length of time unless the mission was extremely important.

Back at the inn, she packed up her belongings, then paid for another night to throw off any potential pursuers. With any luck they would wait for her to return to her room, but she'd be long gone. And finding some answers to the questions that plagued her.

*"You're doing well, Raven. Very well."*

*Scorpion stands beside me as I wolf down a heaped plate of boiled potatoes with chunks of mutton slathered in gravy. I am always fed more than enough; and after this there will be fruit and berries and nuts.*

*I ignore him and continue eating. It has been another long day, and all I want to do is fill my belly and bathe and sleep.*

*"Some say your progress is astounding. What do you think?"*

*"I think," I mumble around a mouthful, "that I'll never trust sorcerers again."*

*"I'm a sorcerer."*

*I meet his eye, raise my eyebrows, then look back to my plate. I know that sorcerers have separate stores for both dawn- and dusk-tide energies, which they refill at those respective times. Part of my training covers what sorcery can and can't do, and I've learned that my dark-tide energy works on the same principle. This ability to draw on and manipulate the dark-tide is one of the reasons I am so valuable to my creators. It is usually only the province of demons from the abyssal realms, and as such is undetectable by normal sorcerers and difficult to defend against. My ability to manipulate objects without touching them has great possibilities, I've been told.*

*I've left my true name and identity behind and become…what? A killer? Not yet, but I think that day is not far off.*

*"It's about time you met the rest of us in the Grim Hand," says Scorpion. "We are all like you, and yet all different. We are a family."*

*I swallow, consider taking another mouthful but resist. My eyes burn for no reason I can fathom.*

Close to the gate in the city walls, Raven paid for a scruffy-looking nag, along with a saddle and bridle that looked like they might fall apart at any moment. She wasn't choosy when it came to horses. Despite its looks, the mount made good time along the packed-earth roads until they reached the edge of the herbalist's village in the late afternoon. Even though it had been years since Raven had passed this way, her memory was sharp. She remembered to take the left fork at a field of sunflowers—though at this time of year the flowers had been rotated out for potatoes—and the right path just after a stone bridge traversing a stream.

As she approached the village, two soldiers left the concealment of some bushes and held up their hands for her to halt. They both wore the standard leather armor of Kroe, and she recognized the badges on their breast that indicated they belonged to an elite squad. Both carried loaded crossbows, along with an assortment of knives. Behind them, in the village's main street, she could now see more soldiers. Two squatted next to a body lying on the dark-stained dirt, and a few more rested in front of a tavern. Judging by the number of horses hitched around the street, there must have been at least a dozen of them. She needed to focus. She should have detected the soldiers earlier as she approached the village, but her thoughts had wandered.

Raven tugged her coat tighter around her and hunched over the saddle. "What's going on? Was the village attacked? I heard there were dead-eyes about. Was it dead-eyes? Is everyone all right? What's that in the street? Did someone die?"

She'd seen enough to know there'd been a fight, but had the soldiers from Kroe been involved, or had they been brought in afterward?

"Whatever business you have here," the older soldier said, "you'd better head back home. It's not safe."

"I came to see the herbalist. Is she all right? I need to see her urgently about my ma. Women's troubles." She gave them a tentative smile and blinked rapidly. The state of her horse should allay any fears they might have about her. It was the mount of a poor person, not a warrior.

"I believe the herbalist is fine," the younger soldier said. He had a hardness about him that Raven recognized as the result of intense training and a willingness to kill.

"The village is off-limits," added the older man. "We have orders to stop anyone from entering."

"Are you sure you can't make an exception?"

The soldiers both stiffened. "Turn around and go back home. We'll likely be done by the morning, so you can return then."

Charming her way through wouldn't work. She would have to try stealth. "All right, then. I'll come back tomorrow. My ma's going to be upset, though."

Raven turned her horse and kept its pace to a walk until she rounded a bend in the road. She gave it another couple of hundred yards before pulling off into a copse of trees. By now the sun was setting and visibility was rapidly diminishing. She dismounted and tied the reins to a branch. The nag whinnied, and she gave it a few hard pats on the neck, raising dust and fine hairs that caused her to sneeze.

If Scorpion had been here, he wouldn't be any longer, not now the place was crawling with soldiers. Her lead had unraveled quickly and now looked to be entirely gone. All her effort had been in vain, and she'd wasted one of the favors Sheelahn owed her.

But who had caused the commotion in the village and destroyed Crooked's apartment? Were they the same person or organization? There was too much she didn't know, and she was in unfamiliar territory.

Once night had truly fallen, she wrapped her scarf around her head and face, leaving only her eyes exposed, and rubbed dirt around them and on her eyelids so her skin didn't shine. As silent as a shadow, she made her way through the trees and around scrubby bushes to the village. Through gaps in the buildings she could see more soldiers carrying torches, and a number of villagers talking to them. The soldiers had stationed guards around the village at regular intervals. She waited long enough to determine they hadn't set patrols; but they likely would as the night wore on and most of them settled into sleep.

She kept her eyes on the darkness at one side of a building fifty yards away and poured her awareness into the shadows surrounding her. Her body and mind melted and re-formed next to the wall. This time the shadow-step didn't weary her anywhere near as much. The orichalcum sphere was doing its job of enhancing her innate talent.

She pressed her back to the wall and waited. She knew she hadn't been seen, but had her burst of dark-tide energy been sensed? There was a remote chance a sorcerer could have been alerted. Caution was her ally now, and she wouldn't rush. Didn't need to. With her artifact back in her hands she was an even more formidable opponent, and the soldiers presented little challenge. But sometimes killing wasn't the best way to get what you wanted.

Two soldiers carrying torches passed the gap between buildings where she was hiding. Raven closed her eyes and froze, waiting for their footsteps to fade. Angry voices reached her, and she decided to risk moving closer. With one eye on the main street and another above her, she climbed onto a rain barrel and pulled herself atop the roof. Only the faint scrape of cloth on wood marked her passage, a sound no one was likely to notice. She edged up to the ridge of the roof on her stomach and made her way down the other side head-first until she could hear the soldiers and villagers involved in the heated discussion.

"He was here in the afternoon," said one.

"Nay, it was the morning," said another.

Raven figured these were the villagers the soldiers were questioning.

"Janner had already gone to the tavern, and you know he don't start drinking until after his missus has left to make her regular delivery to Rangar," the first voice said.

"He does, too!" the second voice replied, and both guffawed like snorting pigs, as if there were a joke in what they'd said.

Raven surmised Janner's missus did more than just make a delivery to Rangar, which might be why Janner drank.

"Enough of that!" said one of the soldiers. "What did the stranger look like? Where did he go?"

"Ugly as sin, he was," the first villager replied.

"Face like it was carved out of soft clay," added the other. "Big nose, too."

"He wasn't tall, but he walked like he was. Had muscles on him same as a blacksmith."

"Arrogant bastard," the second villager put in.

Scorpion had been here! This was better than Raven had dared hope.

"Where did he go?" the soldier asked. "Was he looking for anyone in particular?"

"He didn't go nowhere! As soon as he rode into the village, all hells broke loose!"

"A crossbow bolt missed my head by a whisker!" added the other villager.

"How many men attacked him?"

"Ten."

"More like twenty!" the other man corrected. "They came out of the woodwork and began launching bolts like an army was coming."

"It was ten," the first man said again.

The soldiers' sighs reached Raven's ears, and she suppressed a smile.

"So that was when the ugly man was skewered?" one of them asked.

"No! That's the funny thing. The bolts all missed him, even though he didn't move. They all just zipped past him."

"All except one," added the other villager. "Took him in the shoulder it did. Then he vanished!"

"Sorcery it was." Raven could sense the first villager nodding vigorously.

"Right," said the soldier. "And then the men shooting at him started dying?"

"There was a strange noise—like a banshee wail, but quiet, like."

"A low whistling," added the other. "*Whee. Whee.* And blood spurted from the crossbowmen like they'd been hit."

"But they hadn't. There were no bolts. No arrows. It was sorcery."

"Sorcery," the second villager agreed.

"Our sorcerer found no trace of dawn- or dusk-tide power having been used," said one of the soldiers.

"Well, we ain't lying!"

"Saw it clear as day," the other man agreed.

"So, then what happened?"

"The crossbowmen ran around trying to find where he'd vanished to. A few more ended up dead. Then they stopped dying, and the others worked out the man must have fled."

"So you didn't see if he was going to meet someone?" the other soldier asked.

"No, sir. Like we said, it all happened as soon as he arrived. Like they was waiting for him."

"Where did the crossbowmen go? Which direction?"

"We didn't really see."

"We was hiding by then."

"All right. You two go back home, and don't leave the village. We might have more questions for you tomorrow. And you, bring the tavern keeper to me. I want to talk to him."

Raven kept her head down as the two villagers wandered off, followed by one of the Kroe soldiers. So, Scorpion had been there, and had escaped. He'd swirled the air around him to deflect missiles, and wrapped shadows around himself to vanish. But he'd taken a bolt to the shoulder. Not an easy thing to remove or bandage oneself. The fact he'd only used his dark-tide talents and not sorcery meant his attackers hadn't presented much of a threat. Raven knew Scorpion had strict orders to use his sorcery only in an emergency. That kind of power drew attention. An unknown sorcerer killing people in Kroe would have brought down a heavy hand in response.

Raven edged back up the roof until she could turn around safely, then continued over the ridge. She didn't bother lowering herself to the ground. Instead she looked toward the trees outside the village. There was one that was larger than the others, with darkness gathered around its base. She shadow-stepped to the tree and made her way back to her horse. A short time later she was mounted and heading back to Kroe.

She felt certain Scorpion would recover from the bolt to his shoulder, though there could be complications if the tip had been poisoned like those she'd taken from her assailants on the island. If it was, he'd need help, and fast. The village herbalist probably didn't have the required skills, which meant he'd have to go back to Kroe. Which was why Raven was heading back there too.

As she rode, she considered the fact that she now had even more questions than answers.

Who had attacked Scorpion? And what did they want? If they wanted to kill him, as Crooked had been killed, then why? And were the killers the same people who wanted Raven dead? Or someone else?

# EIGHT

RAVEN KNOCKED ONCE AGAIN AT the door of the Ethereal Sorceress's imposing building. While she was reluctant to use the last favor the sorceress owed her, she didn't have a lot of choices. She had no other contacts in Kroe and needed information fast.

Another gray-coated and black-masked functionary opened the door.

"I'm expected," Raven said, and stepped onto the white and green marble tiles.

The man remained silent, but followed her to the mechanical contraption and allowed her to descend in the elaborate metal cage.

When Raven stepped out, Sheelahn was waiting for her. The sorceress looked exactly the same as she had in Gessa: the sharp-edged robe, and the mask with only inky darkness behind it.

"You are here for your remaining favor," she said, before

Raven had a chance to speak.

"Yes. I need to—"

"It is your last one."

"I know. A friend was injured and—"

"Would you like more?"

That threw Raven. "Excuse me? No. I need to find a man who took a crossbow bolt to the shoulder, possibly poisoned. He's probably in Kroe looking for treatment. He has to keep a low profile, so it'll be an underground healer, maybe someone who works for the Night Shadows, the thieves' association."

"I can already tell you your friend is safe."

"You don't even know who he is!"

Sheelahn's mask stared at Raven. "His name is Scorpion. If I am wrong, I will owe you two favors."

For long moments they looked at each other. This woman was scary, decided Raven, but useful. Whatever trick she had used to move Raven from Gessa to Kroe in less than a day was extremely valuable. Perhaps Raven could prevail on the Ethereal Sorceress to perform the trick a few more times, to any city she wanted. But was she being reckless to put herself into debt with someone so powerful? Maybe.

Bloody sorcerers. After what they had done to her and the others, she'd wanted nothing to do with them. Sheelahn had proved useful so far, but that didn't mean she wasn't just like everyone else.

"He is healing?" she queried.

"Would you like more favors?" Sheelahn replied.

Raven nodded reluctantly. "What would I have to do?"

"Deliver a package for me. Do not look inside."

Raven's eyes narrowed with suspicion. "That's all?"

"Not quite. The recipient may seem strange to you. Or not.

Only you will know."

"That's a bit vague. Strange in what way?"

"Return here once you have completed the task. If you sense anything from him, you will let me know."

"How many favors is this task worth to you?"

The orichalcum mask tilted to the right slightly, as if Sheelahn were considering. "Three."

Three jumps of incredible distance, all for delivering a package and revealing if she felt anything strange. It seemed too good to be true. In Raven's experience, such things often were. Still, it wouldn't hurt to bargain a little, and she was confident she could take care of herself if the task turned out to be dangerous.

"Five," she countered.

"Two," came the reply.

*Bloody darkness!* The sorceress had her over a barrel.

"Two for the delivery, one for reporting on what I feel," she said.

"One for the delivery…two for reporting back to me."

Ah. So the package was almost incidental. It was possible to get Sheelahn to reveal more than she wanted. Her rigid adherence to the strict terms of a bargain had its weaknesses—something that might be open to exploitation. Then again, one trifled with a sorceress as powerful as this at one's own risk.

"Agreed," Raven said.

"Also agreed. The bargain is struck."

A small package appeared in Sheelahn's open palm. By sorcery of some kind, Raven thought, unless she stored all sorts of things under those robes.

The package was surprisingly heavy for its size, and was wrapped in plain waxed paper tied with string. It would be easy enough to open and examine it, then return the wrapping to its original condition, but Raven had already decided not to pry. She was in enough trouble already, without inviting more.

"Who and where do I deliver it to?" she asked.

"The sorcerer Akatta Palek. His mansion is on Short Street in the city of Almeria, Castle Blackstone District."

She knew the city well. Almeria was one of half a dozen fortified enclaves along the coast of the Orgols' kingdom, and was the third closest to the Orgols' capital, Lorestone Citadel. She really didn't want to go back there, of all places, but it seemed she had no choice. In Orgol lands, their shamanistic sorcery might be able to pick up her trail, and then she'd be in dire trouble. This was a risk she'd normally be unwilling to take, but Scorpion's life was on the line. "You'll be transporting me there, I assume?"

"Yes. Akatta Palek is expecting the delivery. You may say you represent me in this."

"All right. Now, I need more information about Scorpion."

"The task first."

"Time is not on my side—"

"It is, if you trust me. Complete the task. Then return to me."

Raven glared at the sorceress, but there wasn't much she could do. Hopefully she could get to Almeria and back relatively quickly.

Sheelahn took Raven to the room with the circle of runed orichalcum set into the granite floor. The sorceress chanted in Skanuric and Raven's awareness splintered as she was scattered across a void. Again there were lights, the boom of thunder, and burning, as reality twisted her.

Raven came-to lying curled on the granite floor. Not *the* granite floor where she'd stood before: another. Her head spun and ears rang, and her chest heaved at the taste of bile in her mouth.

Sheelahn stood there, motionless, as if nothing had happened. "Come," she said.

Raven dragged herself to her feet and staggered after the sorceress, who led her through corridors to another mechanical contrivance. "I'll be back soon," she said.

"My powers will take a short time to recharge. Return after dusk," said Sheelahn.

Which meant the translocation sorcery used the dusk-tide. Raven nodded and filed the knowledge away in case it proved useful.

She ascended and disembarked into yet another room with a checkered floor of white and green marble, to be greeted by another black-masked, gray-coated functionary. The man bowed, then led her to the exit of the strange building.

Outside, the air was arid and scorching, the sun blazing from a clear sky, prickling her skin. Raven squinted and shielded her eyes with a hand.

She managed to hail a covered trap pulled by a varan lizard, and as she headed toward Short Street, Raven considered the package she'd been given. If she kept it in her peripheral vision, she fancied she could see a faint corona surrounding it.

"Short Street," her driver announced.

Raven handed him a coin and disembarked. The street lived up to its name: a short street, crowded with mansions. The Castle Blackstone District had long been home to the ultra-wealthy and powerful, though the castle it had been named for had been sacked and burned in an Orgol invasion centuries ago. Its skeletal ruin had been left as a reminder to all citizens.

Muscled and armored guards stood in front of the flat-faced mansions that lined Short Street. Among them was a skinny woman barely out of her teens, with oily brown hair and a permanent squint.

As she approached, Raven kept her hands clear of her knives, and held out the package. "I'm here to deliver this to Akatta Palek."

"Piss off," grumbled a guard.

Raven swallowed a retort and gave him her best smile. "I'm on the Ethereal Sorceress's business." If they had half a brain, the guards would realize no one would claim to work for Sheelahn unless it was true, or want to meet a sorcerer of Akatta Palek's power unless they had good reason.

At Raven's words, the skinny woman frowned and moved between the guards to stand in front of her. "You're not a sorcerer," she said.

"I didn't say I was," Raven replied.

"Give me the package. I'll deliver it, and you can consider your task complete."

Raven guessed she was probably the sorcerer's apprentice, taking in the valuable lesson of standing around waiting for something to happen.

"No. I am to make sure I put it into Akatta Palek's hands myself."

The woman chewed her bottom lip, probably considering how much trouble she'd be in if it turned out Raven was lying. Then she turned and pushed her way through the guards toward the mansion's main door. "Let her through, you dimwits. If she's lying, the master will deal with her."

The guards sneered at the woman's back as they moved aside. If there was an attack on the mansion, it was unlikely the woman would receive the support she expected, Raven thought.

Inside, she led Raven up a magnificent stone staircase with a decorative iron railing. Raven noted the girl's hair wasn't just oily; she had a mild case of dandruff.

"You should treat the guards with more respect," Raven volunteered. "You might need them to watch your back one day."

"Curb your tongue," the woman snarled. "You'll speak only when asked a question."

That was fine by Raven. There was no helping some people.

They walked down a corridor, the apprentice's boots tapping on polished timbers, until they came to a door no different from all the others they had passed. The apprentice uttered a cant under her breath to open the door.

Inside, a man in a severe black coat sat behind a large desk piled high with papers. He had short, iron-gray hair and eyes of deep blue. A red kerchief poking from a pocket was the only color he wore, and his only jewelry was a ring of gold. The square face of the ring was divided into four smaller squares; each segment containing a Skanuric rune.

"There had better be a good reason for this interruption," he told his apprentice.

"This woman claims to be on the Ethereal Sorceress's business, master."

"And she wouldn't say that unless it were true. Was that your logic?"

"Er…yes."

"I suppose I should give up expecting better of you. You're dismissed."

The woman's mouth sagged with disappointment. She turned to leave.

"Wash your hair," Raven said, and the woman gave her a startled look. Raven just winked and turned back to the sorcerer. Whatever Sheelahn had expected to happen hadn't yet. Raven didn't know whether to be grateful or disappointed.

Akatta Palek waited until the woman closed the door before speaking, and in those few moments Raven felt a tug such as she'd never experienced before—as if she knew this sorcerer somehow, and there was a kinship between them, an attraction. She kept her face impassive, though her mind roiled. This must be what Sheelahn had hoped for, but Raven had no idea what it meant.

Akatta gave no indication that he felt the same urge. He clicked his fingers. "Bring the package here."

Raven placed it in his waiting palm. The sorcerer stared at it for an instant before sitting it on the desk in front of him.

"You have not tampered with it?"

"No."

"Discretion and a lack of curiosity are valuable traits in a servant."

She wasn't a servant—at least she didn't think so, yet. But Sheelahn's words ran through her mind: *I have need for one such as you.* Raven wondered what she'd been dragged into.

"There's something about you," continued Akatta. "A very faint something. At first I thought you were a sorcerer, but I see you are not. What is it?"

"I don't know. Perhaps it's the touch of the Ethereal Sorceress."

A nod. Pursed lips. "Perhaps. But you look familiar. Or perhaps I've read about you. Are you wanted by the Watch? No…that's not it. I should remember someone as interesting as you. Never mind, it will come to me."

He stood and moved around the desk. Raven almost reached for a knife and her artifact, before noticing he held out a small rectangle of cream-colored paper. A business card.

She took it hesitantly; the closer he came, the stronger her attraction to him. It wasn't right. These weren't her real feelings.

As her finger brushed his, a wave of revulsion flowed through her. It was all she could do to stop herself screaming and fleeing—from the man, the room, the building.

She clenched her jaw and backed up a step. Underneath the attraction, which she could smell now as a physical scent, was another trace: an animal reek, the likes of which she'd only smelled a few times previously—when she was strapped down beside the demon and the sorcerers had conducted their vile experiments on her.

Akatta either didn't notice her disgust, or considered she was merely afraid as was his due.

"If you tire of Sheelahn's employ, come to me," he told her. "She sees something in you, enough to make you her servant. That makes you valuable. And I like to collect valuable things."

Raven didn't trust herself to speak. She nodded and left the room. Once in the hallway she quickened her pace until she almost tripped down the stairs in her haste.

The apprentice was waiting at the bottom and gave Raven a disdainful sneer as she rushed past.

# NINE

"IS THIS A JOKE?" YELLED Blasius Matheo. "This is the news you bring me?" He hurled the crystal glass filled with pearlescent alchemical brandy against the wall. The glass smashed and fragments tumbled across a thick rug, while the green liquid dribbled down the timber-paneled wall.

The bearer of bad news, Hanno Dinnas, stood as still as a statue. He was obviously seething at being dressed down, but kept a tight rein on his emotions. Only a tic under his left eye and the precise tightness of his words betrayed his anger.

"Yes. The man escaped us. But he was wounded—a poisoned crossbow bolt to the shoulder. It shouldn't take long to find him. He has to be in Kroe. We're staking out all the town's herbalists, apothecaries, and physicians. He'll turn up. Then we have him."

"I'm paying you a good deal of coin," Blasius said. "So why is it, when I ask you to kill someone, you end up bringing me excuses instead of their heads? First the woman, and now the man she worked with." He poured himself another drink of the alchemical wine, but it tasted like vinegar. He swallowed it anyway. "Tell me, Hanno, do you want to get paid? Is this the result you promised?"

"I agree that it isn't the result we expected," Hanno said. "However, there must be more to the situation than we first thought. The man, Scorpion, was a sorcerer of some kind. And either the woman had help, or she is a sorcerer as well. We know she doesn't have arcane powers—the dawn- and dusk-tides are closed to her. Yet still she managed to kill most of the group I sent after her, and they were all experienced warriors, though they did hire local help. I've never seen anything like it before. It's interesting—"

"I don't give a bloody ball sack if it's interesting," Blasius yelled. "I want her dead! What are you doing to find her again?"

"We're doing all we can. But once a target is alerted, the difficulty increases significantly. Especially if that person is skilled and has had professional training, which she obviously has."

Blasius stared into his wine. A vein throbbed in his forehead, and he felt like punching someone bloody. "I don't care how many men it takes or how much it costs—I want her found. I want her killed and her head brought to me here, so I can piss on it. Is that clear?"

Hanno nodded. "Once she is located, I will supervise her death myself. I guarantee she will not escape a second time. I'll return when I have something to report." He backed away and left the room.

Blasius let him go, then rubbed his eyes. None of this was supposed to be complicated. Find them and kill them. Job done. Move on to the next problem. But apparently the gods had other ideas. First the woman had slaughtered one of Hanno's elite mercenary teams on her own. And shortly after, the brains behind the City State's elite Grim Hand force had escaped a straightforward assassination and was now on the run when he should be in a shallow grave feeding the worms. It was an unmitigated disaster.

He went to take another sip of wine, but his mouth crinkled in distaste. This whole affair had soured his stomach. He didn't even feel like eating the herb-stuffed piglet he'd had his kitchen prepare.

Hanno might not have seen anything like this before, but Blasius had.

He sat dawn and placed his glass on the desk and removed an artifact from a drawer: a silver cage pressed around a cut diamond. The sorcerer he'd hired to make it had charged him a fortune, but if you couldn't use your wealth to buy what you wanted, then what good was it? He hesitated, clenching the caged gem in one hand, then dropped it into his glass, where it sank to the bottom of the liquor.

*Why do I torture myself?*

*Because I don't want to forget.*

Blasius leaned forward and concentrated on the gem. He had a very slight sorcerous talent, sufficient to trigger some artifacts and that was all. But it was enough. The liquid in his glass swirled and turned clear, then an image of a sprawling estate appeared. It was as if Blasius was looking down on the scene from a high tower. The picture was amazingly clear and lifelike, which was no surprise really. After all, it had happened in real life. The sorcerer had taken weeks to scry back in time, then store the images for Blasius to access whenever he wanted. There was no sound, but he could manipulate the recording to a limited degree: pause it when he wanted, bring closer any details he might care to examine. He had done it all before, many times, and already knew everything there was to find.

There was movement at the far edge of the estate. A man fell backward onto sandy pavers, crimson spraying from his chest and splashing across the ground. The blur appeared, almost too fast to see: a figure clad in black, moving with speed and agility. One moment the image was empty, and the next the figure sprang to life from one of the walls, as if it had been invisible or camouflaged. It streaked down the building toward the side entrance, and the image flickered and changed.

Blasius was now looking at an interior door. His hands gripped the edge of the desk and his breath came in hurried gasps. He forced himself to calm down, and wished he'd poured a separate glass of the wine to drink. The door was ornate, made from a rare, walnut-colored wood. The black-clad figure stepped toward it. From the shape of the torso and legs he could tell it was a woman. A long strip of dyed linen was wrapped around her head so only her eyes were visible, but a braid of platinum hair hung down her back. She moved stealthily, footsteps precise, but carried no weapon. That was something that always troubled Blasius: the guard had been killed, but with what?

The recording shifted to inside the room. Blasius's sister, Madlen, stared out the window, but kept glancing over her shoulder at the open door to her study. With a quick jerk she pulled the drapes almost closed, then peered through the crack. Blasius knew what Madlen was seeing and feeling. Her stomach would be twisted with fear as she noticed that none of the guards were patrolling outside.

She left the window, entered her study, and pulled a bell rope beside her desk. Chimes sounded faintly from elsewhere in the house, but no guards came running. Madlen moved back to her desk, buckled on a knife belt and reached for a crossbow. With a few cranks of its lever it was primed, and she slotted a bolt into the runnel. She skulked to the door, head tilted to listen for any untoward sounds. Her hands gripped the crossbow so tightly her knuckles were white.

As Madlen reached for the door, the dark figure detached from the shadows beside a bookcase. Madlen pivoted, bringing up the crossbow, but the assassin's knife flashed and bit into the meat of her thigh. Madlen screamed and shot the bolt, which missed her attacker and hammered into the wall. The crossbow fell from her hands and she scrabbled for her knife.

The assassin plunged her blade into Madlen's abdomen, angled up to penetrate the heart. Madlen's pale green eyes were wide with shock and her blood poured over her killer's hand. Her lips stretched thin as she attempted to say something, then the life left her eyes and she slumped to the ground, the knife sticking out of her chest.

As it always did, the image brought Blasius almost physical pain, and it felt like a fist squeezed his heart.

The assassin bent and slipped a ring from Madlen's finger, then pocketed it—presumably proof of a successful kill. Then, as it did every time, the impossible happened. The assassin looked directly at Blasius, as if she knew he was watching. For a brief instant, he peered into her soul as she gazed at something that wasn't there. The sorcerer who had scried the incident had assured Blasius that nothing he did had any effect on the past; he was merely reading the echoes of events. But every time Blasius watched the recording, he felt as if the assassin were staring right at him.

He froze the image and examined the figure for the hundredth time, searching for something he might have missed. As always, he found nothing.

He continued the recording, and watched the figure exit the room, leaving bloody footprints on the rug that stretched along the corridor. Then he cut the flow of sorcery and the image faded.

The liquid in his glass returned to its original sparkly green, and Blasius drained it in one gulp, feeling the gem pressing against his lips. He lurched out of his seat, poured himself another measure of the wine, and drained it. He knew from past experience it would be a long night, and he'd be exhausted and hungover tomorrow if he continued to drink, but he was unable to stop himself. He returned to his desk, this time cradling two glasses, and drank from one while he once more triggered the sorcerous vision.

The image of the black ghost who tormented him flickered to life. The ghost who had killed his beloved sister. The demon spawn who had a name: Raven, of the Grim Hand.

He watched again, transfixed, his jaw rigid with anger, teeth grinding.

# TEN

AS I TUCK THE ARTIFACT *into my shirt, its power throbs against my chest, even through the blackwood shavings packed around it in the blackwood box; even though, as an extra precaution, the container has been lined with orichalcum hammered thinner than a sheet of paper.*

*It is smaller than I thought it would be. For a sorcerous artifact sacred to the Orgols, one of seven they'd made thousands of years ago when they'd decided to murder their god and take the divine's power, it should be bigger—in keeping with its significance.*

*"They're on my trail," says Moonshadow. "I have to keep moving. Don't look at it, Raven. Don't let it touch your skin."*

*"Good luck," I reply, already scanning the rooftops from the shadowed alley where we squat.*

*"If you're caught, try to dispose of the artifact somehow. If you're at sea, throw it overboard. Anywhere else…you'll think of something. Down a sewer drain, or get a chicken to swallow it."*

*Moonshadow's jokes suffer under stress. "Was it true? What they told us?" I briefly stop my scan of the surroundings to gaze at Moonshadow. His face is paler than usual, even in the heat of the Orgol climate. Fear, I realize. And he's the mightiest of us all. A powerful sorcerer as well as strong with the dark-tide. My meager abilities are a candle to his fire.*

*"That it can extract a person's soul or essence and merge it into the essence of the person holding the pyramid, to increase their strength and powers, the same way one demon could absorb another? Yes. Why do you think they sent the Grim Hand to steal it? It will be a valuable weapon for the City States."*

*The throbbing of the artifact seems to grow in strength, though I know it is probably only my mind playing tricks. I can guess, from experience, how such an ability will be exploited and abused. My job is to deliver the artifact to my superiors in the Grim Hand, but a sudden fear grips me.*

*"I will delay them as best I can," says Moonshadow. "I may not survive. The Orgols' shamanic sorcery is formidable."*

*"I know. Good luck."*

*Moonshadow stands and jogs down the alley, leaving me alone. I almost cry out for him to come back. What might happen if the City States and their sorcerers, the same people who had abused and transformed all of the members of the Grim Hand, get their hands on such power as the artifact holds? A power that the Orgols had kept secret for centuries.*

*Moonshadow had stolen the potential to make a demigod… perhaps even a god—as long as you had no qualms about killing others and subsuming their powers. And the Orgols would kill thousands if it meant getting their precious object back.*

*I've already paid for a berth on a galleon called the* Reunion, *which is heading north to Kroe, then on to Riem, Sansor, and finally*

*Kyuth. I plan to slip off the ship in Kroe and find a faster ship heading north, rather than wait the several days it will take the* Reunion *to unload and reload cargo.*

*When I reach the harbor, the ship's deck is bustling with activity, and sailors are already untying the thick ropes that hold the galleon alongside the stone wharf. I hurry up the gangplank, quashing the fear-induced nausea that still twists my guts, and make my way to the helm. Captain Amberjack stands there, looking toward the city and the cliffs to either side. He wears a red leather coat with shiny brass buttons, and carries so many daggers that he looks like a ruffian in a street-play. When he sees me, he wrinkles his nose and sniffs. No doubt he thought he would get away without me and keep the substantial fee I'd paid him for passage.*

*"Get below," he snarls. "I don't want you underfoot while we're departing."*

*As I make my way back to the deck, the ship lurches once, twice, then pulls steadily away from its berth. Shouts erupt from the crew, and I look east to where they are pointing. Three tornadoes, the yellow-pink of the sand of the Jargalan Desert, and shining with tendrils of sparkling gold, swirl outside the city walls in a display of immense power.*

*"Orgols!" shouts Amberjack. "More sail, you bastards!"*

*The crew leap to obey as if their lives depend on it—which they do. My heart sinks as I look back at the crowds already gathering on the wharves. One ship hadn't made it away in time, and its deck is now crammed with desperate figures fighting for the last safe spot in the city. The mob prevents the crew from doing their jobs and getting the ship underway. A few brave men and women dive into the harbor and swim in the direction of the* Reunion, *as if they'll be able to catch up.*

*I place my palm on my belly, imagining I can feel the life growing within me. I am going to make it back, I know it! And I think of the other mission coming up—an opportunity too good to miss.*

*Soon, we will both be free.*

Judging from the position of the sun, there were a few hours until sunset. Raven touched the orichalcum sphere hanging around her neck for luck, adjusted her rapier, and shrugged her backpack into a more comfortable position. She moved along a street, baking under the sun's glare. She didn't know where in the city she was going yet while she wasted precious time waiting for Sheelahn to recharge her dusk-tide repository for the return journey, but she did know that she had the feeling she was being watched. It was a sensation she'd felt before: a chill in her gut and in her bones, and she hoped it was only local thieves rather than Orgol spies.

She recalled the artifact stolen from the Orgols she'd kept to herself: a four-sided pyramid, its edges and points as sharp as if honed. It had been made from a strange metal she had never seen before or since: laminated layers of black and crimson and violet that swirled in an intricate pattern.

At the first intersection she spotted a patrol of the Watch. They wore the white cloaks and full-face masks of their calling. One of them turned to look at her. Raven couldn't see the expression behind the white mask. She nodded calmly and continued on her way. Dirty children wearing ragged clothes sat together against a wall, almost in a pile. Raven tossed them a few coins and hoped they bought something to eat.

Once past the patrol, she tugged her hood over her head. Her identity was unknown to them, but you could never be too careful. Almeria was a necessarily small city as water was scarce, and this gave Raven less room to maneuver and less space to hide if she needed to.

Whoever was following her might just be a curious informant looking for a lucky break. If she'd been truly suspected of the Orgol artifact theft, they would have done more than follow her, and the occupants of Almeria would hear her screams for days.

In the square ahead, half a dozen bodies swung from gallows: thieves, rapists and murderers, most likely. Street urchins threw stones at the crows that feasted on the blackened corpses, disturbing swarms of flies that quickly settled back to their task. Raven averted her eyes from the stark reminder of her own possible fate.

She stopped at a shop with wilted plants in baskets on the windowsill, and made a show of examining their small flowers and breathing in their fragrance, all the while keeping an eye on those behind her reflected in the window glass. A slender man in a faded brown coat glanced in her direction then bent to examine his boots. There was a slight bulge down the side of one—a concealed knife, she suspected, with at least one or two more weapons under his coat. It was a hot day, too warm for such attire, and the man had a sheen of sweat on his brow.

Raven thought back... Yes. She'd seen the same man across the street, leaning against a shadowed wall. A few final sniffs of the flowers, and she continued down the street, her pace even and unhurried, her mind running at the speed of a galloping horse. Did the man know she'd worked for the Grim Hand? Or was he simply a thief who'd pegged her as a mark? At least he didn't just want her dead, or he'd have slipped a knife in and been done with it. Or tried to.

Raven turned casually down another street, then another, making sure she was heading toward the harbor. The architecture of this district confused her, with its high stone walls, and the freshly painted houses of the slightly wealthy alongside the crumbling plaster of ill-maintained buildings in various stages of decay. All were clustered together, seemingly at random, with dried weeds poking out of nooks and crannies and atop tiled roofs.

At the next intersection, she stopped, shaded her eyes, and looked up to check the sun's position and see if Browncoat was still following her. He was. She continued her winding route in the direction of the harbor, where Sheelahn's business was located. The buildings became less run-down and better maintained, which was a good indication she was going the right way.

But as she turned a corner, she stopped and ducked back beside a wall. The intersection ahead swarmed with soldiers, and a few white-masked adherents of the Watch. They'd set up wooden crates across the street. The way was blocked. On her account? She couldn't be sure, but she knew the soldiers and the Watch were to be avoided.

Between the street blockade and Browncoat, her gut feeling was that her day was about to go to shit. Damn Sheelahn's delay to the Abyss! She needed to get back to Kroe where Scorpion might be dying and need her.

Raven reversed her path, then hurried down a gap between two buildings. The street eventually opened out into a large market square, the other side of which ended abruptly at a low wall spattered with seagull shit. From the scent of brine and seaweed and tar in the air, she'd found the harbor.

The dirty paving stones of the square were dotted with tables and stalls spread with cheap food: pies, cakes, dried fruit and vegetables, preserved and fresh meats. Flies buzzed around the meat and were brushed away with paper fans. Though it was morning, there were quite a few shoppers of all types: dark-skinned men and women from the south, pale northerners, one or two greenish-cast Illapa women. All looked down on their luck, with patched clothes and dirt-stained faces and hands, but she supposed they must have coin to spare to shop at the market or stay in this city.

Raven hurried across the square, ignored a few half-hearted pleas to purchase various wares. At the low wall, she headed west, keeping an eye on the buildings she passed. She was searching for one in particular; a seedy tavern known to be a meeting place for the types of criminals she'd rather not deal with. But on an occasion such as this, they had their uses. An itch developed between her shoulder blades as she realized the crowd had thinned out. A knife in her back and a shove, and she'd tumble over the harbor's stone wall and into the putrid sludge without anyone noticing. She shuddered at the thought—both of the knife and what was in the water.

A group of five children were leaning over the edge, clutching frayed strings dangling into the murk. Fishing, or attempting to jag objects, she supposed. Most ignored her as she trudged past, but one took notice and begged for a coin. Raven flipped her a silver and the girl's face broke out in delight.

Raven walked with her shoulder brushing the grimy buildings, her ears alert for the rush of feet behind her. To her relief, she recognized the street that opened up before her with its gray-painted houses to hide the stains of the city. Above a chipped green door was a sign showing what looked like a child's version of a chicken with a long neck, except Raven knew the bird was a vulture. She glanced back over her shoulder, but Browncoat was nowhere to be seen. There was no reason for him to have given up following her though.

She knocked firmly on the door. A small window opened in the wood and rheumy, red eyes peered out, looking her up and down.

"Whadayawant?"

Raven held a copper royal close to the opening. "I want in is what I want."

"It's a silver to—"

"It's a copper," she said, voice tight. "Take it and open the door."

The eyes blinked, then she heard a lever slide behind the door and it opened. She handed over the coin and pushed past the man into the gloom of a long, windowless corridor that ended in stairs.

Raven stopped halfway up the stone steps, leaned against the wall and counted. On twenty-one, there came a knock on the door. She smiled grimly and continued her ascent to the fourth floor. Browncoat was still trailing her, it seemed, and he knew this place, otherwise he wouldn't have knocked. That meant he was a local and used to rough situations. Her dilemma was whether to wait and watch and perhaps make use of him; to lose him; or to kill him. For the time being she'd wait, she decided.

The stairs opened up into a large, high-ceilinged room. The walls were painted dark red, and the only light came in from open windows at one end. As her eyes adjusted to the dimness, she made out round tables occupying the floor, with booths around two walls, all positioned far enough apart that low conversations couldn't be overheard from table to table. The patrons conversed in hushed tones, many smoking pipes or thin cylinders of rolled-up leaves that created a white smoky haze above the room.

Raven meandered through the tables, appraising each of the room's inhabitants. At the open windows she paused to look out, pretending to admire the view across the rooftops toward the harbor. Ten feet below was the roof of the adjoining building. An easy drop if she had to escape this way.

After another circuit she chose a table close to the second window and sat with her back to the wall. The booths were too constricting. Raven kept her rapier buckled, shifting the weapon slightly to the side where it would be easier to draw. She surveyed the room again, and picked out Browncoat, who'd positioned himself at a table close to the stairs.

A small, officious-looking man approached her table. Bayvel was his name, a go-between she'd used before in various guises. The inn was a front for his real work.

He rubbed slender hands together and cleared his throat. "My lady, would you care for a drink, or some repast?"

She nodded slowly. "I would. A glass of what's popular; and do you have any honeyed crickets?"

Bayvel's expression changed to dismay. "I'm afraid I don't, my lady. May I suggest some purple nuts instead? The chef roasts them with a touch of cinnamon and cardamom. Quite extraordinary, and particularly delicious."

"They'll be fine."

Bayvel cleared his throat. "Did you hear they spotted an Orgol outside the walls last night? It didn't come in, just stood there, watching. It's not a good sign."

Raven froze for an instant, then affected a look of surprise. Had they known she was coming? Had Sheelahn set her up? This changed everything. "Where there's one, there are more," she said slowly. The Orgols used their Jinnal slaves to conduct their business, mostly trading. If one of the Orgols was here, then there was a high chance it was no coincidence. If Browncoat was an informant and had her marked already, the chances of her leaving alive were slim.

"The last time an Orgol stood outside like that was a few days before the last massacre," remarked Bayvel. "Well before my time, but the tales and histories are clear. People are already getting nervous. Soon rumors will spread and there will be unrest in the streets."

"Riots?" asked Raven. Every century or so the Orgols would attack one of the human enclaves along the coast. Not many inhabitants made it out alive. Some said it was random, to show humans their place in this land, while others thought there were triggers, perhaps disrespect shown to the Orgols. The thought she might have doomed this enclave filled her with dread. There was an outpost of the Evokers here: one of the prestigious sorcerous schools. They might be able to hold their own against a few, but not if the Orgols came in numbers.

"Maybe. But until then, enjoy yourself, that's what I say."

Bayvel turned to leave, but on impulse Raven stopped him. "There's one other thing," she said. "I need to hire protection."

He spread his hands in a gesture of helplessness. "I don't involve myself—"

Raven slid a gold royal across the table. "You do today. I need to talk to anyone you think could help me. I'm looking for someone…dangerous." *If only to use as a diversion…*

"My lady, I—"

"Your regular clientele probably won't be able to help. This is bigger game. I need someone big and proficient, who can keep quiet."

Bayvel swallowed. "And if I say no?"

"You won't."

With a nervous nod, Bayvel took the gold and left. It wasn't long before he returned carrying a cone-shaped glass and a porcelain bowl of purple nuts, his face glistening with perspiration.

"I might have found someone for you," he said in a low voice. "A man who lives near here and is up for odd jobs. Ah… I'll need to give him some incentive to come and see you."

She sipped her drink, a surprisingly refreshing blend of fermented cactus pear with spices. "Any reason you didn't mention him before?"

"He's a little…strange."

Raven handed over a few silver royals. "Tell him to hurry."

"Of course. He's called Mezuum, by the way. He doesn't talk much."

"Sounds perfect."

Bayvel rushed off and spoke to a young girl behind a counter. She nodded and skipped across the room and down the stairs. Raven frowned. The girl was one of four. The others were polishing glasses and mixing drinks, as well as coming and going through a curtained doorway. When they came out, they carried bowls and plates, which Bayvel brought to various patrons. She hoped the girls weren't used for anything unsavory. If they were, it wouldn't go well for Bayvel. She kept an eye on the girls, but they looked happy enough and smiled when Bayvel ordered them around. Smiles that didn't drop from their faces when his back was turned. A good sign, but not enough to convince her there wasn't any wrongdoing. Raven glanced in the direction of the stairs, where Browncoat still occupied his table. As she did, she saw him reach into his own porcelain bowl and place a purple nut in his mouth, munching on the nuts and sipping his drink. She hated sitting around doing nothing; she preferred to act. She chastised herself for a lack of patience.

Movement caught her eye and she looked up. A massive coal-skinned man was standing next to her table, his hands as big as shovels. His hair was black and short, hacked off at uneven lengths, and he wore serviceable pants and a shirt of plain brown. His eyes were a pale gray and didn't blink as he stared at her. Mezuum, she presumed. Maybe a sixteenth-blood Orgol. Perfect. A mongrel accepted by neither humans nor Orgols, with something to prove to both.

Raven indicated one of the chairs at her table. "Please, sit."

The chair creaked under his weight. He placed both hands on the table, palms down, covering most of the surface area. Raven fished around in her purse, placed a gold royal on the table, and with one finger pushed it toward him.

Mezuum's gaze flicked down to the coin, then back to her. He tilted his head slightly but made no move to pick up her coin.

Better and better, thought Raven. Any normal mercenary would have snapped up the gold coin without a moment's hesitation and been prepared to kill his own mother for it. This man, however, knew such a payment meant more than just coin—there was a binding with accepting such largesse, unspoken, seldom realized by those whose thoughts ran shallow. But Mezuum obviously knew he'd be committed if he accepted her generosity.

Abruptly, he stood. "No, thank you," he said in a voice like tumbling boulders, and turned to leave.

*Damn it to the Abyss.* "Wait," Raven said. "Sit. Let me speak. Then decide."

He sat again, placing his hands in the exact same position. Raven thought of and discarded half a dozen lies. They all sounded too far-fetched. What would a part-blood Orgol want? He would be feared by other humans and derided by the Orgols.

A place to belong? A purpose? If he survived whatever was after her, she could cultivate him. Sheelahn obviously had plans for Raven, if she hadn't sold her out, and Raven might need the help of someone such as Mezuum.

She slid another gold royal across the table. "I have resources. Not just coin, but other less tangible things. Information; ways to open doors."

Mezuum grunted, nodded at her to continue.

"But there's a problem."

He snorted.

"Yes," Raven said. "There almost always is. And this one isn't small. I need protection." She modified one of her standard stories. "I'm a treasure hunter and I stumbled across something big in an abandoned ruin. Something to do with the Orgols' shamans. There's another twenty golds for you once I'm safe in Kroe in the north. And there are organizations I know there that would value someone with your skills."

She sat back in her chair. She'd baited her hook; now it was up to Mezuum. The two golds she'd already given him would be more than most people earned in a month; and twenty golds more than most would in a year.

He regarded her as a cat might a mouse—a mouse with a broken leg that knew it couldn't escape. Was he considering killing her and handing her over to the Orgols? She tensed slightly, preparing to defend herself. He'd have a weapon concealed on him, somewhere. Then again, he could probably crush her in his huge paws. But he would find this mouse had sharp claws of her own.

Mezuum smiled when she tensed. He knew what she was thinking. Interesting, but she was in no mood to jump to his tune, or anyone's.

His hand moved, and Raven couldn't help flinching. But his sausage-thick fingers came down on the two gold coins.

"If you don't deliver the rest, I'll kill you," he said.

She let out a slow breath and held her hand out for him to shake. "Fair enough. Let me introduce myself. I'm Dania."

He gave her hand a light squeeze, like someone who knew his own strength and was careful not to break things. She would have to push him to see what his limits were, to determine if there were lines he wouldn't cross. But given he'd been earning coin as a hired heavy, her first task should be easy enough for him.

"There's a man in a brown coat at the table by the stairs," she said. "He followed me here, and I don't know who he is or why he's interested in me. That makes me nervous. I don't like being nervous. Bring him to me."

Mezuum nodded. He left the table and reappeared a few moments later, dragging Browncoat by the scruff of his neck. With a tilt of her head, Raven indicated the bench opposite her, and Mezuum manhandled Browncoat into it, then loomed behind him.

"Bloody hells," Browncoat said, twisting his neck in an attempt to eye Mezuum. "I ain't done nuthin' to you. Just mindin' my own business." He turned to give Raven an insolent look.

Through the open window, Raven heard the faint echo of horns—the city alarm sounding. She tilted her head as the trumpeting continued. There was only one thing that could threaten the city: Orgols. If they attacked, then every ship in the harbor would set sail, mobs would crowd the streets, and her route to Sheelahn would be fraught.

"You can quit the act; it's not a very good one," she said.

"I ain't—"

Raven sighed. "Wearing such a coat in this warm weather

indicates you're concealing multiple weapons. But it also indicates you're not too bright because it makes you stand out. Besides, I saw you following me. You're not very good at it."

Browncoat's face twisted from bafflement to sneering arrogance. "It doesn't matter. What does is that Akatta Palek remembered where he'd seen you before, or rather an image of you. He sent word. You're a dead woman. The Orgols will take you back to Lorestone Citadel and torture you for eternity. And I'll earn a nice reward."

Bloody darkness, that was more information than she wanted Mezuum to know.

"Mezuum, please restrain this man," she said firmly.

The enormous man's meaty paws clamped down on Browncoat, one holding his shoulder and the other grabbing the front of his coat. While Browncoat struggled vainly in the implacable grip, Raven stood and grasped the hilt of her rapier. Screams and shouts of alarm emanated from the street below.

Browncoat tilted his head when he too heard the commotion. "They've come for you!" he said gleefully. "You're a dead woman."

A booming crack sounded at the bottom of the stairs as the door to the street shattered. Agonized screams followed, likely from the man standing behind it. Heavy footsteps thudded up the treads, and the remaining patrons surged to their feet, murmuring in alarm.

A lone Orgol, Raven estimated, and it hadn't used sorcery to batter down the door. With her skills and abilities, and Mezuum's aid, she was certain they could put it down. She'd have time to race to the harbor and Sheelahn's and be long gone before more Orgols arrived.

She drew her rapier, but gasped in awe and dread when the Orgol came into view. He was at least seven feet tall, and his midnight skin bulged with muscles. His cheekbones were as sharp as a knife, and he had a nose that could chop wood. He wore thick leather trousers and a sleeveless mail shirt with glimmering gold links, and he exuded an aura of energy and violence. In one hand he gripped a massive sword with a wide blade.

He froze at the top of the stairs for the barest instant, then his head moved slowly until his black eyes pierced Raven's. He knew she had handled their sacred artifact.

She looked at Mezuum. His mouth was hanging open. "We can take him," she said.

Before either of them could act, the Orgol spoke, his voice deep and thrumming. It was a cant. He hadn't used sorcery to batter down the door because, with his brute strength, he hadn't needed to. Glittering golden and silver light swirled around his immense form to create a sorcerous shield unlike any Raven had ever seen. Golden and silver energy swirled to form the ward, not a sphere, but a polygon made up of dozens of flat faces. She'd learned the different tiers of shields sorcerers could generate in order to know their strengths and weaknesses, from tier one to tier four, but she had no knowledge of what the Orgol shamans used. What she did know was that her orichalcum sphere and her demonic ability to speed it through the air like a projectile would be useless against such a shield.

All she could do was run. She was no match for an Orgol shaman; and Browncoat knew too much about her for comfort. As did Akatta Palek, but she'd deal with him another time.

Raven lunged and buried her rapier in Browncoat's heart. He screamed once and collapsed. She jerked her blade free, slammed it back into its sheath, and hurled herself toward the open window. The Orgol's deep bellow of rage followed her as she leaped into space, slammed into the ceramic tiles below the window and rolled. She was on her feet in the blink of an eye and racing across the rooftop.

Tiles cracked behind her as something slammed into them. She risked a glance back, hoping the Orgol was heavy enough to fall through the roof. He wasn't. He gave another bellow and sprinted toward her. Bloody darkness, he was fast.

Raven pumped her legs as quickly as she could toward the edge of the inn's roof. The next building was about ten yards away—a distance most people wouldn't attempt to leap across—and its roof was slightly higher. Raven jumped and drew on her dark-tide energy to push herself across the gap. She landed hard on the opposite roof. One foot slipped on a patch of dried lichen and she tumbled.

There was a jarring crash of shattered tiles as the Orgol landed close by. Any moment now he would scourge her flesh with sorcery. She was going to fail herself, and Scorpion.

*Tiles.* Raven sent a surge of dark-tide into the roof between her and the Orgol, cracking and buckling the ceramic tiles and sending them flying into the air. If she was lucky, they would obstruct any sorcery the Orgol threw at her as she raced away. But the ploy wouldn't last long; she had to think of something else. And with the alarm raised, all the ships in port would be preparing to disembark, and the streets would be clogged with panicked people.

A seed of an idea formed.

Raven sprinted for the farthest edge of the roof, drawing on more dark-tide and flinging tiles up behind her. The Orgol's heavy tread receded slightly. She risked a glance to her right, and found him running parallel to her, having moved to the side to avoid her tiles. He was smiling. Asshole.

They reached the edge of the roof together. This gap was wider than the previous one, but she could make it. So could the Orgol.

Raven made to jump, but instead of launching herself forward, she let herself fall. There was a window to her left, and a surge of dark-tide pushed her toward it. She shielded her face with her arms as she crashed through the glass and felt burning cuts slice across her skin. She rolled to lessen the impact of landing, then leaped to her feet. A bald man stood in the room, clutching a hunk of bread and cheese in one hand and staring at her in shock.

She barreled through the only doorway and into another room beyond, unlatched a second door, and sped along a gloomy hallway filled with the stench of unwashed bodies. The Orgol would be above her somewhere, trying to guess what she would do. The rooftops were no longer an option as she couldn't outrun him. So, she would keep to the narrow streets and the insides of buildings that would be difficult for the massive creature to navigate.

A staircase appeared ahead and Raven slowed to catch her breath and wipe blood from her arms and sweat from her face. A wall nearby exploded in a shower of splintered wood and dust. Raven didn't hesitate. She leaped over the balustrade to the stairs below. As soon as her feet hit the stone treads she was sprinting downward, using the end posts to slingshot herself around the landings. She entered a dilapidated foyer just as heavy crashes sounded from the stairs behind her.

Outside, she slammed into an unsuspecting woman carrying a basket and sent her tumbling. Packages scattered across the road. Raven mumbled an apology and raced on. The street was busy, and she had to dodge around people and shove others aside, which slowed her pace. Something whistled past her ear, and she ducked. A roof tile struck the wall ahead of her and shattered into fragments, quickly followed by another. She dodged down an alley; the Orgol was toying with her. Asshole, she thought again.

Four-story-high walls shrouded the alley in gloom. Raven raced along, boots stirring the ever-present sands of the Jargalan Desert and treading on garbage tossed out of the windows above. A deep voice snarled a cant behind her.

Ahead, a street split the alley in two. Raven's sharp eyes picked out a dark patch fifty yards along the second part of the alley, and she poured her awareness into the shadows. Her body and mind melted and drained away, then re-formed in the darkness of her destination. Bellows of rage echoed behind her. People shouted and screamed in fear.

Raven careened around another corner into a side street, sprinted for thirty yards, then twisted into another narrow alley. Lungs burning and mouth dry, she pressed her back briefly into a wall, then leaped up to grab a windowsill. She felt a twinge of nausea in her stomach, a forewarning of the toxic effects of using too much dark-tide. She pulled herself up and onto the sill. Her arms stung from the glass cuts and still trickled blood. She couldn't do anything about that now. She jumped up to grab the next windowsill and repeated her maneuver, scaling the wall one window at a time until she hauled herself onto the roof. Hopefully the Orgol wouldn't believe she was stupid enough to return to a setting that was disadvantageous for her.

She paused on the edge, gasping for breath, then ran toward the east. She was close enough to her destination now that she began to hope she might make it out alive.

This roof was flat, and there was a chicken coop with a dozen scrawny birds inside. Smoke plumed from a chimney, and faded rugs hung from rope lines strung between old wooden posts.

She leaped over a low wall and onto terracotta tiles that angled downward—and toppled sideways as her feet slipped from under her. She slammed into the roof, smashing her lip and sending cracked tiles skidding down the slope to shatter in the street below. Hands, arms and lip throbbing with pain, she tried to stand, but the world twisted and she fell again.

Raven made it to her hands and knees, and saw the buildings around her move. Was it an earthquake? No. She was moving. Or rather the building she was perched on was moving. *Bloody darkness.*

The roof swayed, then tilted in the opposite direction. She gripped the tiles hard to stop herself slipping. The Orgol shaman knew where she was, and was trying to bring the building down around her. A heavy pressure clamped over her, pressing her to the roof and preventing her from escaping. She frantically searched the rooftops. There. A chimney casting a shadow.

She drew on her dark-tide and shadow-stepped. As she emerged beside the chimney, the pressure relented—she was clear of the Orgol's enchantment.

Suddenly her stomach twisted and she doubled over in pain. She carried with her a few lozenges, but there wasn't time to delve into her backpack. With a trembling hand she steadied herself against the brickwork and sucked in breaths in a partially successful effort to quell her nausea. She had to keep moving.

Raven sprinted as fast as she could toward the gap between this building and the next, and leaped, arms wind-milling. This time she didn't dare to use a surge of dark-tide to help her across. She landed roughly on the roof opposite and heard a thunderous crack behind her. She glanced back to see the entire building collapse in a heap of rubble, sending a cloud of dust and sand swirling into the air.

She took off again, knowing it wouldn't be long before the Orgol realized she had escaped. Her chest ached and sweat stung her eyes. Her lip already felt swollen. Lightning crackled around her, searing her skin, and she yelled in pain. A booming shout of triumph came from behind.

Ahead, a dozen slender towers rose above the rooftops. Her destination. She almost laughed but couldn't spare the breath.

Raven dashed forward, gathering her strength. Another gap—this one a good twenty yards wide. Luckily, the rooftop on the other side was lower. She sailed across the space and landed heavily on the roof of the Evokers' sorcery school. If they were halfway competent, they would have set sorcerous wards around their building. Nothing had hit her yet, but it was only a matter of time if she stayed up here for long. An Orgol shaman, on the other hand, would instantly trigger the wards.

Raven lurched to the other side of the roof and looked down into a paved courtyard with three twisted trees surrounded by cracked stone. All four walls encircling the courtyard had a covered walkway. She smiled. Plenty of shadows.

She looked behind her. The Orgol barreled across the rooftops like a charging bull, his face twisted into a snarl. She waved at him, then clambered over the edge of the roof and dropped to the courtyard three floors below, sprinting to the cover of a shadowed walkway. An alarm like a banshee's wail rang out, and she felt the air hum as the sorcerers drew on their dawn- and dusk-tide repositories.

The Orgol appeared on the edge of the roof, his dark eyes scanning for her. He'd lost his sword during the chase. When he spotted Raven, he leaped, his strange shield flaring around him. She immediately shadow-stepped back up to the roof, into the shadow of one of the thin spires, and hunkered down. Finally able to relax, she shrugged her backpack from her shoulders and reached into a side pocket. With trembling fingers she removed one of the small waxed-paper packages inked with an "X". She popped the tacky lozenge into her mouth and chewed slowly, tasting sweaty boots and honey. Soon her nausea would subside and her pains disappear.

The Orgol shaman hammered into the ground, and flagstones cracked under his weight. A web of scintillant filaments materialized above him and wrapped his flat-planed shield in violet cables. Sparks erupted where the two forces met. The Orgol shouted something incomprehensible.

Human sorcerers poured from doorways around the courtyard, all with wards in place. Many shouted cants and gestured toward the now-trapped Orgol. A low thrumming set Raven's bones and teeth vibrating. It was time to leave.

She stood, and the Orgol saw the movement and glared up at her. Raven turned and ran across the roof. She arrived at Sheelahn's depot just as the sun set.

*"Moonshadow?" I ask as I enter the safe house in Kroe.*

*Scorpion shakes his head. "The Orgols caught him. And then they tortured him and ripped him limb from limb."*

*I cannot speak, and Scorpion gives me a moment's space.*

*Why the Orgols hadn't come after the* Reunion, *I cannot say. Perhaps Moonshadow led them a merry chase. I like to think so.*

*"Do you have it?" Scorpion asks.*

*"No," I reply. "Moonshadow was unsuccessful."*

*Scorpion gazes at me for a few moments then looks away. "Our superiors won't be happy. They'll run us ragged with more missions."*

*I shrug. "That's what we were made for."*

*I buried the blackwood box containing the Orgols' sacred artifact beside a boulder outside of the city, near a farmstead that had seen better days. I'd had time to think about what it was, what it could do, and the likely result. This wasn't a defensive artifact. It was evil. It could enable a person to turn themselves into a supreme being of sorts, more powerful than the greatest sorcerer ever to have lived. Possibly greater than the gods themselves. No one deserves to wield such immense power. Even with the best intentions, the result would be the same. Power corrupts—as I have seen so many times before.*

"I delivered the package," Raven told Sheelahn.

The orichalcum mask shifted slightly, and the sorceress's black-gloved hands moved to smooth the skirts of her robes. "Did you have some trouble?"

Raven peered at Sheelahn's inscrutable mask, aware that she sported freshly bound wounds. "Nothing I couldn't handle." A nauseous chill swept through her. The Orgols would punish the city. She carried death and destruction with her wherever she went, and it sickened her to the core. "The job's done," she continued. "We should get away from here, if you don't mind."

The sorceress stared at Raven for a few moments. "Agreed. Come."

After another nauseating, mind-bending translocation, Raven gathered herself and took deep breaths until she recovered. This time, the after-effects weren't quite so severe.

"The first part of our bargain is complete," said Sheelahn. "What did you discern from Akatta Palek?"

Raven considered lying, not wanting to get too caught up in whatever game Sheelahn was playing. But the truth was, she needed all the help she could get. And having this sorceress on her side, or at least owing her favors, was a pretty big advantage.

"I had a feeling there was something wrong with him. At first it felt like an attraction, but the closer he came, the more I sensed another layer underneath. It was a sensation I'd hoped never to feel again."

"Did he sense it too?"

Raven shook her head, rubbing her arms. "No. Not that I could tell."

"You are still alive, so you are probably correct."

"This is…about demons, isn't it?"

"Would you like to use a favor to get an answer to that question?"

"No. I know the answer. I was just… Never mind."

"What else happened with Akatta Palek?"

Raven looked at Sheelahn, trying to guess her thoughts. She came up empty. "He recognized me as someone the Orgols were after and alerted them. One came for me, and the city …"

"Will be rebuilt."

Raven couldn't bring herself to think of the hundreds, perhaps the thousands of dead because of her. Was holding onto the Orgols sacred artifact worth such misery and guilt? Was keeping such malevolent power out of anyone's hands justified if it led to so much death?

"Where is Scorpion?" she asked numbly.

"There is a healer by the name of Tristana," Sheelahn said. "She is in debt to some of the gambling houses. To pay off some of that debt, she tends to any Night Shadows' thieves who become injured or ill. I have received information that last night she treated a man with a crossbow wound in his shoulder."

It was a start. "And where can I find this Tristana?"

"During the day, she will be sleeping. At night, she will be in the gambling dens."

Not much help, but enough to go on. "Thank you."

The sorceress reached out an inviting hand. "I have a need for one such as you." The words were an echo of what she had said previously. "People speak of you in hushed tones."

"Who does?"

"Those who know the business of death. They speak of a black-skinned wraithe who shows no mercy. No person is safe, they say, once your eyes are set on them."

"That's not who I am. Not anymore." She had never been like that. She'd killed, but so what? Many people killed, some for as little as a copper. "They don't know me. I never killed for coin."

"I know." The sorceress said again, "I have a need for one such as you."

The words chilled Raven. Sheelahn knew far too much about her.

"I have some business that I need to take care of," she said, stalling. "Then I'll think about it."

"Return to me with an answer."

With a final nod, Raven left the sorceress. Maybe she would return, and maybe she wouldn't. She had a lead on Scorpion now. She would find him and figure out what in bloody darkness was going on.

# ELEVEN

SCORPION RUNS HIS HANDS OVER *my naked body, and I shudder at his touch. I allow him to continue for a few moments before slapping his hands away.*

*"Not yet," I say. "Give me a chance to recover." But secretly I want to let him go on, to absorb as much of him as I can in the time we have. Which will be short, if he agrees to help me.*

*Scorpion isn't handsome: nose too big, features too rugged, black hair stiff like wire. But he is all I have, my only comfort.*

*The rules of the Grim Hand are clear: no intimate relationships between team members. Even friendship is frowned upon. After our transformations, we all swore ourselves to a higher cause—to protect the City States from all aggressors. We are beasts to be unleashed when our masters require it, which is most of the time. We are to keep to ourselves, may not speak about our work, and must disappear for months at a stretch, sometimes more than a year, depending on the mission. And yet Scorpion and I manage to carve out time together, if only rarely. Even if our initial attraction had been physical, a pleasurable way to relieve the stresses of our existence, over time we have developed powerful feelings for each other.*

*If anyone knew Scorpion and I were sleeping together, it would only end one way: with my death, or imprisonment under sorcerous bindings. Since Scorpion is also a sorcerer, he is too valuable to lose. And as my superior, he must make life and death decisions and send me into situations where I might be killed or worse. But that hasn't stopped me, or him. We take a small comfort in each other's arms, and the intoxicating attraction between us has not let us go. I'm not sure I am in love with him, never having experienced the emotion before, but I am happy when we are together.*

*"Are you thinking about them again?" he asks. "Don't. We are what we are."*

*Them. The City State sorcerers who had transformed the members of the Grim Hand. Who had taken away my life, my soul. Scorpion thinks I am the perfect soldier and compliments me on my skill after every mission. Perfect. Perhaps I am. But a soldier? No. The Grim Hand thinks they have broken me, molded me into their toy; but I'm not doing this out of loyalty. I am driven by hate, rage, and anguish.*

*"I can't do this anymore," I say, diving in headlong. "This life, I mean. All the killing. I just can't."*

*"Leaving isn't an option," Scorpion says softly. "You know that. There's only one way out."*

*"I understand we're in this until we're dead, but I also know I didn't ask for any of this…for what they did to me. To us. I can't take it anymore. I have to get out."*

*"I wish it were that simple," he says, trailing a finger up my stomach to circle my nipple.*

*"I have to find a way." I swat his hand away and roll onto my side, regarding his face as he wrestles with what I am saying.*

*"I've been meaning to talk to you about all this," Scorpion says. "I don't think it's fair you're taking most of the risk. If we're found out—"*

*I brush my fingers across his lips, stopping his words. "I agreed to this. To us."*

*"I know. But that doesn't make it right. If you were to die…I don't know what I'd do."*

*"That depends on the manner of my death."*

*"What do you mean?"*

*"The only way I can leave this life is if they believe I'm dead. It's the only way I can get out of their reach, away from any enemies I've made. I'll be free to roam the world without anyone trying to kill me on sight."*

*Free to live my own life, and to keep my own secrets. I'd hide the Orgols' artifact for the good of the world. And the second secret is just for me.*

*"But why, Raven? You were made to be a warrior. Fighting and killing is in your blood now; you have abilities normal humans can't match. What will you do if left to your own devices?"*

*"What will I do?" I echo. "I will live. I want to leave my past and begin anew, without all my history weighing me down. I want to stop killing. Stop worrying that I'll be killed. Is that so hard to understand?" I force my voice to harden. "And you know me well enough by now. If you don't help, I'll do it on my own."*

*He knows better than to argue with me. Scorpion gives an almost imperceptible nod, and I hope that means I won't have to do this alone. I almost tell him then. The real reason I want to get out, to start a new life. But I can't trust him to let me go if he knows.*

*"Faking a death isn't easy," Scorpion says, as he twines his fingers in my hair and brings me closer for an unexpectedly tender kiss.*

*I almost break down then. My eyes well up, and I pull away and wipe them with the back of my hand. Hopefully he thinks I weep with gratitude.*

*"I have a plan," I say, "but you'll need to go over it. And it'll need the right situation."*

*"You'll need a good deal of coin, weapons, and your orichalcum artifact. And a destination where you can be safe."*

*"I have one in mind."*

*I roll onto my back and stare at the ceiling before closing my eyes. Of course, there's a chance he'll change his mind and expose me. After all, it means betraying both his team and his superiors, and putting his own life on the line. If he turns me in, I won't blame him. Betraying everything you are isn't easy. But what option do I have? It tears me apart, keeping this secret from him.*

It was easy enough for Raven to find Tristana. The residents near the most popular card and chance houses didn't mind an extra copper talent or two in exchange for information. Raven learned which was Tristana's favorite haunt and followed her from there at a relatively close distance. She kept her eyes on the back of the stork-thin woman, who seemed to also like expensive silks as well as gambling. From what Raven could see, she had much more success with her fashion than she did at the tables.

The healer didn't so much as glance behind her. If she had any reason to be followed, she gave no sign of it, chatting to street vendors and shopkeepers along the way as if she hadn't a care in the world. Raven couldn't see anyone tailing Tristana either. Then again, if Scorpion's unknown assailants had traced the healer, she'd be dead by now, or on a rack spilling whatever information she knew.

The woman halted to examine some glazed pottery. Raven increased her pace and passed close behind her, then stopped at a nearby corner and leaned against a wall, keeping watch in case she'd missed someone else on the healer's trail. It was difficult to spot another follower in such a busy street, but that's what she was trained for.

The healer finished her admiring and walked on. Raven stepped out to block her way. "Tristana? The healer?"

Tristana's eyes narrowed as she examined Raven. "Yes. My, you're a comely one, aren't you? But I'm very busy today. If you need urgent treatment, I can recommend—"

"I'm looking for the man you saw to last night. He's a friend."

"I don't know what you're talking about." She had a terrible face for gambling—too expressive. Probably why she lost so much.

"He took a crossbow bolt in his shoulder," Raven said. "The bolt was likely poisoned."

"I told you, I have no—"

"Bloody darkness, I know you treated him! I just need to know where to find him." Raven held up one of her six gemstones, a blood-red garnet the size of a thumbnail. "Where is he?"

Tristana's eyes fixed on the garnet. Her tongue darted out to lick her lips. "He told me not to tell anyone."

"He wouldn't have expected me to turn up. As I said, I'm a friend." If this line didn't work out, she could always apply less friendly persuasion.

The healer gave a nod and glanced furtively along the street. "I might be able to contact him. I didn't have enough supplies of the herbs required to flush the poison from his system, so I have to send him more."

If Scorpion required regular treatment, then Tristana must be able to contact him, Raven thought. No wonder she lost so often at cards.

"Tell him Raven is looking for him," she said, handing over the garnet. "You should be able to describe me well enough. I'll find you later, and when I do, you'd better have something for me."

Tristana was leaving a jeweler's when Raven sidled up to her a few hours later. The healer's smile faltered when she realized who was walking beside her.

"I see you've sold the gemstone I gave you," Raven said. "It must feel good to have paid off all those gambling debts. A weight off your shoulders."

"There's not much left over, but…I'll make do."

"A word of advice: give up while you're ahead. Or in your case, when you're even." But Raven knew from the set of Tristana's jaw that she would keep gambling. "What's the news?"

"Your friend isn't in the best condition. The poison was virulent. But he wants to meet with you. There's a café on Dreamer's Street in the Wolf Hill district, toward the docks. It's called the Little Banshee. It's expensive, so the clientele is limited. He'll contact you there, but be prepared to wait."

"How badly did the poison affect him?"

"It's…bad. But with a little luck he should make a full recovery. Unless there are complications. I couldn't do much for the pain, which must have been staggering. I thought his teeth would break from grinding them together, but he didn't even whimper."

Raven nodded. "Our business is concluded. Forget you met me, or my friend. Whoever injured him is still out there somewhere, and you want to stay well away. If anyone asks about your sudden increase in fortune, tell them a relative died and left you some coin. And try to make it convincing—you're a terrible liar."

*Everything has changed for me, as if I have blinked and opened my eyes onto a different world. A world that is filled with love and hope, where I have a future without danger and death.*

*An impossibility, or so I was told after they experimented on me.*

*My past, what there is of it, is filled with enough horrors to last a dozen lifetimes, and I had vowed never to have children. After all, I kill people without knowing who they are or what they have done; and I kill the men and women guarding them, too. What kind of parent would that make me?*

*I am dead inside…my emotions are far away things, as if they have been removed along with my memories, except for anguish and rage. The only spark I feel is with Scorpion—and even then it is a fragile thing that could easily be extinguished if we are found out. I can't let it grow, or even fully share it with him. But now I know I am pregnant, another spark has been ignited inside of me. Long-suppressed emotions bubble to the surface, so powerful and overwhelming I am unable to breathe. I feel the urge to protect. To care. To truly love someone else.*

*I should have told Scorpion I am pregnant. I tell myself I will once my baby and I are safe. But right now, it is too risky. Even though I think maybe I do love him, I can't take the chance that a confession might trigger a chain of events that will lead to disaster.*

The Little Banshee was on the second floor above a moneylender's, and had an outdoor seating area on a bridge that spanned a side street to a building opposite. The patrons sitting there seemed to take delight in observing the comings and goings along the main street, shouting and waving to their friends. It was hardly a discreet place to meet.

Raven made her customary circuit of the streets around the establishment. On one corner, a vendor sold different types of nuts and another hawked woven baskets, while the lane behind the building was seedier, with a few prostitutes and a thin, short man who offered her cravv. She couldn't make out any obvious threats, but there was a lot of activity and it was a nightmare to memorize everyone she came across. She didn't see any suspicious carriages or traps waiting in the street though, and there were no loiterers—apart from the occasional street urchin.

She bought a waxed-paper bag of salted swamp-nuts and scrutinized the café's building while she leaned against a wall to eat them and exchange pleasantries with the woman vendor. The café's second-floor location and its openness to the bridge was a recipe for disaster. Anyone could loose a crossbow bolt from a window across the street, with ample time to get away.

She imagined the name of the café was someone's idea of a joke. If they ever met a real banshee in the wilderness, they would piss themselves with fear. Raven had stumbled across one once, and had no desire to repeat the experience. She'd only escaped by throwing herself into a freezing river swollen with snowmelt, and the banshee's hideously alluring wail still haunted her dreams.

She handed the now-empty bag back to the nut-seller to be reused and, satisfied the café wasn't under surveillance, ascended the narrow stairs and requested a table away from the windows. When a server placed a glass of water on her table, she ordered a hot pea and roasted cricket soup, and took a deep breath. She'd waited more than four years to meet Scorpion again, and the circumstances couldn't have been worse.

She didn't have to wait much longer. As her soup arrived, she looked up to thank the server and found herself staring into Scorpion's homely face. Something sharp was sticking into her side.

He hooked a chair with his foot and dragged it closer. When he sat, the knife he held to her skin remained a constant threat.

"Eat your soup," he said. "We're having a pleasant conversation."

Other than his ashen and drawn appearance, and the roughness of his voice—obvious effects of the poison—he looked the same as always. He might have stepped straight out of her memories. He wore loose brown pants and shirt, and sweat beaded his brow even inside the cool café—but he was the same Scorpion she'd slept with a week before she'd faked her own death and escaped the Grim Hand.

"It's good to see you, too," she said. "After all these years, don't I get a welcoming kiss?"

"That depends. Why are you here?"

She understood his caution. After all, he'd just been ambushed and had almost died. She ate a spoonful of her soup, self-consciously crunching on some crickets and glancing at Scorpion for a reaction. When he remained steely, Raven said, "Someone tried to kill me. Several someones."

"That's not the first time that's happened."

"No. But I see you've had some difficulties as well. I have a lot of questions and no answers."

"How did you find me?"

"I went looking for Crooked, then to the village outside Kroe. I heard you were injured, so I came back here and found the healer who tended to you."

"Found her. Just like that?"

Raven met his gaze. "Which means someone else could find her too. I figured you might need a friend. Which you obviously do, from what I can see."

Scorpion grunted and reached for her glass of water, his hand trembling slightly. He drained half of it in a few gulps. "Who did you pay to find me?"

"No one. I swapped a favor for information about which healers someone might go to if they didn't want to be found. As luck would have it, they found out an injured man had recently visited this particular healer."

"That's fairly specific information. Who gave it to you?"

"The Ethereal Sorceress."

"Bloody darkness! What are you mixed up in?"

Raven considered his question, but there was no good answer. "I don't know. I managed to get her to owe me a favor, and called it in."

"You can't trust sorcerers. Does she have her hooks into you?"

*Yes.* "No. Are you going to remove that knife, or do I have to take it away from you?"

"It stays until I figure out if you're here to kill me."

She gave him a tentative smile. "If I wanted you dead, you would be. You know that. So why don't we dispense with all this drama and you can tell me what you know about whatever's going on?"

Scorpion returned the smile, withdrew the knife, and slipped it inside his shirt. Then he sighed and leaned his arm on the table, closing his eyes momentarily. He was in a bad way. Raven slid the vial of antidote she'd taken from the female assassin across the table toward him.

"I picked this up. It might be an antidote to the poison in your system. Or it might not."

With a frown at her, Scorpion pulled out the cork and swallowed the vial's contents. He cleared his throat and handed it back to her. "Thank you."

"How badly did the poison hit you?"

"Pretty bad. Some damage to internal organs, or so Tristana said. She sewed my shoulder up, but said the other damage isn't repairable. I'm sure I'll be back to normal soon, though."

"Do you know who it was?"

Scorpion drank the rest of her water, then shook his head. "I'm not certain, but I have my suspicions."

"I was outside Crooked's apartment when it caught fire. I suspect it was sorcery."

"Were you seen?"

"I don't think so. Otherwise I'd have been attacked again. Of course, I killed enough of them the first time, they'd think twice about coming at me again. Which brings me to why I'm here. I need to know who's after me, and why. And how they know I'm still alive. The only person who knew the truth was you."

The accusation hung in the air between them like the stench of a fish left too long in the sun.

"I…I'm sorry," he said, voice wavering. "I was careless. Too sentimental. I knew better, but…" His shoulders slumped and his head sank.

She placed a hand on his forehead. He was burning up.

"You need to lie down and get some rest," she said. "Where are you staying? We can talk later, once you've regained some strength."

"Upstairs," he croaked. "The door at the end."

She threw a silver talent on the table—more than enough for the soup—and helped him to his feet. "A trifle too much to drink last night," she said to a concerned server as they left.

They lurched up a set of stairs and shuffled down a hallway. Scorpion managed to get a key out of his pocket, and she took it, opening the door to his apartment. It was sparse, though relatively well kept.

Raven dragged him to the bedroom and sat him on the unmade bed. On the nightstand were packets of herbs and a vial containing oil of poppy. She placed a few drops on his tongue, then removed his shirt, slinging it over a nearby stool. A bandage wrapped his shoulder, with a red stain across the back.

She undid the dressing to examine the wound. It didn't look to have reopened; it was just leaking a little. The flesh around it was discolored, the purple-blue of a bruise, but its edges were swollen with protruding black veins—no doubt from the effects of the poison.

She rewrapped the dressing then went to the door and dropped a bar in place. The only other way into the apartment was through the windows, but all she could do was make sure they were locked and draw the ratty linen curtains across. A quick check of the other room revealed enough food to last a few days: bread and cheese, some dried meat and oranges.

Raven busied herself blowing a brazier back to life, then placed a pot of water on it to boil. She made some tea, then returned to Scorpion. He seemed to be asleep.

She sat nearby, in a padded chair that sagged underneath

her, and kept watch in case anyone tried to break in. While she waited, she toyed with her small orichalcum sphere in one hand and listened to the familiar sound of Scorpion's deep breathing.

155

# TWELVE

I LIE ON A GRASSY *knoll that allows me to see over the top of the wall surrounding the estate. Dew soaks into my dark-gray shirt and trousers, and although the coarse woolen hood concealing my platinum hair itches my scalp, I ignore the discomfort, as I've been trained to do.*

*I'd chosen a spot that was likely to be checked by any patrols, but hopefully the cold, wind and rain keeps them inside. The twelve-foot-high brick walls around the estate add to the sense of invulnerability, so much so that whoever is in ultimate control of security hasn't even bothered to obscure the windows with curtains. I can see right inside the dining room, where the targets are gathered.*

*Five of the wealthiest and most corrupt merchants in Wiraya have assembled for a meeting on neutral ground, at an estate in Kyuth perched atop the sea cliffs a hundred yards from the crashing waves below. Carriages built from rare woods and drawn by horses with noble bloodlines have been arriving since the afternoon, when the first of the targets had pulled up in his Maplewood carriage with its eight almost identical black horses.*

*Every torch around the property has been lit, along with lanterns and alchemical globes casting their unblinking light across the opulent residence and its grounds. The guests have brought their own personal guards. Also at the main gate are a dozen white-masked soldiers of the Watch from Kyuth.*

*A firm hand touches my shoulder and a hard voice whispers, "Raven, Are you ready?" It's Boar, a squad leader in the Grim Hand.*

*I nod.*

*"How many guards?"*

*"A couple dozen outside. Inside, it's harder to determine, but based on a count as they arrived, at least a score. So, maybe fifty all up; armed, armored and competent. Plus sorcerers."*

*Boar pauses. "Let me check with Scorpion and see if he still wants us to go in. I'll come back and let you know."*

*I nod, and Boar crawls back through the grasses until he disappears. He has some way of communicating with Scorpion across vast distances—probably sorcery. I don't know and don't care. If I need to know, I'll be told.*

*It has been almost a year since I last participated in an operation with Boar, Smoke, and Sandviper. Their other team member, Crooked, remains deep undercover in Kroe in the Pristart Combine and unable to join us.*

*My plan is as good as it could be on such short notice, and isn't without its risks, but Scorpion and I are confident I can pull it off.*

*A gathering of such powerful merchants represents an opportunity the City States can't miss—a chance to cut off funding for their opponents, who view the City States as heathen and unworthy of the prosperity they enjoy from their mines and agriculture.*

*And now I'm freezing my nether regions off in drizzling rain, staring at enough warriors and sorcerers to start a small war. And the biggest problem, from my point of view, is the source of the information regarding the meeting: someone close to the Kaile nobility, apparently, and another extremely wealthy merchant. One who probably hasn't been invited. The informant had insisted on an observer of their choosing being present, and the condition hadn't been negotiable. I haven't seen whoever it is—they've been kept hidden by Scorpion. Combined with the short timeframe, the presence of the outsider, and the hint they were doing someone else's dirty work, this hasn't sat well with me or my colleagues. But ultimately, we follow orders.*

*I prefer working alone and making precise, incisive strikes rather than using substantial force, but sometimes it just isn't possible. I check my internal dark-tide repository again, and as with the dozen other times I'd checked tonight it has only slightly diminished due to leakage. The source of power for abilities I barely comprehend, my repository always feels somehow apart, as if not truly mine, and it's confirmation that what was done to me was unnatural. I'll be glad to leave this all behind.*

*I hear the faint rustle of grass as Boar returns. He whispers in my ear, "Everyone's in position and ready to go. We'll execute the plan after a one hundred count. Any questions?"*

*"No," I reply, and Boar moves away to alert the others.*

*I begin my count, hoping I don't have to use too much dark-tide. The herbs and alchemicals in my medicinal lozenges wouldn't be good for my baby…the real reason for the plan Scorpion and I agreed to enact during this mission.*

*As I reach ninety-six, seven silvery streaks arc through the air from a tree eighty yards away, where Boar and Sandviper are concealed.*

*The sorcerers protecting the estate sense it, and a shimmering wall blinks into existence between the streaks and the residence—a ward designed to keep out physical objects and both dawn- and dusk-tide sorcery. But the seven shreds aren't dawn- or dusk-tide sorcery, and they aren't quite physical either. They sail right through the sorcerers' shield.*

*As the shreds penetrate the ward, I send a few pulses of dark-tide power into those I can sense, knowing the others on my team are doing the same. The shreds shatter windows, sail inside. The external wall of the dining room explodes outward as the shreds erupt, showering the grounds with glass and brick and plaster. An instant later I hear the air crack, as if lightning struck right in front of me. The dining room walls are now painted red—everyone gathered for the meeting liquefied.*

*The guards outside stand gaping at the destruction, then either run to the ravaged dining room or toward the tree the streaks had emerged from. Four other guards carrying crossbows run for a group of horses tied just inside the compound.*

*Three men huddle together, one raising a robed arm to point at the tree. Sorcerers.*

*I leap up and run toward the boundary wall. My job is to distract as many guards as possible to give Boar and Sandviper time to escape, then get out of there myself. I use my momentum to scramble up the wall and sit atop it, one leg on either side, then throw a knife at a guard who turns to investigate the noise I've made. I push the blade with a pulse of dark-tide power, lending it speed and accuracy. It flies thirty yards to pierce the guard's eye.*

*I locate another guard and, without thinking, throw and pulse. He drops to the ground too, clutching futilely for the knife in his back.*

*Four mounted horses tear out of the main gate toward Boar and Sandviper. I throw and pulse again, and drop another guard, but someone has seen me and crossbow bolts begin chinking off the wall I sit on. It's time to leave.*

*I lever myself up, wrap shadows around me, and sprint along the top of the wall, away from the building and toward the cliff edge. My guts twist as the ill effects of dark-tide use lash my body. More bolts hit the wall beneath me and hiss through the air ahead and behind, but my luck holds. I drop off the wall and into the shadows at its base, landing hard. I steady myself with one hand on the ground, keeping my momentum, and increase my pace.*

*Boar's voice whispers into my ear, and I shiver. Sorcery. "Three sorcerers are coming after you. Good luck."*

*"Thanks for the warning," I whisper, knowing he cannot hear me.*

*I follow a paved path that curves around sculpted bushes, and ahead see the stairway leading to the cliff wall that is my target. I drop a couple of shreds behind me. If the sorcerers aren't careful, they'll get a lethal surprise. Abandoning my throwing knives, I open the orichalcum sphere and remove the smaller ball. Now is the time to bring out all my resources. If I die without draining my dark-tide repository, it will be my own fault for not having used everything possible to escape.*

*I risk a glance behind and see three man-sized spheres of glowing light speed toward me—sorcerers within their protective wards. I send out two pulses of dark-tide energy and both my shreds crack simultaneously. Foliage tears and pavers buckle, but the sorcerers continue. They must have figured out what happened in the dining room and reinforced their wards. Not good for me.*

*Even as I have the thought, arcane spheres as bright as the sun sail into the sky, bleaching the night white. The shadows I've wrapped around myself rip to nothingness under the harsh glare. As I reach the bottom of the stairs, four guards stand up from behind a short wall, their crossbows trained on me. I throw myself to the ground and release the orichalcum sphere, pushing at it with my dark-tide power. Bolts pass above me, and one slices through my hair and the side of my ear.*

*I look up and see one guard hasn't released his bolt. He points his crossbow at me and smiles.*

*My orichalcum sphere accelerates through the air, wailing like a banshee as it hits him in the chest and continues out the other side. The force throws him backward, and his blood sprays his colleagues. With his dying reflex, he triggers his weapon and sends a bolt sailing skyward.*

*I send the sphere zigzagging back and forth as the remaining guards rush at me brandishing short swords. The sphere perforates all three before they take a dozen steps. Their bodies tumble to the ground, leaking crimson.*

*I call the sphere to my hand and resume my feeble dash away from the sorcerers. My steps are sluggish, my body drained of energy from my dark-tide use. About to stagger up the stairs, I shy away as glittering tendrils of power hammer out of the darkness and turn the stones to molten rock. I hiss in dismay and cover my eyes with an arm as droplets of stone splatter around me.*

*I spot a tree and make for its shadow amid the harsh light of the sorcerous spheres floating above. When I reach the darkness, I stop and turn to look at the sorcerers.*

*Their three silvery wards approach—and strike. Fiery globes rain down on the tree and on me. I shadow-step away. The trunk cracks and splinters as sap boils from inside. Flames slam the ground, turning the grass and plants to ash, hardening the soil until it cracks. Black smoke belches into the air.*

*Out of sight, confident my colleagues think I am dead, I clamber down the cliff.*

Scorpion woke a few hours later as the setting sun was turning the sky orange. Raven studied him from the padded chair where she'd dozed on and off while he slept. He groaned and tried to get up, unsuccessfully.

"I'll help," she said, rising.

"Thanks. I need to piss."

Raven helped him up and jammed a shoulder underneath his, supporting him while they shuffled to a covered chamber pot in the corner.

He glanced at her and nudged her away. "I can do it myself."

"I've seen it before, remember. But don't blame me if you fall and I'm not close enough to catch you."

She sat back in the chair while Scorpion grimaced and growled his way to uncovering the pot, then pissed for what seemed an eternity. When he'd finished, he lumbered back to the bed and sat down with a long sigh. His skin glistened with sweat from the minimal exertion.

"How are you feeling?" she asked.

"Not good. I was supposed to stay in bed for at least a few days. But when Tristana told me someone was looking for me and described you, I thought I should see if it was you."

"And such a touching reunion it was, with a knife sticking into my ribs."

"It has been years, Saskia."

It had been so long since someone had called her by her real name, it threw Raven off-guard. Her chest tightened, and she couldn't breathe for a heartbeat.

"Years isn't that long," she managed.

"That depends on what you've been doing."

Raven let the implied question slide. "Have you been eating?"

"Not much. Mostly drinking water. I seem to be sweating

more than I piss."

"You need to get some food into you. I'll fix something."

Scorpion lay back on the bed and closed his eyes. He was fading. "If I doze off... Tristana is supposed to be coming to check on me."

"She told me she didn't know where you were."

"Of course she did."

His head lolled to the side and his breathing became deeper. Not long after, there was a soft knock on the door. Raven leaped to her feet, a knife in her hand.

"It's Tristana," the healer whispered.

Raven unbarred the door and let her in. Tristana carried a waxed-paper parcel, which she deposited on the nightstand beside the packets of herbs and the oil of poppy.

"More herbs," she explained, then bent to feel Scorpion's forehead and check his pulse.

"How is he?" Raven asked. "Really."

"He's healing, but the poison ravaged his system. He's in remarkable physical shape, though, so that will help."

Tristana seemed satisfied with her cursory examination and edged toward the door.

"How long will he need the oil of poppy?" Raven asked as the healer stepped outside.

"A day or two, depending on how he feels. The pain will be the worst over the first days. If he's not getting better by then, well, he never will. I'll come back tomorrow. There isn't anything you can do for him now other than wait and see. If I had to wager, I'd put my coin on a recovery."

Raven knew how most of Tristana's gambles usually played out.

Scorpion slept through the rest of the day and the following night. Raven, in the padded chair, was able to catch some sleep too. She was used to sleeping rough from her training and missions. Old habits died hard.

When he woke, she prepared some tea using the herbs Tristana had brought and cut thin slices of bread that she topped with cheese and toasted on the brazier. Scorpion sipped the tea and wolfed down the bread and cheese. He looked a little better. Some color had returned to his face, and he hadn't begun to sweat yet.

"Tristana said she'd be back today to examine you again," Raven told him.

"She came yesterday?"

Raven nodded. "Although she didn't stay long, for some reason. Before she comes back, can you tell me what in bloody darkness is going on? I was minding my own business, trying to live my life in peace, and someone tried to assassinate me. I killed almost a dozen of them, but they still kept after me. You were the only one who could have told them where I was. No one else knew I was even still alive."

Scorpion swallowed and met her eyes fleetingly. "A few months ago, the apartment I was staying in was burgled. Nobody knew about the place, I swear it. I'd only been there a month. A neighbor in another apartment sent for the Watch. By the time I returned from the mission I was on, the whole place had been looted." He took a breath. "That's the only answer I can come up with."

Raven could tell he'd left something out. "What did they find?"

"A few journals were stolen, but they were all in code. Someone must have broken it. There were some entries about planning your escape, and a few musings on where you might have gone to ground based on what I knew of you." He winced, still not meeting her gaze. "I'm sorry. They must have worked out you were still alive and tracked you down. It's the only thing that makes sense. As you say, only I knew, and I haven't told anyone." Scorpion closed his eyes, as if the confession had exhausted him.

Raven glared at him. "So, someone found out I wasn't dead, and came after me. Why, though?"

"Not just you," Scorpion said, finally meeting her eyes. "All our other team members have been killed as well. Reports are still filtering in, but it looks like they were all killed on the same day that Crooked died."

Raven's mouth twisted in shock. "Every one of them? Dead?" She couldn't believe it. Someone had managed to eliminate an elite group trained by an organization that only a handful of people knew about. A group with abilities that made regular soldiers seem like children fighting with sticks.

"It was a coordinated strike against every one of us by professional mercenaries," continued Scorpion. "I have no idea how they knew who we were, or where we were. After I heard about Crooked, and reports of the others began to come in, I scrambled for a safe house. Only, it wasn't safe, and they came for me. It was pure luck that I managed to escape. And better luck that I found a decent healer in time. If I didn't heal faster than normal, I would most likely be dead."

"And you have no idea who they are, or who hired them?"

"As I said, the only thing I know for sure is they're mercenaries—maybe from Kaile, judging by their accents and the hand signals they used. Did you manage to get any information about the men who attacked you?"

Raven shook her head. "They had no personal items on them. No identifying marks or badges. They could have been from Kaile. Could have been from anywhere."

"In a few days I should be able to locate some of my contacts and have them put feelers out," Scorpion said. "But we can't rule out that our colleagues might have been killed by someone within the City States."

Colleagues. It was a wretched term for those who'd endured the torture and agony of a transformation that had changed them forever. She had existed in an almost emotionless state. She had to, to be effective. As cold as ice. As hard as steel. There could be no compassion. No second-guessing. These tenets had been pounded into her during her training and before her missions. To be safe and avoid getting hurt, you had to renounce all feelings. But without feelings you were as good as dead. Like the ghouls in the wilderness.

"The City States created us," Raven said. "Why would they want us dead?"

"I don't know. But if they wanted to keep their research secret, the cleanest way to do that is to destroy all evidence. Which also means destroying the results of your work." Scorpion's eyes were losing focus; he was obviously tiring quickly. He took a few gulps of the now-cold herbal tea.

"Did you get the feeling there was anything wrong within the team? Or any hints from higher up?" Raven asked.

"Anything is possible. There are plenty of people out there who would prefer us to disappear. And any exposure of who we are and what we do would be disastrous for the City States. Then again, the attack on you might be a separate issue."

Raven scoffed. "That's unlikely. There are too many coincidences. We need to find out more before acting. Right now, we don't have any targets."

Raven spent the morning nosing around the barracks and training areas in Kroe, where the troops she'd seen in the village were likely to originate from. They were the only source of information she had. Scorpion gave her a pouch of silver talents for bribes, and it was half empty by the time she'd found her way to someone of rank who might know anything. Posing as an aggrieved noble whose business had been disrupted by the soldiers and the curfew, she learned that they didn't know who the injured man was, nor what his business had been in the village. A report she paid handsomely to read for a few minutes had a note stating that the attackers had all disappeared, as if into thin air—which Raven knew could mean anything, but likely sorcery. In her view, they were probably in Kroe, searching for someone who'd been poisoned.

Scorpion said he'd paid Tristana a great deal to keep her mouth shut, but she hadn't hesitated long before jumping at Raven's gemstone. The valuable garnet had cleared the healer's debts, though, so she didn't have a massive reason to squeal right now. Still, they'd be wise to find somewhere else to stay soon.

By midday, Raven decided to cut her losses and headed back to Scorpion's apartment. She knocked at a specific tempo, and he opened up. After washing the street dust from her hands and face, she sprawled into the padded chair, rubbing her eyes and the back of her neck, which had been tense all morning. Subterfuge made her uncomfortable. She'd rather a decent fight, so the outcome could be determined quickly.

Scorpion approached from the kitchen bearing a plate of dried fruit and some nuts. His hand holding the plate trembled, and Raven leaped to her feet and took it off him.

"You're supposed to be resting," she said, guiding him to the bed. "Have you drunk the herbs Tristana left for you? They won't do any good lying on the nightstand."

"I know. And I have. But I need to move around to help me think."

"How do you feel?" she said.

"I've had better mornings. But it's an improvement over yesterday. I only took half a dose of the poppy oil earlier, so I can think clearer. I have a feeling I'll need all my wits about me in the coming days."

"What do you plan to do? You've got people trying to kill you, and you don't know who to trust. Plus, you're getting a bit old now. You're probably losing your edge."

He managed a tepid smile. "Very droll. Listen, I want to thank you for staying. You didn't have to, and it could be dangerous."

"Such a way with words. Anyway, where would I go? You were—are—my only lead."

"You shouldn't stay close to me," he said. "You escaped the assassins, and now you can go anywhere you want. You're still dead, after all."

Raven shivered as a chill swept through her, and rubbed her arms. "I can't. I'd be forever looking over my shoulder, wondering where the next knife or poisoned bolt will come from. I don't want to live like that. I'd hoped I'd left my old life behind after our deception at Kyuth."

"I'm sorry. I don't know how many times I can—"

She cut him off. "It's not your fault. I'm not blaming you."

A muscle in his face twitched. "But it is my fault. I should have known better."

"I... Yes, you should have. You're the one who told me to always expect the worst so you're never disappointed and never caught flat-footed. But that's beside the point. I'm here, and I'm all right. And if someone's still after me, I won't run. I refuse to spend my life hiding in fear. It's either them or me; and so far I've always come out on top. You know what I'm capable of."

Scorpion let out a deep sigh. He looked even more tired, as if her words had knocked the energy out of him. "There's no value in going on a killing spree. We have to figure out why our entire team was taken out. The assassins will still be after me, and you. But I have an idea. There's a bank here in Kroe—Tomlin & Willow—that handles the finances for the Grim Hand. If the City States want us all dead, the coin to pay the mercenaries would have come from there. It's a good place to start. I've previously dealt with a senior manager there, but he's a devout family man. I doubt he'll be willing to hand over their books. But if we can find some other way to see them, we might be able to trace the funds and figure out who's behind all this."

"There are ways to make even a good family man cooperate," said Raven.

# THIRTEEN

THE RULING COUNCIL OF KAILE hadn't warmed to Blasius's offers to buy their favor—he needed their permission to access the ruins—which was why Hanno had to dispose of some of them, but perhaps Blasius hadn't offered enough to them. They were greedy, after all. He'd figured there was no reason to hand over more than he needed to, but in hindsight it mightn't have been the optimal move.

Perhaps his best option now was to offer more in coin and trade. He was rapidly running out of time, having considered a number of scenarios before he'd had Hanno assassinate the councilors. But a bold strike to take out the people in his way had been the most likely to succeed and clear the path of debris. He could have tried to influence the councilors to assign sole rights to mine that section of the mountains, but the Council had their own mining businesses and would want a piece of the action, if not the whole pie to themselves.

So Blasius decided to try violence and subterfuge instead.

But the greediest of the lot, the Patriarch of the Church of Menselas in Kaile, was a tricky one too. He had the backing of the Order of Eternal Vigilance—knight sorcerers. The Patriarch was best dealt with in other, subtler ways, such as scandal—there were rumors, after all. There were always rumors.

A light snow dusted the corpses of the seven dead-eyes. The pale, stick-limbed creatures had thought the team an easy target, probably goaded by hunger due to the slim pickings the mountains provided. Now, their milky blood had splashed across the ground and their eyes lived up to their name, though there had been no change to their boiled-egg whiteness in life or in death.

Hanno Dinnas hadn't even needed to reach for his weapon, and instead had sat atop his shaggy horse while his mercenaries dispatched the creatures with quiet efficiency. One of the men, a short, mace-wielding warrior he'd picked up on the way, strode to each corpse with a grin on his face and smashed its head in, though there was no chance any remained alive.

Brushing flakes of snow from his shoulders and donning his wide-brimmed hat, Hanno clapped his hands together and the muffled sound of his gloves carried clearly in the dead air created by the snow.

The mercenaries finished cleaning their weapons and guided their snow-bred horses until they could all hear him.

"Men," Hanno said firmly, "we'll reach the village of Roisin just before dark. Preparations have been made, and we'll rest up in a barn on the outskirts. There you must leave all personal possessions in the lockbox provided. No one must be able to guess who you are or where you're from. As with every job you do for me, the rules are simple. Do not get friendly with the locals. That goes for comely lasses who want a tumble, or the old man who wants to gossip. Everyone stays close by the barn, unless I give them orders to do otherwise. And there will be no fighting among yourselves. No getting drunk. We're going in and coming out as quickly as we can. You all know the layout and the targets. Are there any questions?"

"Are you sure we can't tumble any of the women?" guffawed the mace-carrier.

Hanno looked to Achim, the leader of the team. Achim gave the newcomer a clip across the ear. The man cursed and glared at him, and Achim stared back silently. Few were able to withstand such a look, and the chastised mercenary averted his eyes, grumbling to himself.

The rest of the men sat silently, snow drifting between them. Achim shook his head.

"Excellent," Hanno said. "I'm sure I don't need to tell you again how important this mission is. You are the best of the mercenaries I've gathered. The pay for this job is triple the usual rate. Remember that, and what it'll buy you. Do your best and look after each other. Achim?"

"You heard him. Let's get moving."

The warriors, led by Achim, trotted off down the path beaten through rocks strewn around the hills at the base of the mountains. Barely wide enough for a wagon, many had met ill luck on wintery treks by straying from it and finding themselves tumbling down slopes, or worse yet, falling into empty space over a cliff.

Hanno pulled an orichalcum disk from his pocket and thanked the gods it didn't need contact with his flesh. If he removed his gloves in this weather, he'd be risking frostbite. He gave the rune-covered disk a frown filled with distaste. The artifact was useful, he'd give it that, but dealing with sorcery was repulsive and too often led to unpleasantness. Despite the communication device's helpfulness, he couldn't help thinking Blasius Matheo could use it to track his location at any time. It wouldn't surprise him if the merchant could hear, or even see, through the device without Hanno knowing. He made a mental note not to say anything Blasius wouldn't want to hear when it was nearby—which was almost always.

He exhaled onto the black circle in the center to warm it up, then grimaced before licking the metal. It tasted like any other metal, but Hanno couldn't rid himself of the feeling that the ancient artifact had taken something from him.

He sniffed in the frigid air and glanced around him, wary of any more dead-eyes, though any others would know their brethren had been slain and likely have fled.

Blasius's hard face appeared in the circle Hanno had licked. He was chewing something, but spoke through the mouthful. As always, the sorcery that allowed him to see Blasius made Hanno shiver.

"What is your status, Hanno?"

"The first team is on its way, sir."

"Outstanding work. Any update on the missions you failed?"

Hanno ground his teeth in frustration. "My contacts are looking into every avenue, but so far they've come up empty. Scorpion hasn't shown up at any of the reputable healers."

"Then look at the disreputable ones."

"We're doing just that. There's a high probability that he's dead. He was wounded by a crossbow bolt coated with a usually lethal poison."

"So your men say. I'd prefer certainty over guesswork, wouldn't you?"

"As you say, sir."

"He's still alive. Mark my words. He's out there somewhere. I can feel it in my plums."

At the thought of the big man's gonads, Hanno grimaced. "Sorry," he said quickly. "It's cold here. We're still searching for him and assuming he's alive. I have another four men on their way to Kroe as we speak. We will be ready when he surfaces."

"And the infernal woman?"

"She is a bigger problem, I'm afraid. Although she doesn't have any bearing on our operation here. She has disappeared. We've combed the island, and the ones around it, in case she went to ground there. But she'd have to have evaded our search and that of the Watch there, who want her for the murders. I think we should abandon our hunt. Our best option is just to wait until she surfaces."

"Hanno, Hanno, Hanno, I believe I was quite clear. Do not halt your search. Put more resources into it if you have to. I don't care. But I want her. I want her head. I don't care how long it takes or how much it costs. She isn't going to get away this time. I want your best men on it. And women too. Their only job is to find her for me. Is that understood?"

Hanno nodded, even though the chance that they'd find an expert such as Raven had proven to be was minuscule. He'd have a better chance of marrying the long-dead Queen of Niyas. He could argue the facts with Blasius, try to convince the single-minded fool that the probability of killing her now was approaching zero; or he could charge the dupe his exorbitant fee, plus expenses, and continue searching indefinitely.

"It is indeed, sir. As you said, my best warriors are on the job.

I'm sure it's only a matter of time. Whatever we need to do to find her, we will."

"Then we understand each other."

Blasius's scowling face disappeared from the artifact, and Hanno hastily tucked it back into his pocket. He had other similar devices for communicating with his various lieutenants, but nothing that made his skin crawl like this one.

Or perhaps it was just Blasius.

# FOURTEEN

I STUMBLE FROM THE CARRIAGE *and press a silver into the driver's hand. Another cramp rips through me, and I clasp my hands around my bulging belly. My breath steams in the early morning air, and the scent of freshly roasted meat from a nearby butcher makes me gag.*

*"Miss, are you all right?" the driver says, descending from the carriage. "Do you need help?"*

*I brush his hands away and stagger to the open doors of the hospital. I came here a few months ago to make sure it was up to my exacting standards. As I step onto the polished marble floor, warm wetness trickles down my legs. A woman behind a counter notices and rushes around to help.*

*"I think my water's breaking," I say. I clutch at the soaking fabric of my skirt and feel heat in my cheeks at the spots of translucent pink fluid on the floor.*

*"You don't say," the woman replies. "Do we—?"*

"I've paid for a birthing in a month's time. The baby is early."

"Oh my. Here, come with me. What's your name?"

"It's Carina. Check your records."

"Let's get you seen to first."

As we pass the counter, the woman rings a small silver bell. A few moments later, another woman joins her, with a third moving to take over the counter position. All three women have their hair tightly pulled back and wear identical brown skirts and shirts.

They find an empty room and help me onto a hard bed covered with a waxed canvas sheet. It isn't the most comfortable, but it is probably easy to clean. Three alchemical globes in wall sconces provide a bright light, and I have to squint.

The first midwife disappears, while the second one bustles about, lifting my head and placing a pillow underneath, then hitching my skirt up to remove my underclothes. As she busies herself taking towels from a cupboard, another contraction rips through my abdomen and I gasp. My stomach loosens, and a gush of pinkish water spreads between my legs across the canvas sheet.

The first midwife returns carrying a steaming kettle. She is accompanied by a healer. The second woman breathes a sigh of relief.

"It's early," I blurt. Sweat pours down my face. "Will my baby be all right?"

"Don't you worry, your baby's going to be just fine," the healer says. She holds a hushed conversation with the two midwives, then one of them steeps some tea while the other wipes up the mess between my legs.

Another contraction tears at me—a sharp pain in my belly, as if the baby is trying to claw its way out. I moan, and the healer holds a hollow wooden cone to my bulging stomach and places her ear to its narrow end. As she listens, a frown creases the woman's forehead.

"What's wrong?" I gasp.

*"Nothing. Don't you worry. Everything will be fine."*

*Another tearing wave of pain rips through me, and this time I scream. I try to hunch over, my hands reaching for my stomach, but the two midwives grab my arms. My vision blurs with tears of pain. The healer drops some yellow liquid into a cup of the tea.*

*She brings it to my lips and commands, "Drink this down. It will help your muscles relax. If you don't, it could go ill for you and your baby."*

*I do as I am told. Another contraction hits, but already the medicine has taken the edge off the pain.*

*The healer grasps my hand and gives it a reassuring squeeze. "The pain will lessen now, and you'll most likely not recall the birth afterward. Try to relax. Everything will be fine."*

*As the healer keeps talking, the world around me grows fuzzy. I feel as if she is floating in water. The healer's voice grows fainter and fainter, then fades altogether as the room turns gray.*

Tristana came into the kitchen and set a leather satchel down on the table. Raven followed, keeping her eyes on the woman, and picked up a thick piece of dried meat from a plate. She chewed the end off. It was actually quite good, with plenty of spices rubbed onto the meat the way she liked it.

"How is he doing?" she asked.

"He's slowly improving. He's doing far better than I expected, but there might still be internal damage we don't know about. The wound hasn't gone rotten, and he says the pain has receded, though I think he's lying. As far as it goes, I'd say he is a very lucky man. Being hit by a poisoned bolt like that should have killed him."

Raven took another bite and chewed thoughtfully. "He's still weak, though. How soon before he can travel?"

"Travel? Quite a while. He can walk around for short periods now, but you must have seen how it tires him out. Maybe in a few days he can leave the apartment—if he doesn't exert himself. Riding would be out of the question, but a carriage or trap would probably be all right. He won't be fully recovered for at least a month or more. Considering I thought he was a dead man when he turned up at my door, I'd say it was a miracle. He should make an offering to his god."

The gods and goddesses had abandoned Raven and the rest of the Grim Hand long ago. What she'd been through, what they all had, proved it. Raven divided Tristana's estimate by four to account for Scorpion's accelerated healing. Maybe a week, then. "Good. We can't stay here much longer."

She and Scorpion had outlined a sting operation to pressure the banker from Tomlin & Willow, Ralnar Bryel, to cooperate. It was risky: show and bluff, with no substance other than what the mark believed. But the consequences would be very real for Ralnar if he didn't give Raven and Scorpion what they wanted.

Tristana made her farewells, and Scorpion called out to Raven from his bed.

She entered the room to find him sitting up with a grin on his face. There were some people whose smile made them less attractive. Scorpion was one of them, except to her.

"Let's move on Ralnar tonight," he said.

"Are you well enough?"

"You'll be doing most of the work. How hard is it to confect outrage? I can do that standing on my head."

"Let's hope it doesn't come to that."

Dressed in a plain brown shirt and long skirt, with padding underneath to provide added bulk, her hair secured under a linen shawl and lines drawn on her face, Raven looked like an older woman who'd had a hard life. Her orichalcum sphere was snugged out of sight under her shirt, and she had a narrow knife strapped to her thigh. She tucked a shallow basket filled with posies over her elbow, and entered the Priestess and the Cauldron, an upmarket tavern that Ralnar visited nightly for a tipple on his walk home from Tomlin & Willow bank.

Scorpion sat on a bench across the road, smoking a wooden pipe and looking for all the world like a laborer avoiding returning home to a nagging wife. As Raven strolled along the street, he gave her a slight nod.

Raven entered the tavern quickly and, when no one stopped her, scanned the room for Ralnar. The banker sat alone in a booth, nursing a glass of amber liquid in one hand and scribbling in a notebook with the other. Before she could be thrown out for hawking her wares without permission, Raven hustled over to him. The banker didn't look up as she approached, nor when she stopped next to his booth.

She dropped her basket on the table with a thump and palmed an open vial of a strong intoxicant usually used to treat insomnia. She'd also added a narcotic that would cloud Ralnar's memory.

He looked up at her in annoyance.

"Flowers for your wife?" crooned Raven. "Posies for your mistress?" She began to place posies onto the table, making sure to reach across and position some at the far end.

A scowl replaced Ralnar's frown. "Who let you in here? This is a place for quiet reflection after a hard day's work. Remove these flowers at once and be on your way!"

Raven doubted Ralnar, sitting at his desk all day, had done a hard day's work in his life.

"Just a few silvers for a posy," she said. "Your wife will look kindly upon you, good sir." Out of the corner of her eye she saw a burly man shuffle around the end of the long bar and hurry toward her. "Just buy one, please, sir. You won't regret it."

Ralnar's face flushed, and he grabbed several of the posies and shoved them back into the basket. Raven pretended to help, getting in his way, and took the chance to pour her alchemical concoction into his drink.

As she slipped the vial back into her skirt pocket, she felt a firm hand grab her shoulder. "No hawking allowed in here," a gruff voice said.

Raven turned to the burly man and nodded meekly. "I was just leaving."

Out in the street, she dumped the basket and flowers in an alley and moved to stand a few dozen paces from Scorpion, where she could keep an eye on the door of the tavern. Not long after, Ralnar walked out on unsteady legs. The bouncer had hold of one arm, supporting him, but the banker waved him away. Ralnar walked slowly along the street, pausing frequently to lean against the wall. Raven followed a dozen paces behind, and Scorpion strolled down the other side of the street, directly opposite Ralnar.

When the banker stopped and leaned both hands on a wall, his head lowered, feet shuffling as if still walking, Raven scooted forward and clutched his arm. A couple walking toward them glanced over curiously. Raven gave them a smile and mimed a drinking motion. The couple sniffed and hurried past.

"Ralnar!" exclaimed Raven. "Here, let me help you."

"What?" He peered at her, eyes bleary. "Do I know you?"

"Oh yes," she replied. "Very well."

"I'm not sure… I-I'm not feeling well. Is there a trap nearby I could hire?"

Ralnar wobbled, then staggered. Only Raven's tight grip on his arm prevented him from falling.

Raven heard a whistle from behind as Scorpion summoned the trap he had waiting. It stopped nearby, and Scorpion came to help Raven bundle the banker into it. A few moments later, they were on their way to a nondescript apartment Scorpion had arranged.

With Raven doing most of the heavy lifting, they carried Ralnar up the stairs, then let him fall onto the bed Raven had made up earlier with linen sheets and a woolen blanket. The room also contained a dresser and wardrobe, and a table positioned underneath a window with floral curtains. Raven had added a few extra touches for authenticity—shoes and boots by the door, a chipped vase filled with half-wilted flowers, a bowl with wizened apples and dried dates. After all, she was supposed to be playing a single woman trying to make her way in a harsh world.

They stripped Ralnar of his clothes. Raven took a monogrammed handkerchief from one of his pockets and tugged his family ring from his finger. She tucked both items into the pocket of a dress and hung it over one of the table's chairs. She then stripped to her underclothes, and she and Scorpion surveyed the room to make sure they hadn't forgotten anything. Scorpion gathered up her flower seller's disguise, while Raven removed the make-up on her face with a cloth moistened from a bowl of water. She slipped a knife under the edge of the mattress in case it was needed.

"He'll be waking soon," she said to Scorpion. "You'd better leave."

After he'd gone, Raven perched on the edge of the bed. She hated these kinds of tricks, but in some cases it was the quickest and easiest way to get what you needed. With any luck, this would be the last time she ever had to employ such methods.

When Ralnar stirred, Raven slid into the bed beside him and positioned herself suggestively: an arm around him, one leg between both of his. When Ralnar failed to show more signs of life, she poked him in the ribs. He jerked and made a snuffling noise, then groaned as he half turned. His hand moved to clasp Raven's thigh.

"Viola," he muttered, "I'm not feeling the best. Perhaps—"

"Is Viola your wife?" Raven asked.

Ralnar jerked as if stung, then threw Raven off and stared at her with wild eyes. He uttered a gasp of horror, and rolled out of bed, hitting the floor with a thump. He stood, then realized he was naked, and dragged the sheet from the bed to cover himself. His mouth opened and closed like a fish's.

Raven gave him a timid smile. "You weren't so shy earlier."

"I…who are you?"

Raven frowned. "What do you mean? I love you, Ralnar." A little over the top, but he wouldn't be thinking clearly in this situation, and would still be suffering lingering effects from the drug they had used on him.

Ralnar shook his head and glanced frantically around the room like a trapped animal. "This isn't happening," he muttered. "I would never—"

"What are you saying?" Raven kneeled on the bed, extending a hand to him. "After what we did together…how can you pretend you don't remember? Come back to bed. We're good together."

"No!" he shouted. "We were *not* good together. I don't remember anything."

"Don't say such things! You're hurting me."

"I don't know who you are! Or where I am."

"You're here, with me. And that's all that matters."

"No, it isn't. I'm married!"

Raven got off the bed on the other side from Ralnar. She didn't want him lashing out at her. "I know. But you said you would leave her for me." She took Ralnar's handkerchief and his ring from her dress pocket. "See? You gave me presents."

"Where did you get those? You stole them!"

"I didn't! You gave them to me when you professed your love."

"I did no such thing. Hand them over. You're deluded. A conniving witch!"

Ralnar found his clothes and tugged them on, still attempting to hide his naked form with the bedsheet. Eventually, after much cursing, he made for the door, his shirt untucked and boots unlaced.

"The Watch will hear about this!" he shouted at her over his shoulder. "You'll be put in prison. And don't sell my belongings—I'll pay you for them. I'll send a man to deal with it."

Raven let him go, suddenly weary. He wouldn't tell anyone about her, she knew. He had too much to lose to become embroiled in a scandal. That's what she and Scorpion were counting on. A part of her hoped they wouldn't have to ruin him to get what they wanted.

They waited two days before springing the final stage of the plan on Ralnar. Raven lingered outside Tomlin & Willow bank at midday, when the junior employees filed out for their midday meal. She knew Ralnar would leave around the same time for a quick lunch. She concealed her hair under a hood, but made sure to tie Ralnar's kerchief around her neck and wore his ring on her finger.

As he hurried down the building's marble steps, head down, brow furrowed, Raven moved to intercept him.

When he saw her, his mouth twisted in distaste. "Get out of my sight, you filthy harridan," he snarled.

Raven was beginning to feel less sympathy for him. "We need to talk."

She made to grab his sleeve but he brushed her hand away. "Get out of my sight!" His voice had risen in volume and he glanced around in case anyone had heard. He took Raven by the arm and she let herself be led down a side street. "You can't come here," he said, looking around nervously and licking his lips.

"Someone came to me. They know about us."

"There is no us! Wait, who came to you? What did they say?"

"They know about us, about what we did. They want something from you, or they'll tell everyone about us: your wife, your children, the people you work with. Everyone."

The blood drained from Ralnar's face. His fingers tightened around Raven's arm. "This cannot happen! I'll be ruined. What did you tell them?"

"That we're in love."

"We're not! What else did you say?"

"Nothing. They knew everything already. They said they'll hurt me if I don't do what they say. And that your wife and children would get hurt too."

She didn't like using his children, but Ralnar and his family should come out of this unscathed. As long as he saw sense and didn't kick up a fuss.

"Who were they? Tell me!" he said.

"I don't know. They told me to meet you today, and said they'd be in contact with you afterward. I shouldn't have come after the way you've treated me. But I couldn't bear the thought of you or your innocent family coming to harm."

"Never speak of my family again!" he hissed. "This is outrageous. I'm going to the Watch. See if I don't."

Raven decided it was time to make her exit. Her part was played out, and Scorpion would take over from here.

"You've treated me cruelly, Ralnar. I don't know what schemes you're embroiled in, and I want no part of them. These thugs were serious, and I'd advise you to give them whatever they want. Otherwise you and those you love will get hurt."

Before he could respond, Raven yanked her arm from his grip and hurried away.

Scorpion intercepted Ralnar that evening on his way home from the bank. After stewing all afternoon on what Raven had told him, the banker was ripe for the picking.

Raven kept a watch on them as they argued, then Ralnar nodded and led Scorpion back to the bank.

Raven heard the key turn in the door lock. When Scorpion entered, she placed the knife in her hand back on the dresser beside the bed.

"Good news?" she asked.

Scorpion grinned, though his face was pale and drawn. "Yes, but I'm starving. Wait a few moments." He busied himself cutting two slices of bread and cheese, and chewed hurriedly, also sipping on a strong, dark beer that Tristana had recommended. Once he was sated, he brushed his hands and sat on the bed. "All right, I might just have figured something out. Ralnar keeps meticulous records, and the money trail was difficult to trace, but I managed to work out a few things. I found out who ordered the transfers; and best of all, someone who's been moving money to a private account, stealing from the City States. There's a complex web of transfers to and from people and organizations we know of: the City States, and someone high up, and another account whose ownership has eluded me so far. And it all revolves around the last mission you were on, where you faked your death."

"In Kyuth? They were a bunch of rich, corrupt merchants. No one would miss them." She sat back in the padded chair. "I don't understand. How does this tie together?"

"I don't have all of the information, but I do know that our strike in Kyuth should have rid the world of some nasty characters who profited off others. And the money they funneled to those who would do the City States harm would have ceased. But it looks like not all of the merchants died, or their business weren't disrupted sufficiently. According to notes in the margins of Ralnar's ledgers, one has emerged, wealthier and more powerful than before."

"So did we only make things worse?"

"I don't know. Possibly. What I do know is the account manipulating all the money through Ralnar's bank belongs to was Merab Varko."

"You're joking? She's a Gold Commander in the City States combined military."

"She's been promoted to Emerald Commander now. And I wish I were joking." Scorpion shook his head in disbelief. "I don't want to believe it was Merab Varko. She's highly respected, and so powerful that she probably thought she'd never be exposed. Very few people know about the Grim Hand, but she does. A directive came down a month before everyone was killed: someone wanted a list of our people and all their possible locations. It's happened before, so I didn't think the request was unusual, but now, in hindsight, I can see the timing was suspicious. A few weeks after I made my report, everyone else was dead and I barely escaped alive."

Raven met his eyes. "That's not enough to prove anything."

"Since when have you required proof?" he countered. "Varko has betrayed all of us, and the City States. And for some reason she wanted the Grim Hand dead. Perhaps killing all of us is one of her first steps. If we're all dead, we can't be sent after her."

"The safest thing would be to eliminate the best resource the City States have," agreed Raven. "Why would she want to kill me though? What did I do to her? It doesn't make sense. Maybe I was still a potential source of information too. That's the reason she wanted me dead."

"I agree. There's something we're missing. My guess is they looted my belongings to see if I had anything they could use. And they broke the code I used in my journals, which put them on your trail. It had to be Merab Varko who requested the report on the Grim Hand—the bank documents show how deeply she's enmeshed in all of this. I want to kill her, but that might not be for the best. She'll have designs within designs, and no doubt she'll have covered her tracks, just like we would."

"We can do it, you and I. Kill Varko and then disappear," suggested Raven.

"We can't. We need to find out what's going on. The survival of the City States might depend on it. Just killing Varko is the wrong course and you know it."

Raven did know it, and that was the reason she'd never have been able to take over Scorpion's role as leader of their group of killers. Sometimes she allowed her emotions to get the better of her, especially anger and hate.

"Do you ever think of doing the same thing I did and getting away from it all?" she asked him. "You could leave this life behind."

"It isn't so easy for me," he replied. "I don't take part in direct contact missions, so I can't make it look as if I've been killed, like we did with you. And I'm a sorcerer. You can disappear into a crowd, but to another sorcerer I'll always stand out."

"So, you have thought about disappearing?"

"Sometimes. And then I wonder what I'd do instead of this. There's nobody and nothing to go home to. I don't even remember my home. Hells, I don't even know my own name like you do. I don't know anything other than this life."

"You were hit with a poisoned bolt. What if you just vanished and never resurfaced? Maybe this is a chance for you to get out?" Raven's head swam with thoughts of a new future with Scorpion by her side. Would it even be possible? Had too much happened to change them over the years? "If everyone thinks we're both dead, we could go anywhere. Maybe we could head west to Ivrian. Or even farther west." She paused, heart hammering in her chest. "You'd have someone to come home to then."

Scorpion didn't speak for several heartbeats. "My greatest regret about helping you leave was that I'd never see you again. It was hard to let you go. But you said you didn't want to live a life where you're always looking over your shoulder. I'm the same."

Raven wanted to say more, but the words stuck in her throat.

"I'll recover," he added, when she didn't reply. "Then I'm sure everything will work out."

She nodded and went into the kitchen, leaving him to rest. Her eyes were moist, and she wiped them with her sleeve. Years ago she would have chastised herself for being weak, but now she knew tears for what they were: a sign she was still human.

# FIFTEEN

I STAND AT THE GRAVESIDE, *muscles tense, skin sheened with sweat, barely able to keep myself upright on wobbly legs.*

*At the bottom of the hole lies a cloth-wrapped bundle.*

*Amelia.*

*Grief again bubbles up from its simmer and I hunch over, trying to keep it contained. If it erupts, I fear I will throw myself in with my baby. Tears course down my cheeks, running into my mouth and dripping from my chin. I don't have the strength to wipe them away. My body shakes with sorrow and rage.*

*Why did this happen? Why my little Amelia? Am I undeserving? Am I cursed?*

*The gravedigger, a thin man wearing dirt-stained clothes, begins shoveling earth on top of my baby, and I jerk upright and place a hand on his shoulder.*

*"I'll do it," I say.*

*He leaves, mercifully. I move as best I can, feeling like my limbs are planks of wood, and begin to shovel the mound of loose earth. A worm wriggles on top, and I almost collapsed at the thought of it burrowing its way into my baby.*

*I kneel and grab fistfuls of damp earth, letting it fall over the tiny bundle in the hole. I try to remember what god or goddess I should pray to, but I can't think of any.*

*My sobs start again, and this time I cannot stop them.*

*I get to my feet and resume shoveling the cold earth over my baby Amelia.*

When the sun set the next day, Scorpion felt well enough to replenish his dusk-tide repository. Raven could feel her own dark-tide repository slowly leaching of energy, but with her orichalcum sphere to enhance her abilities she should be fine until the next full-dark, when she could build up her power again.

Soon after dark, Tristana came again to check on Scorpion. She did her usual healer things: looked into his mouth and ears, listened to his chest, shone a lamp into his eyes, and made him walk around the room stark naked. Raven suspected this last was for the healer's benefit and not for his. She couldn't blame the woman. Though his face wasn't much to look at, the change Scorpion had gone through had sculpted his muscles and made his body hard. But if Tristana had seen Raven without her clothes, she would have been shocked to see the raised lumps on her back and shoulders. She'd overheard the cursed sorcerers speculating they might be the beginnings of horny spikes taking root. Maybe Tristana would think they were some sort of disease.

Maybe they were.

"You're healing remarkably quickly," said Tristana.

Scorpion glanced at Raven. "Good clean living. No drinking and no drugs. Plenty of healthy food and water."

Tristana grunted, unconvinced. "I'd say you're well enough to get out of this apartment. A careful walk around the nearby streets will do you good."

"Is there anything he shouldn't do?"

"Drink anything alcoholic. His internal organs were damaged by the poison and it'll take some time for them to recover. Also, no running or carrying anything heavy. He might feel a lot better already, but he'll tire quickly."

"I'm right here," said Scorpion. "You can talk to me."

"The shoulder looks to be healing exceptionally well," said Tristana. "You're out of the woods, I'd say. Try to avoid getting shot with a poisoned bolt again and you should be fine."

Scorpion tugged his pants back on. "Thank you for taking care of me. If you hadn't, I wouldn't be standing here. I owe you more than coins."

"I didn't do it for altruistic reasons," replied Tristana. "With what you've paid me, plus the garnet from this woman here, I've cleared my debts and begun to think about giving up gambling. Maybe we're even."

Tristana approached Raven. When the healer reached out to grasp her hand, Raven froze. More memories flooded her mind: so strong they blocked out the present. *A firm, warm hand enfolding mine—a giant's. Comfort. I trust this person without reservation. Soft skin and the scent of baked bread.*

"Excuse me?" came a voice.

She shook her head and the room swam back into view. A wave of longing washed through Raven. Homesickness. How could she be homesick for somewhere she couldn't remember? A family she had no recollection of?

Tristana was looking at her, concerned. The healer spoke slowly. "I just wanted to—"

Raven realized the healer still held onto her and she snatched her hand away. "I'm sorry. It's nothing. A memory." The truth, but a memory of what? It had to be hers, it was so familiar, but she didn't recognize it. "I'll be fine. I need some water."

She stumbled to find a cup. Scorpion and Tristana exchanged low words, and then the healer left.

Afterward, Scorpion made himself more herbal tea and sat on the bed, seemingly lost in thought.

"We need to get to Danelin in the City States," Raven said. The traitor Merab Varko had to be their focus. Raven knew Danelin well, as did Scorpion. It was where they had undergone the sorcerers' infernal experiments, and then completed their training after being tested for various newly acquired demonic abilities.

"It will take an age to get there," Scorpion said. "In the meantime, she will forge ahead with her plans and we'll be at an even greater disadvantage. It's too risky."

"We'll be careful. I feel in my gut that this is the right path to take."

"What if you're wrong? And we're operating way beyond our usual scope. We don't normally make these kinds of decisions."

"We do now," Raven said flatly. "Instead of someone we don't know and have never seen making the decisions for us. And Varko's a bloody traitor! She tried to kill us, remember."

Scorpion remained quiet, his jaw working. Eventually he spoke. "What if I refuse to go?"

"Fine," she snapped. "I'll go alone. I'll deal with the traitor myself."

She would return to the Ethereal Sorceress and ask for her help to get to Danelin. It would use up another favor, but she would be two thousand miles north before the next morning.

Scorpion stared at the ceiling for a moment, then let out a loud sigh. "You know I'd never let you go alone. Not now that we've found each other again. I know a weapon smith who'll produce what we need for a few gold talents and look the other way. He has no idea who I am or what I do."

"Good. That's a start. I have some gemstones, but I'd like to keep them, if possible, for when this is all over. It's hard to start a new life if you're begging for scraps."

"That I can arrange. I have letters of credit, plus some stashes hidden away. The one in the house outside of Kroe is probably lost. It's too risky to go back there. One day someone will make a surprise discovery. No one knows about the credit, or where the stashes are. Although now I'm concerned someone else could con the information out of Ralnar."

Raven glanced at Scorpion's clothes. She'd washed most of the blood out and repaired the tear at the shoulder of his shirt, but they still looked too noticeable

"Then get dressed and we'll get out of here. I won't be comfortable until we're gone permanently and Tristana has no idea where we've gone. She brought you some new clothes, by the way." Raven gestured at a string-tied bundle on the kitchen table.

Scorpion made his way over and burst out laughing once it was untied. He held up a shirt that was never going to fit his massive arms and chest.

"You'll need some more clothes," Raven said.

"Tomorrow. I'll get us some coin and see this weapon smith as well."

"We'll buy you clothes tonight. It'll give us a reason for being on the street. If you need to rest, we'll hire a carriage."

Raven left Scorpion to lumber down the stairs and made sure

she was first into the street. She did a quick check to see if there was anyone suspicious hanging around, but it looked fairly quiet. Even though the curfew had been lifted until midnight, it seemed people preferred to keep off the streets at night.

She noticed Scorpion grimace in pain as he stumbled down the last few stairs.

"Are you sure you're all right?"

"A few twinges, but it's fine. The pain isn't going to go away for a while yet, so I'd better get used to it. It's always a struggle, and tonight we don't really have to be out."

Soon they'd found a clothing store and stocked up for the both of them. By that time Scorpion was sweating and breathing heavily, and he asked Raven to carry their purchases. She hailed a carriage and they made it back to the apartment, with Scorpion taking a lot longer to ascend the stairs than he had coming down.

He staggered to the bed and lay down, sweating profusely. At least it wasn't all over the new clothes. Raven prepared more herbal tea and some bread and cheese. She'd hoped Scorpion would be well enough that they could eat out somewhere, even if it was only from a street vendor. Being cooped up in his apartment had her on edge.

After draining a cup of the tea and requesting another, Scorpion propped himself up in the bed and gave her a wan look. "I'm afraid I'm not as strong as I'd hoped."

"You're well enough to get out of here. I don't trust Tristana."

"You don't trust anyone. Neither do I. Part of the life we lead, I guess."

The next morning they caught a carriage into the main district of the city, Sourhill, where the military barracks were located. It was also where many of the nobles and wealthy merchants made their homes. Raven remembered there had once been a petition to change the name to something more palatable, but it hadn't ended up happening. Maybe the rulers of Kroe had a sense of humor.

The Simorga Sea Bank had opened its doors at dawn, and there was a steady stream of customers going about their business. Scorpion disappeared inside, and Raven waited in the square outside, nibbling on a stick of roasted grubs sprinkled with spices purportedly from the lost southern depths of the Jargalan Desert. Or so said the enthusiastic vendor. It looked and tasted like pepper and salt to her, though nothing more was needed to enhance the nutty flavor of the grubs.

She kept her eye on the people crossing the square, as well as those patronizing the food vendors and stall holders. They were probably all living completely normal lives. Raven felt a stab of jealousy and wondered, for probably the umpteenth time, what it felt like to be normal, to experience life without all the horror and death she'd seen. Then she shook her head to clear her thoughts. There was no point dwelling on what she couldn't change. The past was just that. "Ever forward" had to be her motto. She was treading a path of her own now, which was all she could do.

After what seemed like forever, Scorpion strolled out of the Simorga Sea Bank carrying a leather satchel over one shoulder. He showed no sign of weakness as he descended the steps, and even his color had returned. If she hadn't seen for herself the terrible state he was in a few days ago, she would never have believed he'd been injured and poisoned.

She strode toward the nearest main street and nodded at the

driver of a single-horse trap waiting there. The woman nodded back. Good. Raven handed her a few copper talents and waited for Scorpion before boarding. He gave the driver a district and street name, and they were off.

"Did you leave anything?" Raven asked.

He shook his head. "I cleared it out. I figure it's better with us than somewhere that might be hard to get to later."

They fell silent as the carriage weaved through the swarming streets. It wasn't long before it stopped, and the driver turned to speak to them.

"Street's just there," she said. "It's too narrow to drive down."

"Thank you," Raven said as they disembarked, but the woman drove off without replying.

"The weapon smith's about fifty yards down," said Scorpion.

"How well do you know him?"

He shrugged. "As well as you can know anyone."

Which meant not at all.

They ambled along, taking their time, pretending an interest in the other shops crowding the street while keeping alert for anyone shadowing them.

At the weapon smith's Raven eased through the door first. A bell attached to a string above her tinkled, and a woman behind a counter toward the back glanced up from a ledger. She wore a too-tight red shirt that showed off her ample cleavage. Raven wondered if she was why Scorpion knew this weapon smith's so well.

Hanging on the walls were every type of weapon imaginable: from straight and curved swords to needle-like and wide daggers; maces and flails; long spears for thrusting, and some with shorter shafts and longer blades for skilled warriors; simple and recurve bows; basic crossbows and more expensive composite contraptions.

"Anything specific you're looking for?" the woman asked.

"Is Ivar here?" Scorpion said. "I was hoping to see him."

The woman gave a heartfelt sigh, as if he'd just asked her to complete a momentous task. She turned and shouted through the doorway behind her. "Ivar! Someone's asking for you. And no, I don't know what they want." She returned to her ledger, nibbling on the end of her metal-tipped wooden pen.

"Who is it?" came a gruff voice.

The woman looked at Scorpion expectantly.

"Finn," he told her.

"It's Finn," she shouted.

"Tell him to come out back."

The woman waved them through and returned to her important work. Raven followed Scorpion through a small office with a desk and some drawers, and into another room where a goateed man with thick spectacles lounged in an armchair, staring at the ceiling.

"Ivar," Scorpion said, "it's been a while. What are you doing?"

"Thinking. Doesn't take much skill to bang out the short blades and spears the military want these days, so I have time to come up with new ideas."

Ivar stood and peered at Raven. She noticed he held a polished wooden cane in his left hand, and his leg was slightly crooked.

"How's business?" Scorpion asked.

"Boring. Unless I'm making a special order. Those I can get excited about. I assume you want something special? Maybe for the woman here. She a warrior?"

"You could say that. New assistant out the front?"

That answered Raven's question.

"Caught the old one stealing from me! Can you believe it?

I took the poor waif in, fed and clothed her, warmed her bed, and that's how she repaid me." Ivar rubbed a hand through his thinning hair. "What are you after?"

"Knives for me, blades a foot long, and a chest harness for them. Inconspicuous."

Ivar nodded. "Difficult to make foot-long blades inconspicuous, but I'll do my best."

"And a couple of smaller knives for her." Scorpion indicated Raven. "And I'll need a special alloy mixed and set in small blocks."

Raven's ears pricked up. Scorpion was talking about shreds, she was sure of it. The method of their manufacture was a closely guarded secret, and the Grim Hand doled them out with parsimony.

"Same as last time?" Ivar said.

"You remember the metals and ratios? I wrote them down for you."

"Better than that, I still have some left over. Five of them. As I recall, you said you were coming back for them, but you never did."

"Sorry. I got caught up with work. You know how it is."

"I do indeed. These Kroe soldier asses wanted me to visit their southern defenses and come up with siege engine ideas. I went, of course, was paid for a holiday, and then told them there was nothing wrong with what they already had. Always looking for something new and innovative, they are, as if it would kill someone deader."

"I'll also need some of the alloy cast into small balls, about the size of a thumbnail."

Ivar grunted, and his eyes narrowed. "And what are they for?"

"Never you mind."

"Well, that won't take too long. I can melt down one of the blocks, if you like, though it'll mean one less of them."

"That's fine. The sooner the better."

"A few hours should do it."

"Perfect."

Ivar opened a couple of drawers and pulled out the big knives Scorpion wanted, along with two smaller ones and a harness. He placed the weapons atop a crate. "These beauties were commissioned by a noble who thought his dueling practice made him a decent warrior. Ended up dead a few days later and never collected them."

"He lost a fight?" Raven asked.

"You could say that. His wife found out he was cheating on her and tripped him out of a fourth-floor window. Said his foot got tangled on the edge of the rug." Ivar shrugged. "She's rotting in a dungeon now, I suppose."

Scorpion and Raven examined the knives. Hers looked nothing special, though they were a good size and weight for her. Scorpion's were big and heavy, and would be able to turn aside a sword or weightier weapon. Raven preferred not to get that close.

"How much for everything?" Scorpion asked.

"For you, because you're a friend, twenty gold talents."

Raven suppressed a wry smile. It was an outrageous sum. But they were also paying for discretion.

"A deal," Scorpion said, and he and Ivar shook hands. "We'll be back for the blocks and balls later."

He took a few coin bags out of his satchel and counted out the twenty talents, then sheathed the knives and strapped the harness under his coat. He was moving freely enough, Raven noticed, and didn't seem to be in any pain. Raven's knives went into his satchel as she didn't need them at the moment. They were spares in case things went awry and she lost the knives she was already carrying.

"We'll find our own way out," Scorpion said.

"Nice doing business with you," Ivar replied. "I'll get to work."

In the street, Raven stopped a woman eating a freshly-baked bread roll and asked directions to the bakery. They spent the next few hours sipping tea and nibbling on pastries until Scorpion headed back to Ivar's. He returned shortly after, his satchel looking slightly fuller.

"Are you going to tell me what the balls are for?" Raven asked.

"Something Moonshadow was working on. The shreds are fantastic, but they're heavy to push with the dark-tide, and not many have that innate talent. Yours was the strongest out of all of us. They can't be thrown through solid matter either; you need an opening. But if these balls are propelled fast enough, they can penetrate timber."

Raven nodded her understanding. "And what was a safe place becomes a deathtrap. Moonshadow always was the smart one. Hopefully he's in a better place now."

Guilt rose in her, and she wasn't sure why. She hadn't killed Moonshadow, the Orgols had. But she had lied to Scorpion and his superiors about him, telling them Moonshadow hadn't passed on the Orgols' artifact to her.

"I can't move objects like you can," Scorpion said, "so you can have them. All except two."

"What are you going to do with those?"

He grinned at her. "No idea. But they might come in handy."

Raven turned right into an avenue and set a brisk pace to burn off some of her nervous energy. Her rapier swung energetically at her hip, and she grasped the hilt to steady it. As she passed a tavern, she briefly debated entering to buy a bottle of spirits but decided against it. Strong drink helped to deaden her emotions, though it was almost impossible for her to become inebriated. Another side effect of her change.

As they turned into another street near the sorceress's building, Scorpion grabbed her arm from behind.

"Raven."

She twisted out of his grip. "Let go."

"All right. All right. But slow down. We should be heading to the docks to find a ship north."

"No. I have a better plan." As the words left her mouth, she noticed two carriages in the street up ahead. She slowed. The street was strangely deserted for this time of day. "Carriages. Drivers are up top, but the curtains are drawn and they're not moving."

"Bloody darkness."

"Are you sure you're up to a fight?" said Raven.

"I'll have to be."

As Raven drew a knife and a shred, chaos erupted around her. Seven warriors emerged from an alley and came rushing up the street at them. Raven pushed Scorpion toward a pile of crates and threw herself down behind a rain barrel just as crossbow bolts whistled through the air near them. She heard a shouted cant and sensed an arcane surge from Scorpion. Two melon-sized burning spheres materialized overhead then arced away. She tugged a couple of poisoned bolts from her belt pouch. Tossing them into the air, she poked her head up to get a view of the warriors and sent two pulses of dark-tide energy at her bolts, propelling them in an arc overhead.

Scorpion's sorcerous globes hammered into the men and broke apart into cascading flames. But each attacker was now inside a spherical protective ward, and the conflagration did no harm.

Shit.

Raven kept her eyes exposed for another instant, enough to send two more dark-tide surges ahead to propel her bolts with blistering speed, to ensure her missiles struck home. The two front men had their arms raised, as if they had expected to be immolated and were surprised to find they were still alive. Both were still encapsulated by a complex sorcerous shield, which would keep out physical objects and heat at the very least. But her bolts were wrapped in a shroud of dark-tide.

The missiles penetrated the shields as if the physical protection didn't exist, and slammed home into chests. The men went down hard, and the remaining five scattered, seeking shelter behind crates and barrels.

"They have a sorcerer with them," she said, drawing her rapier.

"I know. Sensed his workings after I sent mine."

"Can you locate him?"

"Maybe. And maybe we don't need to. We can take these warriors out, and he'll run. He's here to support, not to directly engage."

"How do you know?"

"Fire isn't raining down on us."

Raven ducked her head around the barrel just as Scorpion lobbed a shred up the street. She waited a moment, then the block erupted near the entrance to a side street. Its nail-like shards of darkness sprayed in all directions, most fading to wisps after a dozen yards in the harsh sunlight. But a man staggered out from the side street, clutching the side of his face, which was painted red with blood. She tossed up another bolt as a fourth man emerged to drag his injured colleague away, surged it outward, and his head erupted as the missile hammered through his skull with devastating force.

She leaped over the barrel and ducked into an alley, then pressed her back against the wall just by the corner. It was too risky to shadow-step in broad daylight. Too many reflections, too much chance for it to go wrong. Unless she could find a patch of deep shadow… She shook her head. Focus.

Two bolts clipped the corner and ricocheted down the street, just missing the crates Scorpion was hiding behind. He leaned back and threw another shred. Raven felt his surge and the thunderous detonation, then Scorpion ran in a crouch to her old position behind the barrel.

Raven edged closer to the corner. As Scorpion arced a few more scorching globes toward their assailants, she glanced back down the alley and up to the roofline in case more attackers were there. All clear. She tucked her shred back into her pouch. Her rage, which had been subsiding, now burned white-hot inside her. She took out two of the smaller shred balls and her pea-sized artifact sphere.

"No," Scorpion said. "Let's go."

*Bloody darkness.* He was right, but she couldn't stop herself.

She sprang from her cover and into the street. Crossbows plinked in front of heads poking over makeshift barricades. She pulsed the two shred balls at the carriages with as much force as she could muster, then shadow-stepped into the darkness of an alley behind their attackers. As she re-formed, her shred balls hammered into the carriage walls and passed through. She sent dark-tide surges into them, and two cracks like splintering trees rang out. The carriage curtains ruffled, as if caught in a breeze, and tiny holes appeared in them. The carriages rocked slightly, and both drivers jumped to the ground.

Raven took her eyes off the carriages and found the remaining three men. All were in sunlight and focused on the crates and barrel they thought Raven and Scorpion were using for shelter. She gathered her dark-tide power and set her strongest demonic talent—moving objects—loose.

She flicked the matching pea sphere into the air and propelled it toward the nearest man. It screamed through his stomach with a wail close enough to a banshee's to make no difference. Bright crimson spurted across the street as his companions looked up, seeing him drop and finding Raven staring at them.

Too late.

She propelled it again, arresting the sphere's flight and twisting it back. It cut down a second man, and with more surges she sent it into the last, bursting through his chest. With a final push it returned to her hand.

Then Scorpion was grabbing her arm, dragging her back down the street. By the carriages, one driver opened a door and vomited onto his shoes at the sight inside.

"The sorcerer is still around somewhere. Let's go," urged Scorpion.

She jerked her arm free and glared at him.

"Think for a moment," he said. "Soldiers will be here very soon, and the Watch. We need to get out of here."

Raven looked at the six dead men around them, and the wounded man still wailing and clutching his ruined face. Then she took in the carriages and nodded. Strangely, flames were coming from inside, and smoke billowed from the windows.

"All right." She sheathed her rapier, which she hadn't even used.

They sprinted down an alley and made a few random turns. Scorpion uttered cants under his breath, and Raven assumed he was keeping a watch out for sorcery and preventing anyone from scrying them. They ducked into an apartment building, keeping to the ground floor, and found an exit on the other side.

"That was stupid," said Scorpion. "You know it's risky to shadow-step in broad daylight."

"The alley was dark."

"It was foolish."

Scorpion was right, but her anger had overridden her common sense. "The balls work well."

"Someone's following us," said Scorpion grimly.

"Sorcery?"

"A little. Plus skill. They're traveling across the roofs above us."

"If they bring in soldiers and the Watch, we're done for. Come on, Scorpion. We're going to pay a visit to the Ethereal Sorceress."

"At what cost? I don't trust her. I doubt she'll jeopardize her business interests to protect us."

His breath was becoming labored, and Raven wasn't sure how long he'd be able to keep up their pace.

"How do you think they found us?" she asked.

"Either Tristana told them, or they followed her to us."

"At least she'll die debt-free."

"That's not funny." Scorpion's mouth twisted in pain, and she saw his face was sheened with sweat.

"No, I'm sorry. How are you feeling?" she asked.

"I need to stop running, but we don't have a choice."

"Then I guess my plan is the only option."

Sheelahn stood, as she always did, at the end of the green-carpeted hallway, wearing her multilayered robes and orichalcum mask.

"You bring trouble to my door," she chirped in her birdsong-like voice.

"I'm sure you can handle it," Raven replied. "I want to use another favor."

"And your companion?"

"He comes too."

"No."

Raven's mouth dropped open. "What?"

"The bargain was between you and me; no third parties."

"Then I want a new bargain."

"What do you have to offer?"

Raven wasn't sure she had anything that Sheelahn would want. Would the sorceress care that someone high up in the City States had probably killed almost everyone in the Grim Hand? Probably not.

"Akatta Palek has inquired after you," the sorceress added before Raven had thought of a reply.

Scorpion groaned. "Bloody darkness, Raven, what have you gotten yourself into?"

Raven waved at him to be quiet. "What did he want?"

"You. He was quite impressed that you escaped the Orgols. For a second time, I believe."

"He offered me a job." And was likely after the sacred Orgol artifact she'd stolen. You could never trust sorcerers.

"As did I."

That's what Sheelahn was after. Twice before she'd said she

had need of Raven.

"I have a heaped plate at the moment," she said. "And once it's cleared, I'm not sure where I'll be or what I'll want." Except she did know.

"You have found me easily enough when you have needed to," Sheelahn replied. "I repeat my offer: I have a proposal for you. Are you not intrigued? Did your experience with Akatta Palek not cause you even the slightest interest?"

She meant the sensations that had come to Raven when in Akatta's presence. Raven didn't want anything to do with yet another sorcerer, but right at this moment she couldn't afford to put Sheelahn off-side. "When I'm free of my current complications, I'll make a decision."

"I would like an answer."

"I cannot give you one," Raven said.

"Not even in return for information pertinent to your current situation?"

Raven thought furiously. She needed Sheelahn now, and the sorceress knew it. If they had to travel to Danelin by ship, it would take too long. In addition, if the sorceress refused to help them and they had to go back outside, she didn't like their chances of survival. And now, it seemed Sheelahn had information they might need.

"A compromise, then," Raven said. "I'll perform one more mission for you once my business is concluded, and we'll see if we're suited to working together."

"Raven," growled Scorpion in warning. He knew as well as she did that sorcerers had a way of digging their hooks in and never letting go. Hells, he was one himself.

"Agreed," said Sheelahn. "Our bargain is struck. A cluster of ancient ruins have been discovered in Kaile, in the mountains to the east. And not only that—a rich seam of orichalcum was also uncovered in the same area. Ensorcelled orichalcum is rarer than hen's teeth. All the old mines ran dry decades ago, and supplies of the metal plummeted while demand rose. Sorcerers covet it for its ability to hold sorcery and its superior strength and corrosion resistance."

"So the price increased," Raven said.

"Exactly. A new source of the metal is probably the most valuable discovery of the last few decades. Along with the ruins and whatever artifacts they hold, there's a great deal of coin to be made from that area. More than a great deal. Whoever owns the orichalcum seam can ask whatever they want for the metal. And people will pay. The ruins and the orichalcum seam were confirmed by a group of surveyors. Once they'd sent their report back to their employer in Sansor, they were all killed. There was nobody left alive to let out the secret out of the new discovery. The government in Kaile didn't know anything about it, and neither did any of the sorcerer schools. I had an agent on the surveying team. Their death is unacceptable."

The death of her agent, or the loss of information about such a valuable discovery? "What does this have to do with me? Or the deaths of the Grim Hand?" asked Raven.

"The City States had an agent working for one of the merchants who knew about the find. One placed fairly high up. Merab Varko, an Emerald Commander in the City States Army. She was behind the money transfers and has siphoned a great deal of coin into her own pockets."

"Our mission in Kyuth," said Scorpion to Raven. "The secret of the ruins and the orichalcum seam should have died with them, or at least sent the merchants' plans spinning out of control long enough for someone else to take the reins. Presumably the City

States. If this is true, then it wasn't about protecting the City States. Our bosses decided it was in the City States' interests to disrupt the merchants' cartel and keep the find quiet. They think they can exploit the ruins and the orichalcum seam from the other side of the border."

"Or rather, Merab Varko thinks she can," Raven said. "But the secret didn't die, did it? At least one merchant in Kaile knows. The only thing that makes sense is that they're trying to wrest the discoveries from the City States, with Varko's help. That settles it then, we need to confront Varko and find out what's going on."

# SIXTEEN

MERAB VARKO DESCENDED THE MARBLE steps of the
Citadel in Danelin and nodded to the four guards on duty. Only
the sergeant nodded back; the others continually scanned the
street for suspicious activity. There hadn't been an assassination
attempt on a commander of Merab's rank for quite some time,
and the last dozen or so had been by more subtle methods such
as poison and sorcery. Still, you never knew, and she wasn't alive
today through carelessness.

A Citadel carriage waited for her, drawn by four horses, the
driver a well-known servant of many years. Merab rubbed
her eyes then ran a hand through her short-cut hair—she
was tired from yet another long day of solving problems that
shouldn't have made it to her desk, and bickering with the other
commanders about various operations and designs they had on
the boil. Today had been an especially shit day in a bloody shit
year. Retirement was looking better and better, but in her line of

work there was usually only one way to retire, and that was to be buried. Unless you had a creative plan.

Over the last few months Merab had cultivated an ever-increasing manner of forgetfulness, and had made deliberate small mistakes in her work. Her superiors had expressed concern, and Merab had laughed them off while still managing to nurture their apprehension about her advancing age and competency. In her mid-fifties, she wasn't exactly old, but a loss of cognitive ability at such an age wasn't unknown. If she played it just right, she might actually be able to retire alive in a year or so. And then she'd go south, to somewhere warm. Maybe an island with a beach and some luscious natives to fulfill her desires.

The carriage dropped her off at her comparatively small mansion in North Wedge, the best district in Danelin. After her husband had died some years ago, she'd laid off most of the servants, only retaining a housekeeper who came a few times a week, and a manservant whom she'd since dismissed a short while ago. The more she saved those gold talents, the more she could enjoy herself when she was gone from this place.

She fumbled with an alchemical globe, which brightened immediately and cast lurid shadows across the walls and floor. And lit the figure of a woman standing at the bottom of the main staircase. Merab reached for her knife, even as she took in the lithe curves under the woman's tight-cut pants and shirt. It wasn't the girl she'd taken to bed the other week, was it? She'd been expensive, but worth it. Maybe she'd come back for more.

A blow to the back of her head sent her tumbling. She gasped, and found herself staring at the polished floorboards, fighting to catch her breath. A muscled arm wrapped itself around her neck and squeezed. Merab struggled, but she had no strength and the room blurred.

She regained consciousness slowly, but didn't let on she was awake. She opened her eyes a sliver and confirmed the hard surface she was sitting on was one of the guest chairs in her study. She liked to make her visitors uncomfortable. Someone had drawn the curtains, and most of the room was in darkness. There was only a faint radiance from an alchemical globe atop her desk, and a warm glow from a brazier behind her. She took a few deep breaths. She had some gold stashed away, and they could have it if that was all they wanted. Or, if they were foreign agents, she might still get away since she never kept any of her work at home.

A shadow in the corner moved, and Merab clamped her eyes shut. "I haven't seen you," she said, keeping her voice calm and firm. "If you leave now, I can't identify you. There's gold in a false bottom of the topmost left drawer in my desk. Take it all. If you're not interested in coin, then you must know who I am and the resources I command. There is nothing of value for you here. Leave before you get in over your heads."

She coughed when she'd finished, her throat dry. She wanted water but wasn't going to ask for it.

"Merab Varko, Emerald Commander in the City States combined military. Weren't you a Gold Commander not so long ago?" It was the woman. Her voice was warm and raspy, sensual even.

Merab shrugged, or tried to. The ropes around her arms, legs and chest restricted her movement. "What does that matter? What do you want? Who are you?"

"I'm one of the Grim Hand," the woman said. "One of the team you treacherously condemned to death, and whose lives you took gold for. Your real job is running covert operations against foreign countries and forcing people through horrifying sorcerous transformations for your own benefit. And we know you're up to your neck in corruption and worse. We know about the ruins and the orichalcum."

"I don't know what you're talking about. What is the Grim Hand? What deaths? I'm in charge of supplies here in the City States. Logistics. I don't know what you want from me."

A slap rocked her head to the side and made her ears ring. Her teeth cut her lip and she tasted blood.

"Stop with your lies," the woman said. "Your guilt is plain to see. You are a traitor to the City States; you betrayed those who went through the Abyss for you. They faced death constantly for you, and you pissed on them. There's no point in continued denials. They will just make me angrier than I am right now. And you don't want to see that."

Merab opened her eyes and studied the woman's toned figure, her face, her midnight skin. Bloody hells. It was her. Raven. But she was dead, wasn't she?

Raven smiled. "I see you recognize me. So you know what I'm capable of. Are you afraid, Merab? You should be."

She felt an urgent need to piss but held it back. "I swear, I don't know what—"

Another slap rocked her head, and her cheek erupted with pain. Blood filled her mouth, and she coughed and spat it onto the floor. She hadn't even seen Raven move.

"Don't you understand?" Raven continued. "Unless you tell me what I want to know, you're dead."

Merab tongued a tooth, felt it wobble. Raven…she still couldn't believe it.

"Did you take the artifact?" Merab asked. "The Orgols are still looking for you. Give it to me and I'll make sure you're safe from them."

"I didn't take it," Raven replied. "But we're here on other business."

Merab couldn't tell if the woman was lying. The Cabal would find out the truth, one way or another. Her attention was caught by another figure emerging from the darkness into the dim light. A large muscled man. Merab felt the blood drain from her face, and her body trembled.

"Scorpion," she said. He was meant to be dead, too.

"Let's not play silly games any longer, Merab," said Scorpion coldly. "We have questions for you. And you have the answers. You know what we're capable of, what we've been trained to do. We have no mercy. No conscience. All such feelings were scoured from us during our ordeal. If you don't cooperate, we'll brutalize you until you wish you were dead. Then we'll do it some more. So, why did you do it, traitor? Why did you betray the Grim Hand?"

Merab swallowed, tasted sour spit thick with blood. "I didn't know Blasius would authorize killing all of you. How could I have? It wasn't my idea!" A lie, of course. Blasius was a tool, useful only for his wealth and power.

"So, you admit you're on this merchant's payroll. What did you think he was going to do?"

"I don't know. He's the wealthiest man in Sansor and has his fingers in just about everything, including the Night Shadows and underworld crime. I thought this was all about money. But once I'd taken his coins, he kept asking for more. Eventually I just did as I was told. But I didn't authorize the Grim Hand to be killed."

"You didn't care to know what was going on. You didn't want to face the truth," said Scorpion.

Merab remained silent. Had they already made their minds up

to kill her, or was there an opportunity to get out of this?

"Answer him!" Raven shouted. "What did you think would happen?"

Merab shook her head. "I've said all I'm going to. Your loyalty is to the City States. You know you can't hurt me. We're all just trying to survive, and to make the world a better place for our people."

Scorpion moved behind her. Merab tried to twist her head to keep him in sight, but the ropes prevented it. Metal clinked on metal as Scorpion did something with the brazier. Then the big man appeared again, holding an iron poker. Its tip glowed orange with heat.

Merab licked her lips. Surely they wouldn't…

She jerked her head back as Scorpion brought the glowing tip toward her eye.

"I'll start with your feet and work my way up," Scorpion said casually. "There's no point trying to hold anything back. I'm telling you, everyone breaks in the end. Everyone. But before I begin, I'm going to give you one last chance. Why did you betray us? Why did you want us killed?"

Scorpion had to be bluffing. He had no proof. And he couldn't torture an Emerald Commander and expect to get away with it. Merab clenched her jaw and said nothing. The Tainted Cabal would do far worse than these two could if they knew she'd betrayed them.

Scorpion turned to Raven and jerked his head in the direction of the door. "Stay by the entrance and make sure we aren't interrupted."

Raven gave him a short nod and looked at Merab. "I wish I could say it was nice to meet the woman behind so many of the missions I completed, but I can't."

She disappeared behind him, and the door clicked shut. Merab heard the creak of a single floorboard as she walked away, then nothing.

Scorpion moved closer, his muscled presence filling Merab's vision.

"I'm innocent," Merab said quickly. "For god's sake, stop and think about what you're doing. Don't throw your life away." She could hear her too-high voice filled with pleading. "If you do this, there's no coming back. The City States will hunt you down for your crimes."

Scorpion came down the stairs and joined Raven in the foyer. His face was grim, and he reeked of burned flesh and sweat.

"She's dead, the maggot."

"And the body?" she asked.

"We'll leave it. They'll check on her when she doesn't arrive at work tomorrow morning."

"We need to get as far away as possible, and soon," she added. "They'll put the Watch and the military on high alert, and any strangers will be fair game."

He nodded. "We're done here anyway. She spilled her guts and told me what we need to know. And all that will die with her, including her information on the Grim Hand. This Blasius's full name is Blasius Matheo, and he won't have Varko's help any longer.

"Varko did tell me a little more, before she died. Our mission in Kyuth where we wiped out the merchants, where you disappeared… Apparently the other merchants all hated Blasius and wanted him pushed out. We were Varko's tool that night, not the City States'. Now Blasius has the lion's share of the wealth: selling artifacts from the ancient ruins, some which are sorcerous, along with the raw orichalcum ore."

It figured. There were always those who thought only of themselves. "But it still doesn't explain why they're going to such lengths to kill me." Raven opened the front door a crack and peered out. "It looks clear. Let's go."

"Where to? The harbor?"

"There's no point us staying here in Danelin," she said, leading the way outside. "And we need to execute the next step in my plan. So, like it or not, we have to prevail upon the Ethereal Sorceress again. But first we need to find somewhere to spend the night. I don't want to approach Sheelahn when I'm tired. She's dangerous."

He didn't reply, just locked the door, and they made their way up the street, Raven hunched slightly against the evening chill.

"What did else did Merab tell you?" she asked.

"Some sob story about how Blasius threatened her only daughter. The thousands of gold talents she got paid were secondary, supposedly. She was lying."

Raven snorted. "Most likely. What about Blasius?"

"He knows about the existence of the Grim Hand. And according to Varko, Blasius was the one who wanted us all dead. Varko said she didn't give Blasius Crooked's name or location though. It still doesn't really add up. We're missing something again, and I can't think what it might be."

"So Crooked's death isn't on Blasius's head?"

"Doesn't look like it. A coincidence, probably. It looks like someone figured out Crooked's identity was a cover and decided to take him out."

"Dead is still dead."

"Merab also said the City States are aware of something happening in the mountains east of Kaile. I think we can safely assume it has to do with the ruins and the new orichalcum find."

"Are the City States doing anything about it?"

"Not according to Merab. But there could be others inside the City States taking coin from Blasius. All Merab knew was that whatever's happening in the mountains has gained enough momentum that it can't be stopped."

Raven waved down an empty horse-and-trap and gave directions to the other side of the city, where Sheelahn's business was located. Once they were in the right district, they'd find a place to stay the night. They rumbled along streets, and buildings passed in a blur as Raven became lost in thought.

"You're quiet," said Scorpion after a while.

"I didn't ask for any of this," Raven replied. "Not to be part of their experiments, nor to be a member of the Grim Hand. I just did what I was told until it was too much for me. And I found a way out. A way to finally be free of this life."

She would do what she had to return to that life. She might not like it, but she'd get the job done. Then she'd deal with Sheelahn, and Akatta.

Raven paid for a decent-sized room at a sizable upmarket inn named The Candle. The woman on duty, a pleasant and professional matron, didn't blink when Raven told her Scorpion was her manservant and they'd be sharing a room. For a few extra copper talents, the inn provided buckets of hot water to wash up in, and also a local news sheet.

Once the door was locked, and they'd checked the room for

spy holes—none—and cleanliness—excellent—they felt they could relax. Soon after, two serving girls lugged steaming buckets of water inside and deposited them next to a small copper tub, barely large enough to sit in. Raven opened a floor-to-ceiling balcony door and stepped outside to look at what she could see of the harbor view in the dark, while Scorpion handed the serving girls a copper each and shooed them away, despite their protests that they'd be happy to assist with "your lady's" bath.

Lights on the water caught Raven's eye, and she watched them move slowly toward the docks. It would be a nice view come morning, but they'd likely be gone and wouldn't get to enjoy it. When she returned inside, locking the balcony door and drawing the curtains, Scorpion was lying on the enormous bed, an arm over his eyes.

Raven undressed quickly, then sat in the tub and poured a bucket of hot water over herself. She savored the feel of it on her face and skin, then set to scrubbing away the dirt and sweat of the day's activities.

"I want to wash too," said Scorpion. "So don't use all the hot water."

Raven caught him glancing at her naked body before he rolled onto his side and averted his eyes.

"I'm almost done," she said. "And there's plenty left for you. Living on the island on my own, I got used to not using much water. It's a hassle to heat."

She dried off using one of the towels provided and wrapped it around herself. There were also strips of rough linen cloth and various pastes and powders for cleaning your teeth. She was delighted to find a sage and salt powder that she hadn't used for years.

"I'm finished. It's all yours," she said, rubbing her teeth as she walked over to the bed.

Scorpion removed his shirt on his way to the tub. The wound in his shoulder was now only a scar. If Tristana had seen it, she would have been amazed.

Raven sat on the bed and perused the news sheet. Above the fold was a story on the fight between Raven and Scorpion and their unknown assailants. The news sheet got several details wrong: the body count was twice what it had been, and it was described as an attack on the good people of Kroe by a foreign power, and hence on all of the City States. It finished with an appropriately outraged spokesman for the Watch saying they would increase their vigilance and the City States would not be cowed by such inexcusable acts. Raven had long ago learned the news sheets contained mostly fiction, but there were facts in there, if you could tease them out.

She brushed her damp hair back over her ears as Scorpion reappeared, a towel around his waist. He sat on the bed, and she handed him the news sheet.

After scanning it, he snorted and handed it back. "There should be a law against misrepresenting facts and spreading lies."

She shrugged. "The news sheets just want to make coin the same as any other business. The people that matter know the truth. I mean, everyone matters, just some more than most," she corrected herself.

"Do you think the Ethereal Sorceress might have some information on Blasius, and more on what's happening in the mountains in Kaile?" Scorpion asked.

"Probably. It wouldn't surprise me in the slightest."

"That's another reason to see her, then, although I don't like it. What will she have you agree to this time?"

Raven shook her head. "I don't know. But let's not talk about it tonight. There'll be time enough tomorrow."

He took her recently injured hand in his and gently rubbed the scar. "You need to stop the skin tightening up. Maybe there's an ointment we can buy."

Raven kneeled on the bed and moved closer, until she could smell his freshly washed skin. Her head was higher than his from this position, and she looked down at his unique face. He didn't move, his eyes locked onto hers.

"If I could go back and make my choices again," he said, "I'd escape with you. At the time, I thought I was protecting the people I cared about, but all I really care about is you. I'm sorry. Whatever happens, I'll do the right thing this time. We have a second chance, and that almost never happens to people like us."

She brought her lips down to his, felt her damp hair brushing his shoulders. His lips parted, and as her tongue found his, memories of their previous trysts washed over her. Raven slid a hand under his towel and he groaned. Her heartbeat quickened as a wave of familiar sensations flooded through her, and then his firm hands removed her towel. She descended into a sultry delirium, her senses and body craving his touch, which she'd never expected to feel again.

Raven left Scorpion asleep in the bed and wandered over to the window. She hadn't been able to sleep: guilt kept her thoughts jumbled and mind restless. Long dormant feelings she'd thought buried had rekindled inside her. Her attraction to Scorpion was stronger than ever. Was it possible they might have a future together after they'd dealt with Blasius? Could they settle down somewhere and make a normal life together that didn't involve constantly looking over their shoulders, being on the run, or killing? She knew their chances of surviving their current situation might not be good, but the image of a happily married life seemed almost achievable.

Except for the unresolved issues between them.

Raven hadn't told Scorpion about her—their—baby. Poor Amelia. She thought of her every day, of what could have been. And every day her heart squeezed with the pain of losing her. But the past couldn't be changed, so what was the point of telling him? He was better off not knowing the truth.

She was responsible for Amelia's death, and she couldn't bear the thought of telling Scorpion. If she'd looked after herself, and the baby, properly, Amelia wouldn't have died.

# SEVENTEEN

I WAKE, COUGHING. SMOKE FILLS *my room. My eyes sting and stream tears. I grab my doll with scraggly yellow hair and clutch her tightly.*

*"Mama!" I yell.*

*Thumps and a curse sound from the other side of my door. That scares me. Mama almost never curses. I slip down off my bed as my door opens. Mama's hands grab me, and she lifts me into her warm arms.*

*She rushes through the house and out the back door to the street. Outside, the air is clear and I can breathe, but my lungs burn and I can still smell smoke. I look around and see a flickering orange glow and hear a crackling, roaring sound. Behind the glow, a tower rears into the sky.*

*"It's the bakery," Mama says. "It's on fire. But we're going to be all right. Don't be afraid, Saskia."*

*And I am not. I'm always safe with her.*

Raven woke before dawn, as she always did, after finally managing to nod off. Scorpion had left the room, and she heard his footsteps returning as she dressed. He entered bearing a plate filled with cut fruits and crispy pastries.

"The kitchen is open early and I thought we could use a decent meal to get us started," he said.

He had a news sheet tucked under one arm. Raven gestured to it. "Anything I should know?"

"There's no mention of Merab Varko, and another story of our little incident. Apparently it's the most newsworthy thing to have happened in quite a while. There's speculation the city is riddled with foreign agents and saboteurs."

"I'm not surprised Merab isn't in there," Raven said. "They'll want to keep her role in the Grim Hand secret. No one will know anything's wrong until her house comes up for sale. The good news is that it's unlikely she told the City States you're still alive. You're just as dead as the rest of the team. That means we're both free of the City States. If that's something you'd want."

Scorpion didn't answer, just placed the plate on the bed and munched on a pastry. It oozed something orange, probably mashed peach. She'd missed pastries on her little island. But she'd missed Scorpion even more.

She tugged her shirt over her head and stood there under his frank appraisal.

"There's time before we have to leave," she said as she walked over to him and her fingers tangled in his hair.

They hailed a trap before the sun rose and ignored the strange look the driver gave them when Raven stated their destination. As usual, the Ethereal Sorceress's masked doorman let them enter, but this time he gave Raven a short bow.

"You are expected," he intoned.

Scorpion glanced at Raven, a concerned look on his face.

They descended to the green-carpeted hallway and saw the sorceress waiting for them.

"I didn't think to see you so soon," she said.

"I thought we were expected?" Raven replied.

"At some time. It has barely been a full day."

"Our business here is done."

"To your satisfaction, I hope?"

Raven shrugged. "As well as can be expected. I need another favor."

Sheelahn inclined her head. Raven couldn't tell anything from her orichalcum-masked face, even with the cross-shaped opening.

"Granted. I will add it to your ledger," Sheelahn said. "Thus is our bargain struck."

Any price would be paid further down the track, Raven knew, hopefully with a few quick missions. Assuming she and Scorpion emerged alive from this situation. If Raven died, Sheelahn had struck a bad bargain. But that was the price of doing business, she guessed.

"We need to travel to Kaile," she told the sorceress.

"As you wish."

"And we need information."

"Another favor? Your tally is growing, and you have not attempted to repay me yet."

"Soon," said Raven, nervous that she was getting in too deep. Whatever she had to give in return would undermine her plan to resume a quiet life for a while. But that wouldn't happen if she was dead, either. "I can't work for you until I've done what's needed now."

"Very well. What information do you seek?"

"The latest news on Kaile; if you know of anything untoward happening there. And if you know someone named Blasius Matheo."

Sheelahn paused, as if searching her memory, but Raven had the feeling she was doing more than that.

"You refer to the discovery of the ruins and orichalcum, of course," said the sorceress. "Among other things, someone has cleared a large patch of land near the ruins and is building a compound there. Mercenaries have removed many of the local people. The few that remain are in hiding."

"People have been killed?" Raven echoed. "To what purpose?"

It was Scorpion who answered. "To scare them. To keep them away from the sites."

"Precisely," said the sorceress. "In addition, there have been a number of deaths in Sansor. Some councilors who believed the mines should be owned only by nobles or the government."

"We should go to the mountains," Scorpion said to Raven in a low voice. She didn't think whispering would make any difference as to whether or not Sheelahn would know exactly what he was saying. "Whatever is happening there is critical to Blasius's plans. He expects to make a lot of money from the ruins and the orichalcum discovery. If we can disrupt whatever's going on, we'll hit him where it hurts. In Sansor, he's invulnerable.

But if we can get him into the mountains…"

She shook her head. "I still want to head to Sansor first."

"You are going to kill Blasius Matheo?" asked Sheelahn.

For the first time, Raven wondered if the Ethereal Sorceress was partnered with Blasius, who must surely do business with her at times… Maybe Raven and Scorpion were already compromised. But why offer as much information as Sheelahn had already?

"We merely want to talk with him," replied Raven.

"Do not presume to lie to me," said Sheelahn. "It is good you wish Blasius Matheo dead. I will miss his business, but someone else will take over exploiting the ruins and orichalcum. It is inevitable. Blasius Matheo does business with the Tainted Cabal, and that I cannot abide."

Raven's eyes narrowed. "Akatta Palek is Tainted Cabal, isn't he?" She knew it, somehow, as certain as she knew her own name.

"Correct."

"And you are part of an opposing organization?"

"Also correct. Events have moved swifter than I had anticipated. Deals struck. Partnerships formalized. We are the Order of the Blazing Sun."

Raven raised an eyebrow. "That's a little ostentatious."

"It is a name. Names may not mean anything, or they may mean everything. You must answer my offer soon. There is no avoiding sides in this war."

"I must deal with Blasius first," said Raven.

"You'll never get within striking distance of Blasius Matheo without help," said Sheelahn. "He has the best protection wealth can buy, including sorcerers."

"I'll find a way," said Raven. "No defense is without its weaknesses. Especially with our talents. He might be rich, but he bleeds like everyone else."

"No," said Scorpion. "It would be suicide. You've already died once. Don't die for real this time."

She regarded him evenly, hands on hips. "It's just like any other mission. The question is whether I do it alone or with your assistance. He's after me, and he hasn't stopped. It's him or me. That's the end of the matter. So we need to figure out his plan. It has to be related to the ruins and the orichalcum, otherwise why kill the surveyors that confirmed the discovery? There's a chance we can use that against him, or to draw him out."

"That's too difficult. You'd need a long period of surveillance to break through his security team, and even then you probably wouldn't be successful."

Raven sighed. "Very well. I can't come up with anything better. We disrupt whatever Blasius has going on in the mountains and see how he reacts."

"I also have information that could be of use," said the Ethereal Sorceress.

Scorpion gripped Raven's arm as they descended the wide steps from Sheelahn's building in Sansor. "That was again a horrible experience," he said with a shudder.

"It gets easier," she said, then grinned. "Hard to believe, I know."

In the main street, he hailed an open-topped trap and directed the driver to a stockyard just outside the city. "Our first priority is to buy some horses and gear and get moving," he told Raven. "It's probably a few hundred miles from here to the mountains, then we still have to locate the ruins and the orichalcum find."

In the end, they paid over the going rate for two shaggy moose.

Sometimes the beasts' antlers blocked their rider's vision, but they were cold-weather tough, and capable of fighting back if any of the creatures that inhabited the wilderness attacked. They also bought saddles and reins, then picked up provisions at a market close by.

Ignoring the hostler's warnings about traveling without guards, they rode off to the east. A river flowed north-west from the mountains to the coast, and they would make better time if they rode south-east along it. It would provide them with fresh water, and there should be settlements along its length too, for shelter and further provisions. Though at some stage they'd have to brave the wilderness and risk encountering the dead-eyes or other monsters that lived there. Not an insignificant risk, but both Raven and Scorpion were confident they would be able to handle whatever happened.

As they traveled, Scorpion occasionally smiled in Raven's direction. She assumed he was thinking about their newly reawakened feelings for each other, and perhaps even a shared future. For her own part, she felt content just being with Scorpion, even though they were heading into danger. Even on the island she'd known there was something missing from her life, some indefinable factor that prevented her from attaining true happiness. She didn't know if she loved him, but what she felt was deeper than just attraction.

By the eighth night, they were well into the mountains. They stayed in a village that had an air of disorder and poverty. The owner of the village's only inn—a single-story building that had clearly first served as a warehouse—informed them that a tribe of dead-eyes had killed almost the entire village a decade before, and it had never recovered. People now feared the place had bad luck and hesitated to make it their home.

They paid to stable their moose in a tiny barn, and decided it was best if they stayed with their mounts for the night. Just before dusk, Raven went out and purchased more provisions, at half the price they'd cost in Sansor. She also bought a large portion of fried rice with river fish from an old woman, with a promise to bring the bowl back in the morning. She shared the meal with Scorpion, and after her first mouthful realized why there had been others waiting to buy the old woman's food—it was delicious.

"What's the plan when we get there?" she asked once they'd finished eating.

Scorpion fished around in his saddle bags and came up with a dark-green bottle, which he uncorked and handed to her. Raven took a swig and smiled with appreciation. Alchemical wine was expensive, but she supposed they might as well live the good life while they could. In a few days they might both be dead.

"We scout the area during daylight," Scorpion said, "see what we're up against. If there aren't any surprises, anything we think we can't handle, we'll kill as many of the mercenaries as we can as soon as the sun goes down. And try to take one alive, so we can question them. Preferably someone in charge rather than a foot soldier."

"We'll need to leave someone alive to report back to Blasius too," Raven added.

It took another few days to get close to their target. They set up a concealed camp beneath a well-positioned overhang from where they could see the track and a good deal of the surrounding countryside. There was no running water, but they had enough canteens to last for a few days.

In the few hours before darkness descended, they rechecked their weapons. Scorpion divided up the shred blocks and small shred balls, giving the lion's share to Raven.

"I'll mostly use sorcery," he said.

Raven hesitated, but squirreled the shreds away. She thought he might be giving her an advantage in case it all went to shit, but she also knew he couldn't concentrate on his dawn- and dusk-tide sorcery at the same time as the dark-tide they'd all inherited during their transformation.

"We're well set up," she remarked. "We should be able to handle whatever we encounter."

"And what is the first rule of combat?"

The old lesson brought a smile to her face. "To never be overconfident. It probably means even more now. After all, there are no others after us. We're all that's left of the team."

"And if we fail, then the Grim Hand will go unavenged."

Raven pursed her lips but remained quiet. The team had been Scorpion's life until very recently, but she had left it years ago. His need to avenge the Grim Hand burned hot, but she barely cared. She just wanted Blasius dead so she could—so *they*—could have a chance at a normal life.

Scorpion unrolled two blankets and made a bed on the soft dirt underneath the overhang. "No fire tonight, I'm afraid."

A bitter wind had grown stronger over the last few hours, and if they weren't protected it would have chilled them to their bones. "We'll find a way to keep warm."

"It'll be a long day tomorrow. And a long night."

"I'm ready."

In the morning they left their moose under the shelter of the overhang and filled their backpacks with food and water. When they made their move, they'd conceal the packs somewhere safe so they could move swiftly and precisely.

Their target was a few miles from their overnight camp. Dawn broke halfway through their trek there, and soon they could see smoke from cook fires. Before they got too close, Scorpion called a halt so they could catch their breath and run over their plan.

"It's best to be careful," he said. "They may have set traps around the site."

"Unlikely," Raven said. "No one's supposed to know they're here. My guess is they'll have a watch positioned on the track leading in, and the occasional patrol in case of intruders or dead-eyes."

"They'll have sorcerers too," said Scorpion. "They have to. They can't risk getting wiped out by a tribe of dead-eyes or a pack of ghouls. If you see someone with a talisman, kill them. If someone only has a dagger instead of a sword or spear or crossbow, kill them too."

"Understood." Talismans were concentration aids for sorcerers, and usually hung from their belts for easy access when they performed their calculations and cants.

"Any questions? Things I haven't thought of?" he asked.

"No. Time to get the job done."

They moved out toward the target site, pushing through thick brush and then into a slightly less vegetated rocky area. The terrain was excellent for scouting as it offered areas of dense undergrowth, along with rocky outcrops perfect for hiding behind and for cover in case of missile weapons or sorcery. Sporadically they stopped and listened for any sounds out of the ordinary. Only the wind and the occasional bird call reached them.

After a good few hours of stealthily examining the area around the site, both Raven and Scorpion had committed to memory various escape routes and hiding places. There didn't look to be any traps laid around the perimeter, although there could be some closer to the newly erected buildings.

They stopped for another break, and ate bread to fill up, followed by nuts and dried fruit for energy. In a few hours the sun would set. If they could get closer when the dusk-tide washed over the land, they had a good chance of spotting any sorcerers who were outside to replenish their power. If there was only one, they would mark them and the building they were in. Two or more, and their best chance was to take them out while they were distracted. That would mean losing the element of surprise, but it couldn't be helped.

They rested separately. Raven would have liked to snuggle close to Scorpion, but protocol existed to keep you alive and this way, if one of them was discovered, the entire mission wouldn't be compromised. They dozed until the sun touched the horizon, then used hand signals to indicate they were both ready. From now on there would be no talking unless absolutely required.

Raven drank half a canteen of water then relieved herself before they moved out. She clutched a shred in one hand and the smaller of her orichalcum spheres in the other.

Scorpion held his talisman—a simple stick with notches carved into it at unequal intervals—and a shred in his other hand. His large knives were strapped to his chest harness and could be drawn in an instant.

Fifty yards from the site, Raven caught a glimmer in the grass and stopped abruptly, raising her fist and crouching down. A wire had been strung between two trees at waist level. She followed it and found a cow bell tied to one end of the wire. Not the most professional alarm system, but sufficient to announce the approach of dead-eyes or ghouls. She didn't deactivate it in case someone checked.

They continued, keeping to the long shadows and maintaining as much cover between them and the target as possible. A short while later, they lay in tall grass beside a boulder, peering at the site.

There were three large tents with double poles and guy ropes pegged to the ground, and five smaller single-poled tents. A few of the ropes were held down by rocks instead of pegs, which showed the ground was rocky and probably uneven underfoot. Smoke poured out the top of one tent—probably a makeshift kitchen based on the pile of firewood stacked on one side. Thirty yards behind the tents was a picket line, to which a dozen or so shaggy moose were tethered.

There were two buildings under construction: timber frames, with walls and roofs partially completed. Three wagons filled with lumber stood nearby. Some distance from the tents was a screened-off area, which could only be the jakes. To the right of the buildings sat another wagon, this one loaded with what looked like chunks of rock: probably orichalcum ore. Next to it was a squat brick structure and a pile of coal, along with metal implements and a crucible atop a low table of thick timber.

Raven and Scorpion lay motionless, conserving their energy and waiting for the sun to completely set. As they watched, two leather-armored warriors bearing spears exited one of the smaller tents and made their way along a dirt path already worn into the ground. Occasionally they heard shouts and laughter from other tents, then there was the clang of metal on metal as someone rang a chime. A rotund man came out of the kitchen tent and tied the flap back to reveal a table holding several pots, a large tray filled with sliced bread, and a stack of mugs.

Men and women filed out of the smaller tents to eat. The ratio of warriors to workers was about one to one; Raven counted twelve in total. They all deferred to one man, who had to be in charge. He was tall but not muscular, and wore a sword on his belt. While he ate he was joined by another man and a woman, and all three talked animatedly—perhaps about the day's progress. To Raven's irritation, none of the men or women stood out as a sorcerer, and not a single one left the evening meal to partake of the dusk-tide. Either there was no sorcerer with the group—which was unlikely—or they hadn't used any dusk-tide sorcery during the day and therefore didn't need to replenish their repository just yet.

Two of the warriors finished their meal, then began a slow walk around the tents, before widening their patrol circle. One held a lantern; and at intervals the other moved ahead to let his eyes adjust to the darkness so he could scan the perimeter. The rest of the men and women moved into the tents for the night.

Two fires were left burning, and they stood out against the inky backdrop, along with lanterns inside each tent. Raven and Scorpion would wait until the lanterns were extinguished and the fires had burned to coals before making their move. Both moons were in the night sky but only as slivers, which meant there was good cover for tonight, and full-dark was on its way.

The warriors on patrol rested their spears against their shoulders and talked at low volume. They were sloppy and not paying enough attention to the darkness outside their campsite. Clearly they didn't expect any trouble. That was a plus for Raven and Scorpion. Twelve, plus the two who had left to guard the approach to the site, made it fourteen against their two.

When the last flame had died, Raven and Scorpion rose and

moved together toward the site. Where the long grass stopped and the ground became rocky, they split up. Scorpion darted across open space and crouched behind one of the lumber-filled wagons. Raven focused on her own task: to take out the patrolling warriors without alerting anyone else in the camp.

When the lantern-bearer stopped and the other moved ahead, she made her way through the camp and around the pool of light spread by their lantern. A shred surge would be overkill, and also too loud. It would give them away, as would the screech of her orichalcum artifact if she used it. A knife or the thrust of her rapier were better tools for silent work.

Raven took out a poisoned crossbow bolt and tossed it toward the lantern-carrying sentry, sending the missile on its way with a surge of dark-tide power. There was a faint hiss and a fainter groan, then the lantern clattered to the ground as the warrior holding it fell.

"Kartin?" whispered the remaining sentry.

Raven sprinted up behind him and drove her rapier into the base of his skull, severing his spine. He gurgled and convulsed, and she felt hot blood run down her blade as she lowered his corpse to the ground.

Somewhere close to Scorpion, a cry of alarm rang out. *Bloody darkness!* There were no other patrollers, so he must have been discovered by sorcery. Raven saw him run from behind the wagon to the side of one of the partially constructed buildings, but the damage had been done. A bright light shone from one of the smaller tents as the sorcerer inside erected an arcane shield.

Raven arced a shred toward one of the large tents and sent a surge of dark-tide into it. A thunderous crack split the night, as if an invisible bolt of lightning had struck the camp. Shards of solid darkness peppered the tent, and there was a cry of agony.

As men and women poured from the other tents, she hastened to Scorpion. "What went wrong?" she asked.

"I was probing for any sorcerers and got caught. Something must have alerted them. It happens."

"Do you know how many there are?"

He shook his head. "At least one."

"I could have figured that out myself. Remember, we want the leader alive."

Raven split away from Scorpion just as a woman shouted and pointed toward them. It was dark and they shouldn't have been seen, so this marked her as a sorcerer. Whistling crossbow bolts followed the woman's gesture, so Raven shadow-stepped to the other partially built building. She kept low and ducked around the back, then made her way to the end to look at the camp. Someone splashed oil onto the two fires and the logs caught quickly, sending light across the camp and black smoke into the sky. Raven could see that the warriors had taken cover behind whatever was available: a couple of barrels and some crates. But there wasn't enough to protect them all, so some must have vanished into the night. She cursed inwardly.

As she watched, a man surrounded by a sparkling sphere emerged from another tent. So, there were at least two sorcerers in addition to the guards. If they were halfway competent, they would cause trouble. If they were skilled, then Raven and Scorpion might have to flee and attempt to catch them unawares another time.

Something fell from the sky and landed in the fire closest to the tents. Raven sensed a surge of dark-tide just as the fire erupted into shadowy spikes. Blazing oil-soaked logs flew in all directions, some landing on the tents, others leaving flaming paths as they rolled across the ground. The light they spread revealed the entire camp, and Raven smiled. A nice move by Scorpion. Her grin broadened as flames crept from the logs onto the tents.

A hoarse voice shouted commands, and two warriors scrambled to douse the tents. Raven tossed up a pair of bolts, and with two dark-tide surges sped them toward the camp. Her missiles struck both warriors, and they collapsed before they could extinguish the flames.

The campsite was in chaos. There were already five down, which left eight, mostly non-warriors, and the two sorcerers, plus the leader. The priority now was to kill the warriors who'd had the foresight to conceal themselves in the darkness.

Raven heard a shout and a thump from Scorpion's direction, then incandescent globes spiraled into the sky, banishing the darkness and bathing the campsite in radiant light. *Bloody sorcerers.* Raven concealed herself in the nearest pool of shadow, which stood out starkly against the bleached ground.

The sorcerers voiced manic cants and more globes rose into the sky, burning with a furious, hissing crimson. They flew with an eerie howl before plummeting toward their targets. One slammed into the building beside Raven, cracking the timber and sending jagged, burning chunks of wood exploding outward. Another globe hit the ground, followed by two more. They were targeting shadowy areas—where any attackers could be hiding.

Another globe came arcing through the night toward her. She focused on a darker patch over by a protruding boulder and poured her awareness into the shadows. Her body and mind melted away, then re-formed just as the scorching globe hammered into her previous hiding place, sending gouts of fire splashing across the timber.

A wave of weariness swept through her. There wasn't enough

time to recover from her dark-tide surges. She peered around the boulder to see men with crossbows zigzagging in all directions. Some of those she'd discounted as non-warriors obviously had weapons training. And when your life was at stake, you did what you had to. She of all people understood that.

Three more orange globes rose into the sky, one bearing toward her, one to a spot where Scorpion might be, and another to where she wanted to move next. *Bloody darkness.* A shred wouldn't work: the sorcerers both stood within perfect spheres of sorcerous energy.

She drew a deep breath and bolted from cover, searching for another hiding spot. Bolts whirred past, and she pushed all around her with the dark-tide to deflect any that were on target. Immediately her head spun and she stumbled. *Keep moving.* A dip in the ground provided a modicum of cover, and she threw herself into it, but the warriors were coming and the sorcerers had likely already targeted her.

She crawled farther along the depression, rapier still in hand, until she could poke the top of her head out. Starkly illuminated figures approached swiftly, and a bolt thudded into the ground right beside her. She had to move or she'd be in a great deal of trouble, but there weren't a lot of options. Focusing on the shadows by one of the large tents, she shadow-stepped behind the warriors and sorcerers. The move wouldn't give her much respite. They were professionals and would immediately search elsewhere for her.

She crouched at the corner of the tent. Shouts of alarm and the sharp detonation of a shred told her Scorpion was still alive—and why wouldn't he be? A skilled warrior and sorcerer, with innate dark-tide talents bestowed by his Grim Hand transformation, he was the deadliest among them all. Raven's knees were weak, and her hand shook as she sheathed her rapier and drew a knife. She took a few deep breaths to try to steady herself. She was already feeling the effects of using her dark-tide power, and the situation was still a mess.

A scream sounded, followed by another. Raven heard the closest sorcerer curse and begin a cant. She gripped the hilt of her knife and peeked around the corner. Both sorcerers were still shielded, their arcane spheres humming with energy. Their illumination globes floated over the campsite, banishing shadows. But there were multiple shadows spread behind the sorcerers. Which gave her an idea—if she could manage it without killing herself.

Raven squatted to make her profile smaller, and shadow-stepped *inside* the closest sorcerer's shield.

The woman sensed something was wrong immediately. She gasped and turned, just as Raven drove her blade into her side. Blood gushed over Raven's hand as she pulled the knife back and severed the woman's throat, cutting off her scream. The shield around them winked out, but at the same time Raven's knees buckled and she felt her gorge rise. *Not now.*

The other sorcerer stared at Raven with revulsion and anger. She smiled at him, then shadow-stepped inside his shield. One, two, three thrusts of her knife into his back, and he dropped lifeless to the ground.

The sorcerers' incandescent globes vanished, plunging the campsite into almost darkness. Though the fires were still burning, everyone was now night-blind. Which was just as well, as Raven felt herself falling. She landed across the dead sorcerer and struggled to pick herself up, to no avail. Her stomach rebelled and acid stung her throat. She managed to suppress the urge to vomit and crawled in the direction of the nearest tent. Whoever of the enemy remained would hide and wait, or regroup here by the fires. Her whole body shaking, she managed to drag herself inside the tent. Dirt and dead grass clung to her hands and her blood-coated shirt and knife. For long moments she couldn't do anything but breathe and hope she wasn't discovered.

Outside, she heard movement and some low-pitched voices, but nothing else. No sorcery, no shred detonations, and no panicked alarm. Scorpion was either dead or injured or keeping a low profile. She needed to move, to do something to help him, but her head pounded, and she shivered as sweat dripped from her.

Taking a waxed-paper lozenge from her pocket, she was relieved to see it was one of the stronger painkillers marked with an "X". She unwrapped the lozenge and shoved it into her mouth. The unwholesome flavor mingled with the sweat dripping down her face, adding a saltiness that made the taste worse. Against her better judgment, she found another dose marked with an "X" and ate it as well. The after-effects would be terrible, but this was no time for short measures. Immediately, a numbness spread through her and her nausea subsided.

A thunderous crack sounded outside: a shred. Raven bared her teeth in a smile.

Booted feet clumped toward her. Someone breathing hard. They cursed. Not Scorpion. Then she heard a gurgling moan, and a body thumped to the ground.

As far as Raven could tell, their targets had lost at least ten, which left four. She hoped their leader was still alive.

There was another shout. A woman's scream, abruptly cut off. Then the camp fell eerily silent, except for the sound of someone sobbing in the distance. A less than clean kill by Scorpion. Maybe he was slipping.

Raven managed to drag herself to her feet. She wiped the dirt and grass and blood from her hands onto her trousers. Dizziness washed over her, but she remained standing and forced herself to take deep breaths as quietly as she could. Her exhaustion felt as if it were far away, almost as if it were someone else's.

Readying a shred, she looked out of the tent flap. She caught a glimpse of Scorpion: he was kneeling beside a barrel close to one of the fires. His face dripped sweat, and there was a dark stain on one trouser leg. He was whispering under his breath, but stopped and shook his head, before starting again. She could tell he was as tired as she was.

But as she watched, strength flowed into her limbs—a false strength from the medicine, and temporary, but it would suffice for now. Raven stumbled toward the kitchen tent and found cover behind the table, which had been tipped over. She peeked around its side. Something glimmered about fifty yards away— and a bolt slammed into the table, its barbed tip emerging half an inch on her side.

Scorpion looked over at her, and shook his head. His sorcery was spent. The hard way it was, then.

She leaped to her feet and over the table, racing in the direction the bolt had come from, zigzagging to avoid any more missiles streaking toward her. Motion caught her peripheral vision, and she dashed toward it. The man she'd marked as the leader was running along the track that led away from the site.

He must have sensed or heard her pursuit, because he turned and loosed another bolt. Raven flung herself down and rolled, yelping as her arm banged into a stone. The bolt hissed through the air above her. A surprisingly accurate shot under the conditions.

She jumped up again and raced toward him, her booted feet thudding into stones and hard-packed earth. He drew a wicked-looking blade, almost as big as Scorpion's daggers, and crouched into a knife-fighting stance. Raven groaned. She was in no condition for a one-on-one fight, even if she had the advantage of a rapier against the man's knife. And if she used the dark-tide, she'd regret it.

It couldn't be helped.

She removed her smaller orichalcum artifact from the larger sphere, and with a flick sent it pulsing toward the man. It hammered into his leg. Bone cracked and blood spurted, and he pitched over with a grunt of pain and surprise. Raven sent a pulse of dark-tide to bring her sphere back to her hand, then sank to the ground and vomited.

A flickering orange light approached, and a strong hand gripped her shoulder. Scorpion had followed her. He was carrying a torch, which meant he was confident everyone else had been taken care of.

She spat to clear her mouth and nodded toward the leader. "We need to bandage his leg, and yours too."

Scorpion hobbled away to find their backpacks. Raven took some time to recover her wits, then returned her attention to the leader. He'd managed to crawl a dozen yards, leaving a bloody trail behind him. She walked over, placed her boot on his wounded leg and leaned her weight on it.

A howl of pain escaped him, and his hands grasped onto dirt and grass.

"You're not going anywhere," Raven said quietly. "Roll over and let me see how much damage there is."

The man's eyes remained squeezed shut, and his breath came in short gasps. Snot dripped from his nose. Raven disarmed him of a few knives and a garrote that doubled as a fancy necklace.

"Put both hands on your wound to stop the bleeding,"

she said. "We'll wrap it with a firm bandage, but you'll need a physician. I suppose Blasius will pay. In any case, whatever you're doing here is over."

He didn't react to the name. When she looked down, she saw he'd passed out.

# EIGHTEEN

AFTER RAVEN HAD EATEN ANOTHER lozenge, she and Scorpion laid the wounded mercenary beside the blazing fire. After a time, he groaned and opened his eyes. His face was illuminated by the fire's flames and also by a lamp sitting atop a table a short distance away, and Raven saw him take in the dead bodies lying around the camp—his mercenaries, and the men and women Blasius had sent to accompany them. Nevertheless, he kept a tight rein on his emotions. Only a tic under his right eye betrayed the fact that he was under great stress and in immense pain from his shattered leg.

Raven's eyelids were drooping from the effects of her medicine, so she let Scorpion take the lead. He approached the mercenary leader from behind, while Raven stepped directly into the man's vision, letting the light of the flames paint her skin with flickering orange.

The mercenary blinked. "You!" The word came out as a hoarse

croak.

"I see you know who I am," she said, "so there's no need for introductions. Who are you?"

He didn't respond.

Raven gave Scorpion a curt nod.

"Let me be clear," said Scorpion, stepping into the mercenary's vision. "We need answers from you. If you lie to us, we'll leave you to die out here. If you're lucky, the cold will get you. If you're unlucky… Well, let's just say the dead-eyes don't treat their captives well."

The mercenary nodded, but his eyes were hard. If Raven had to guess, he was longing to drive a blade into both her and Scorpion.

"Who are you?" Scorpion asked.

"Hanno Dinnas," came the answering croak.

Raven sniffed. She'd heard of him. A professional. Highly sought after and commanding an exorbitant fee.

"I know of you," said Scorpion, his eyes narrowing.

Hanno licked his lips. "I'm famous. And wealthy."

"Not for much longer," said Raven.

"Who were the people with you? They weren't all mercenaries," Scorpion said.

The mercenary glared at them. His breath came in gasps and sweat trickled down the side of his face to drip onto the earth.

"You must be in a great deal of pain," Scorpion said. "You're in bad shape. Unless you make it to a healer within a day or two, you're done for. Answer my questions and we can make the pain go away." He held up a clear vial filled with a cloudy yellow liquid. "Oil of poppy. We might even be able to do something with your leg so you come out of this alive."

Dinnas looked down at his leg. Scorpion had splinted it while he was unconscious and wrapped a bandage around it. They wanted him to live, or to survive long enough to provide some answers.

"If we think you're being truthful, you'll get some oil of poppy and we'll take you to the nearest village in one of the wagons," Scorpion continued. "From there you're on your own, but I'm sure you have enough coin to persuade someone to take you wherever you want."

Dinnas coughed, and tried to shift his position, but couldn't manage it. When he spoke, his voice was still hoarse. "Most of them were working for me. I employed one of the sorcerers. The other was on loan."

"And what are you doing out here in the middle of nowhere?"

"Running an operation."

Scorpion grunted. "What were the objectives?"

"Guard this site, and make sure word of what's here didn't leak."

Raven broke in. "Why the extra men and the sorcerers? A few skilled warriors could handle things out here. I could have completed the mission on my own."

"A village close by found out what was going on. We were supposed to make it look unprofessional," Dinnas said. "Lots of attackers. Lots of arcane bolts flying about, causing damage to the buildings and workers. That sort of thing. The idea was the attack would be blamed on feuding merchants or councilors in Sansor who didn't hold the same views as my employer."

Scorpion frowned. "Why, though? Why make it messier than it needed to be?"

"I don't know."

"But you have some ideas?"

Hanno shook his head.

He did, thought Raven. But in a foolish show of bravado he was putting up some resistance.

Scorpion moved closer. "You're lying to us. It looks like you need a reminder. You only get the oil of poppy for being a good boy. Or it's this."

He drove his fist into the mercenary's shattered leg. Dinnas screamed until his throat was raw.

Raven and Scorpion waited patiently until the man came to his senses again. When he opened his eyes, she was nibbling on some nuts and dried apricots, and Scorpion was drinking water from a wooden cup.

Scorpion placed his cup down. "I hope you don't need another reminder. What was the reason for making the attack messier than it had to be?"

Hanno licked his lips and drew in ragged breaths. He probably needed water, but he was likely too proud and stubborn to ask for it. "I… I was just told to do it. I don't know anything else."

Scorpion exchanged a glance with Raven.

"Why did Blasius hire you to kill the councilors?" Raven asked, changing direction.

It was obvious her question and the knowledge it contained surprised Dinnas. His eyes flicked to the vial in Scorpion's hand, and Raven could tell the moment when his will broke. The tension left his frame and his eyes closed for a few heartbeats. He wanted to hold out but didn't have the strength. He couldn't stand the pain anymore.

"A little of the poppy oil," he begged.

"Answer the question first," Raven told him.

"It was to do with the ruins and the orichalcum here. They were intransigents—they refused to approve Blasius's claim to the area. With them dead, new councilors will be appointed, and Blasius has his hooks into all the likely candidates."

Scorpion carried the vial toward Dinnas, and he eagerly opened his mouth. Scorpion dripped a single drop onto his tongue.

"Only one?" Dinnas said querulously.

"For now," Scorpion said. "You'll get more later. Were you and your team behind the attempt on my life outside Kroe?"

"Yes."

"And on Raven in Gessa?"

"Yes."

"And you killed the members of the Grim Hand?"

"I was paid to."

"Why the Grim Hand?"

"You murdered his sister, and he cannot forgive nor forget."

Raven folded her arms across her stomach in reaction to the sudden chill that coursed through her. Her past had come back to hurt her, but…she'd been responsible for killing someone's beloved sister. From what this Blasius had done so far, she knew he would never leave her alone.

"If that's the case, I can't live in peace until he's gone. We can't. Blasius has to die."

Scorpion looked at Raven, then back to Hanno. "Who was she?"

Hanno uttered a weak laugh. "Like me, you've killed so many you can't remember them all. But it wasn't specifically you, it was her. Raven. Blasius hates you. No…that's not a strong enough word. There was a woman, Madlen, at an estate east of Sohrah."

Raven recalled the mission. She saw again the woman's pale green eyes, wide open in shock and agony. "Yes, I remember."

"He found out you killed Madlen. That Scorpion planned the mission, and others of the Grim Hand were involved too. He'll keep after you until he kills you. Whatever the cost of that, he'll pay it. Nowhere is safe." Hanno fixed Raven with a glare. "I'll pay for my failure too. He'll have me murdered, or just throw me in a cell and let me die slowly, painfully. Maybe it's for the best. I have no desire to live a life on the run, even if I do manage to walk again."

Raven shrugged. "I've had people try to kill me before. As you can see, I'm still standing. Now, back to the questions, and then maybe you can have more poppy oil. Where is Blasius now?"

Hanno grinned, though it looked more like a grimace. "You'll never get to him."

"Others thought the same thing, and they're dead. Where is he?"

"Safe in his mansion in Sansor. His guards are the best he can afford, and he's one of the wealthiest men in Kaile. Blasius is powerful, and powerful people gather enemies. His guards deal with an assassination attempt every week or two."

Raven stared at him then took the vial from Scorpion and stepped forward. She gave Dinnas a few more drops of the poppy oil. He swallowed it hungrily. When the full force of the drug hit, he would probably lose consciousness.

"No security is perfect," she said, gripping his jaw. "If there's one thing I've learned, it's that every target has a weakness. I want you to think for a bit, then tell me how you'd get to Blasius if you were hired to assassinate him."

Dinnas shook his head. "It's impossible."

"All right," said Scorpion. "Let's get you out of here."

The mercenary laughed. "I failed Blasius. Even if I somehow survived these injuries, he'd kill me. Give me the rest of the poppy oil and leave me here to die."

Raven understood Dinnas. He couldn't face a future in which

his leg was amputated and he became helpless against the bright knives that would come for him. At least with the poppy oil he'd die without pain. But they hadn't gotten all the information they needed yet.

She shook her head. "Sorry. Your luck has deserted you today."

Dinnas moaned. His body shivered and his eyes darted all over the place. "I know Blasius's weakness," he gasped. "Promise me you'll give me the vial and I'll tell you."

"All right. You have a deal. Our bargain is struck." Raven's mouth twisted as she realized her words were an echo of Sheelahn's.

Dinnas managed to raise his uninjured arm to beckon to her, before flopping back down. Raven leaned over him, and he spoke softly into her ear.

She turned to Scorpion. "We should get out of here. There might be reinforcements on the way to construct the mining equipment for the orichalcum."

"The vial," Hanno gasped.

Raven held it out, but the effort to raise his arm to take it was too much. She placed it into his hand and pressed his fingers around it, then helped him raise it to his lips.

"Die, if you want," she said. "But you must drink it yourself."

He managed a minute nod of gratitude and tipped the contents of the vial into his mouth. A few drops were enough to numb even the most intense pain and likely render someone unconscious. The entire vial…well, it wasn't recommended.

Hanno's lips moved, and Raven caught a faint prayer to a god she didn't recognize. After a few moments he began to speak, soft words that barely carried to Raven's ears, drawn from the mercenary by pain and delirium. His eyes opened and he stared straight up at the stars.

"It's too late, Mama," he said. "Where has my life gone? Dying. Alone except for the corpses. Freezing in the mountain air. If I had known this would be my end, would I have made the same choices? Could I have been someone different? Someone better than who I became?"

Raven shifted, uncomfortable that she was privy to the last sacred words between a dying man and whatever deities he worshiped.

# NINETEEN

"WELL?" DEMANDED BLASIUS. "DON'T JUST stand there, mute. What's going on?" He frowned as he stared into his sorcerous orichalcum disk, seeing the new mercenary he'd hired, Kane, swallow and glance over his shoulder. Hanno hadn't responded to Blasius's attempts to contact him, so he had been forced to spend more coin to confirm his suspicions that the mercenary leader and his men had failed.

"Sir, they're all dead."

*Bloody imbeciles.* "Dead how? Are you blind as well as stupid?"

"It's hard to tell. Something's eaten them. Probably dead-eyes. They've been stripped of flesh down to the bone, and their large bones cracked open for the marrow. I…there's signs of a sorcerous fight. Patches of dried blood everywhere. Other than that, there's not much to go on."

Blasius threw the orichalcum disk across the room. It bounced off the wood paneling—leaving a dent—and came to rest on the thick rug. The black circle in its center looked like an accusing eye.

Veins throbbed in Blasius's neck and forehead, and he bared his teeth at the imperfection the disk had left in the wall. "Shit-eating whoresons!" he shouted.

His plan to secure the orichalcum seam and the new ruins was in pieces, and he could feel the assets slipping from his fingers. He had lost the element of surprise. The disappearance of so many mercenaries could not go unremarked, which meant his enemies would pay for information, and soon his designs would become known. The scavengers would circle, and everyone would want a bite of his find until all he was left with was whatever he could hold onto by force.

Assume the worst, his father had always said to him, usually after thrashing Blasius with his fists to hammer a lesson home. He had been a pig and a savage, but he'd also been possessed of an innate cunning that had served him well.

Blasius had to assume someone had found out about the ruins and orichalcum and made their own play for the valuable assets. His plans had been compromised. When he found out who had ruined them, they would rue the day their mother had squeezed them out.

He strode over to his stained-glass window and looked out over the city. He needed to throw more resources at this problem before his designs totally unraveled. An opportunity such as this—the orichalcum discovery, the untapped ruins—came once in a lifetime, and he wasn't about to let it slip from his grasp.

Hanno's mercenaries were the best that coin could buy. Whoever had sent a superior force to kill them had to be extremely powerful. Maybe it was the Pristart Combine; they had meddled in his affairs in the past. Or perhaps the City States, who made it their business to interfere everywhere they weren't wanted. Or had the Ruling Council of Kaile somehow learned of his plan and moved against him?

He just didn't know enough, despite his very well-paid web of informants. And that lack of information made him uneasy.

Blasius moved to a side table and poured himself a glass of alchemical wine to soothe his agitation. Anger was a weakness. He drained the glass, felt the familiar burn of liquid in his mouth and throat. By the time its warmth spread through his stomach he was calm.

He'd been through many fires before, and each one had changed him, forged him anew. From his early days risking all his coin on trading ventures to the loss of his first ship in a sudden squall that had almost bankrupted him, he'd always emerged victorious. He just needed to think through this hiccup and find a new way to reach his end goal.

The Ruling Council of Kaile were still reluctant to side with him. Perhaps his best option now was to pay more, both in coin and trade. The Council had their own mining businesses and would no doubt want a piece of the action at the new site. He just needed to make sure they didn't try to take the whole pie for themselves.

With the recent deaths of several of the councilors, it wouldn't be long before Blasius's puppet councilors were in place, and the balance of power more easily shifted. Then the entire Council would be more pliant going forward. After all, what was prosperous for Blasius was prosperous for Kaile too. Of course, Blasius would retain the lion's share of the profits of the mine, as was only just, but there would be plenty of coin to go around. And once the orichalcum mine was fully operational, the taxes the Council collected from it would rapidly pay off the debts their ineptitude had run up over the years. And Blasius and his web of companies would go from being the dominant player in Kaile to taking on the whole of Wiraya. A heavyweight that could no longer be ignored.

Blasius moved to his desk and sat down with a sigh. It should have been a week of triumph for him! And there was now a possibility his entire design was in tatters and defeat was staring at him with its cold hard eyes.

He could not let that happen.

There were others he could turn to, now that Hanno and his useless mercenaries had failed. The Tainted Cabal could be persuaded to help, though Blasius was reluctant to become entangled with the secretive sorcerers again. He would give the idea more thought. For now, he had to find a way to get the councilors to come over to his side—and an impressive party and display of wealth should do the trick.

# TWENTY

A SMALL GATHERING OF ADMIRERS had congregated around Raven's table at the Card and Coin, Sansor's infamous gambling establishment—not only because of the low-cut, black silken dress shot through with silver threads that clung to her like a second skin, but because she was playing for noteworthy high stakes.

The house had a reputation developed over more than a hundred years, and had become a playground for the wealthy and powerful in Sansor—and indeed, in all of Kaile. People came here to gamble but also to be seen: nobles, merchants, councilors, and those famous for being famous.

Alchemical globes illuminated each of the four opulent levels. Guards patrolled the floors and tables and positioned themselves at exits and on the wide marble staircases that joined the different levels. Solid goldenwood beams held up the ceilings, and each floor was tiled in a different color and pattern. Raven was on the third floor and wouldn't get to see the fourth unless she spent months earning a place there with gold coins, skill, and amusing conversation.

She watched the other card players place their bets, then, after a few moments of feigned consideration, slid another gold across the table to the dealer. Many eyes lingered on her, and although it was part of the plan, she had to suppress a shiver. She felt naked without her usual weapons concealed on her person. All she had with her was a short blade hidden in the buckle of her wide belt, in case of emergencies; and her orichalcum sphere, which hung from her neck. Its value alone would send rumors circulating.

The revealing dress accentuated her skin, which she'd considerably lightened with a tincture. Her hair had been dyed blue-black, brushed until it shone, and then intricately braided with silver chains from which dangled small diamonds. She'd even consented to a light touch of make-up to highlight her sharp cheekbones, widen her eyes, and give her lips a reddish tinge. She fidgeted with the neckline of her dress, self-conscious and irritable, and wanting to get out of the outfit. But it was essential to stay in character if she wanted to succeed.

She had arrived an hour earlier, and her initial stake of fifty gold talents had grown marginally to fifty-seven. Now, she leaned back in the upholstered walnut chair and stretched her neck, using the movement to scan the crowd. Her eyes passed over Scorpion without stopping and Raven acknowledged a new arrival with a nod and a smile before tilting her head to the side.

"Such luck must be a gift from the gods," murmured the man from beside Raven.

She met the man's eyes. He was attractive, though a good few decades older than her. "Perhaps you forget. No sorcery is allowed in the Card and Coin. Though luck can hardly be seen as an arcane power. Tonight, some men will find themselves luckier than others."

She turned back to the card game, a variation of Malice, where teams could be formed or disbanded on the go. When the dealer finished shuffling the cards, Raven glanced at Scorpion where he stood next to the bar and saw him jerk his head to the left.

Their target was here. Raven rubbed her earlobe to signal she understood.

The dealer coughed discreetly to bring Raven's attention back to the hand. She flashed him an apologetic smile and studied the three cards she'd been dealt and the two the dealer had placed face up. As luck would have it, she had two Emperors, and another lay in the dealer's draw. There were five of each card type in a standard deck of sixty-five, which meant there were two more Emperors floating around somewhere. The odds were minimal that someone else had also drawn two. It really was her night, if she cared anything at all about gambling. She pushed ten gold talents forward and heard the spectators around her gasp at the size of her additional wager.

Raven flashed a brief smile at the card player to her right. From the pile of gold talents stacked in front of him, she knew he was wealthy. He pushed forward some of the golds to match her wager.

A blue coat sleeve brushed past Raven's ear as someone deposited a stack of five golds next to hers—a side wager. She forbore glancing behind her to see who'd made the bet, but hoped it was Arborn Meyvant, their target.

Meyvant was a rising star of the theater in Sansor. The theater's latest production, *The Inveigling of the Moon Goddess,* had sold out sessions for the last six months. Raven suspected it had something to do with the titillation of having a goddess suborned and defiled that brought wealthy theater-goers back for more. That, and the fact the actress playing the part of the moon goddess was stripped naked and whipped on stage in front of hundreds of degenerate spectators.

Arborn Meyvant was in his early twenties and exceedingly handsome. His current play's success had propelled him into notoriety and wealth, and he was frequently seen at the Card and Coin. Arborn was an avid card player, as well as a lecherous partner-hopper who favored a sort of love-play that involved pain as a sexual stimulant. Raven's appearance had been tailored to entice the actor: the dress that clung to her fit body; the leather boots and belt that would appeal to his preferences.

According to Scorpion's information, Arborn Meyvant was rumored to share Blasius Matheo's bed. And tonight, Blasius was holding a soiree at the Rose, a building atop a wooden pier in the harbor, and Arborn had been invited. True to form, he'd come first to the Card and Coin, to see and be seen, and to scratch an itch to play cards for an amount of coin a poor person would kill for.

The dealer drew another two cards: The Chariot, and the Two Moons. Raven frowned and toyed with a few of her gold coins.

Almost immediately, her rival moved ten more golds forward. Raven matched it with ten of her own. With so much at stake for each player, it would probably be one of the highest hands of the night.

"Are all bets placed?" said the dealer.

Raven and her rival nodded.

The dealer withdrew both the players' cards from the lacquered boxes in front of them. Each box had a small black curtain on the dealer's side through which they could place and withdraw cards when required, but no one else except the player could see their cards. Raven's rival had an Emperor, which was inferior to Raven's two.

A murmur rippled through the crowd gathered around the table.

The other player stared at Raven's cards and his face went red. Giving her a tight-lipped smile, he rose and bowed before leaving the table. He forgot to take his drink with him.

The dealer took two of the gold coins for the house, then pushed the rest of the pile across the table toward Raven. He handed the side-wager winner a gold and a handful of silvers: two golds less ten percent.

"Thanks, Keld," she whispered under her breath. The practice from their games, and his card tricks, had come in handy. She hoped the old fisherman was well, and had finally asked the widow Reena out.

Raven handed a gold coin back to the dealer as a thank you. He mumbled something, eyes bulging in shock. A few in the crowd clapped lightly in approval. Raven scooped up the remaining coins and deposited them in a calfskin pouch she removed from her clutch-purse.

"A spectacular hand," a male voice whispered in her ear. "Old Jesal will feel the loss of those golds. His wool and weaving business has had a few setbacks recently."

Raven stood and met Arborn's eyes, then brushed his cheek with her lips as she responded with a whisper of her own. "I thank you for the compliment. So, he was a merchant. Golds easily come by are easily lost. He'll recover."

"And where do your golds come from? I haven't seen you here before."

Raven shrugged and offered a coy smile. "Here and there. More there than here. Men seem to leak coins when I'm around."

"I daresay they do." Arborn moved closer and placed a hand on hers. He wore black leather pants and a white cotton shirt, unbuttoned to his navel to show off his lean, hairless chest and firm stomach. Two chains hung from his neck, one platinum and one gold, and both his nipples had been pierced with plain orichalcum rings. A bright red coat with gold details at the cuffs and collar set off his tawny coloring and his golden hair, which was cropped short. "Perhaps I can buy you a drink?"

She could see the hunger in his eyes, and it revolted her. She let her gaze slide down his bare chest and linger on his crotch. "Why? Do you think I look bored?"

He didn't react, except for a predatory smile. She grabbed his forearm and dug her nails into his skin until his eyes widened and he gasped.

"Do I need to teach you some manners?" she said. "Wait for me. I need to freshen up first."

Without waiting for a response, she released his arm and made her way through an appreciative crowd, many of whom raised their glasses in acknowledgment of her performance.

As she glided toward the ladies' room, she passed close to Scorpion and murmured, "He swallowed the bait."

"Don't enjoy yourself too much," he murmured back.

The ladies' room was a small chamber with mirrors lining one wall, and a few lounges and armchairs standing on thick rugs. Two scantily-clad women, one with curled blonde hair and the other mousey brown, looked up at her as she entered.

Once Raven had finished her ablutions, she took a few moments to steady herself in front of one of the polished bronze mirrors.

"You look stunning, dear," remarked the blonde.

"If we looked half as good as you, we'd make our fortune, then do what we want rather than what we need to, to survive," the other woman said.

Raven gave the two a closer look. Their dresses showed a couple of faded patches and repairs, and their perfume was on the cheap side. She knew that once women like this got on a downward spiral, it was hard for them to arrest their fall. She made a quick decision and handed them her purse. "There's almost seventy gold talents in there. Split it between you."

The women's eyes widened. The blonde gave her a quizzical look, while the other frowned.

"What do we have to do to earn this? Kill someone?" said the blonde.

"The going rate for an assassination is far less than that, depending on how good you are, of course. But anyway, I'll ask nothing in return. I will give you some advice, though. There will be an uproar in the commodities markets shortly. You know what they are? Good." Raven lifted her artifact and they both gazed at it. "Orichalcum. A big find will be announced soon. The current market price will plummet. Have a legitimate trader write some promissory notes for you both to sell orichalcum in a few months at the current price. Your seventy golds will likely be worth a great deal more once the upheaval settles."

"So we'll be rich?" asked Mousy Hair.

"You already are. If you follow my advice, you'll be extremely wealthy. Do some good with it. But that's up to you." Raven turned and left them sitting there. She'd already delayed too long.

Scorpion noticed the missing purse immediately. "Where's your gold?" he said as she walked past.

"I gave it away."

He grunted. "To whom? A beggar, or a scam artist masquerading as one?"

"To someone in need," she replied, and made her way back to the card tables.

Arborn watched her as she approached. He'd taken the seat of the merchant she'd beaten, and the crowd around the table had thinned. The dealer drew his final card and Arborn glared at it: The High Priestess.

"It seems you took all the luck with you when you left," Arborn said wryly to Raven. His eyes drifted down to her breasts.

"I don't believe we've been introduced," she told him.

"I am Arborn Meyvant, the actor. Perhaps you've seen one of my plays?"

"I can't say that I have."

When his eyes tightened, Raven thought she'd made a wrong move, then his mouth softened and he shook his head ruefully. "Perhaps you'll have the chance to see what I can do later tonight."

"Perhaps," she said. "If I don't become bored and leave."

"I'm sure I can accommodate your desires. I'm on my way to a friend's celebration, down on the harbor. It's very exclusive and promises to be a party to remember. I'd like you to join me."

"How do you know I'm here alone?"

"An actor knows these things. All were impressed by you, yet no one dared approach. And I find you extremely interesting," he added, his voice wavering slightly.

No doubt he was thinking of what would come after the party, when he had her in his private rooms. Raven knew her hook had been swallowed.

"As it so happens, I am alone," she said. "As it seems you are. How fortunate."

He took her arm and escorted her through the gambling room toward the main exit. A man followed close behind; a bodyguard, Raven assumed.

"And what is your name?" Arborn asked as they walked.

"I was wondering when you'd ask. I am Karina Vedis. A somewhat successful trader and entrepreneur."

"From the Jargalan Desert to the south, judging from the color of your skin," he said. "Which, I might add, is quite exquisite."

"Thank you. Yes, my origins are in a wild land that brings out the worst in all who live there. Luckily, I have been able to tame my urges. Though occasionally they get the better of me."

Arborn grinned and offered his hand to help her into the carriage his bodyguard had waved down. Once Raven and the actor were seated, the bodyguard rode up top with the driver. Raven had to stop herself shaking her head. The guard wasn't very good; or perhaps he thought no one would attempt to assassinate a mere actor.

Arborn slipped his arm through hers and sat so close, their thighs touched. To anyone observing they would look like lovers.

"So, what do you entrepreneur, Lady Vedis?"

"Just Karina, please," she said, holding back her revulsion. "I endeavor to separate coin and valuables from those who have grown old and weak. Mostly men. It is rare I get to meet a real man such as yourself."

He grinned again. "There are few of us around, that's true. Seldom do physical perfection and intelligence mingle, as they have in my case, and in yours."

Six guards clad in black woolen pants and gray coats met Arborn and Raven at the steps up to the pier. In addition, Raven could see the local Watch patrolling the streets to make sure the residents of the underworld, such as the Night Shadows, didn't get any ideas about robbing the gathering of wealthy guests.

Bulges underneath the guards' coats hinted at concealed weapons, and more than one wore brass knuckledusters. All six moved with grace, despite their bulk. Obviously well-trained and dangerous, probably ex-military and experienced in actual combat. They recognized Arborn and ushered him past, along with his bodyguard, but they asked Raven to halt, and one of them patted her down for weapons. They even searched her clutch-purse, which contained only a few coins, two crystal perfume vials, a silken scarf, and her medicine.

"I know how many coins are in there," Raven told the guard doing the search, a grizzled man with a short beard.

He smiled thinly. "We wouldn't steal from a guest. What are these small waxed-paper packages? And I don't recognize some of these coins. Where are they from?"

"The lozenges are for my personal recreational use, if you take my meaning. And the coins are from the savage south. Arborn here will tell you, it's a land rife with danger and intrigue."

"Of course," Arborn said to the guard. "Beyond the Jargalan Desert the wilderness is harsher than you could imagine." He turned back to Raven. "Only the strong, and the beautiful, survive."

She inclined her head in acknowledgment.

The guard grunted, handed back Raven's purse, and waved her through. The party was being held on the second floor of the building, which had the best view of the harbor. An elderly gray-bearded man ascended the steps ahead of them, and Raven recognized him from her and Scorpion's surveillance as Frewer, the head of Blasius's security team.

At the top of the stairs, which were made from thick wharf

timbers, stood another two guards. Their faces remained impassive as Raven and Arborn passed. Scorpion would be lurking somewhere close by in case something went wrong, and now he'd seen her enter, he would move to his next position.

Inside, six musicians played a lively tune while a few dozen of Sansor's wealthy and elite mingled. A score of alchemical globes illuminated the vast room with an unearthly glow, bright enough to see by, but low enough that the harbor was still visible out of the massive clear glass windows. Stewards wearing cream coats and bearing trays of wine-filled glasses and various delicacies glided between the guests. Raven saw pickled butterflies dusted with crystalized honey and resolved to try them as soon as she had the chance.

Two of the gray-coated guards were stationed at the center of each wall, and Raven noted another two wandering casually around the room. When one turned to reply to a question from a guest, Raven saw a talisman at her belt. So, there was at least one sorcerer to deal with.

Arborn grasped two glasses filled with a yellow alchemical spirit and handed one to Raven. "This is a pearlescent alchemical brandy. Blasius adores it, and even though it's hideously expensive, he doesn't mind giving it away. Really, he could give away a ruby in each glass and not notice a drop in his wealth. I heard he spent a few hundred thousand on his mansion overlooking Sansor. Imported marble from Manela. Glazed tiles from the kilns of Atya. Rugs created by the most skilled weavers in Riem."

"Between you and me, it looks like piss," Raven said, holding her glass up to the light.

Arborn looked shocked. Raven chortled, and after a moment he joined in.

"Really, Karina, don't let Blasius hear you say that, or he'll be most upset. You are a demon!"

Raven shivered, cringing inside at Arbon unknowingly giving voice to her worst nightmare. "I hope not, or you're doomed! Speaking of our host, where is he?" Raven sipped the brandy, pleasantly surprised at the peachy taste that danced on her tongue.

Arborn peered around the room. "I believe he's over there, next to that table filled with an excellent array of delicacies. He does like to eat. But he also works off any ill effects, unlike most merchants I could name."

"Will you introduce me?" Raven said. "And once the formalities are over, we can move on to other, more interesting activities."

They approached the table, which probably would have been sagging, if it hadn't been reinforced. Raven counted three whole roasted pigs, plates heaped with dripping honeycomb, bowls filled with fried fish the size of her little finger, at least ten different meats sliced thin enough to see through, berries coated with hard toffee, a plate of what looked like slugs in a brown sauce, and more pickled butterflies dusted with crystalized honey. Blasius had four of the slug-like creatures skewered on wooden sticks in one hand, and was munching on a fifth, judging from the empty skewer he tossed to the floor.

Blasius regarded Arborn with a grin as they approached. His pet sorcerer stood a few paces behind: a woman with a mistrustful expression.

"I thought I'd left word with my guards that you were to be roughed up and tossed into the street if you dared show your face here," Blasius said to Arborn.

He clasped Arborn in an enthusiastic hug, and Raven noticed him grind his groin into the much younger actor's. To each their own, she thought. If it helped her get what she wanted, she'd undress them both.

"I heard the drinks were free for ladies tonight, so I brought someone I could sponge off," Arborn said, laughing.

Blasius eyed Raven appreciatively. The corners of his mouth turned up in a smile. "And where did you find this magnificent creature?"

Raven had no fear of being recognized. Her skin was much lighter than her natural color, and her hair was black instead of platinum. Besides, Blasius believed she was a thousand miles away. She thought he looked similar to his dead sister and once more remembered the woman's face as she drove her knife into her heart. Madlen, that was her name.

Raven smirked back at Blasius, indicating that she knew she was being treated like a piece of meat and it didn't bother her. At the same time, she wondered what her chances of escaping alive would be if she grabbed one of the wooden skewers from the table of food and drove it into his eye. She could dive out of a glass window and into the harbor, and easily hold her breath underwater until she was out of range. But it was the sorcery she couldn't counteract, and that knowledge stayed her hand.

"This is Karina Vedis, a trader and entrepreneur," Arborn told Blasius. "Karina, this is Blasius Matheo, Sansor's premier merchant and trader, and perhaps soon to be one of the Ruling Council."

"I'm honored," Raven said as Blasius took her hand in his limp grasp.

"A pleasure to meet you, Lady Vedis."

"Karina, please. This is a wonderful place."

"I'm pleased you like it. I see your glass is empty. Arborn isn't very considerate. What would you like to drink?"

"More of this pearlescent brandy, I think. It might look like piss, but it tastes like peaches."

Blasius chuckled at her comment, but she could see in his eyes she'd irritated him. That was fine by her. She wasn't here to impress him. She was here to kill him.

"Karina, please," muttered Arborn, trying to rescue the situation. He raised his own empty glass, and a cream-coated steward hurried over. Within moments, all three held half-full glasses of the yellow liquor. Arborn raised his glass in a toast. "To chance acquaintances."

"To unexpected change," Blasius replied.

"To getting roughed up," added Raven.

This time, Blasius's laughter reached his eyes, and Arborn looked as if he'd like to take Raven to the nearest private, or not so private, room and have his way with her.

All three sipped their brandy, and this time Raven let it linger on her tongue. If she made it out of this alive, she might just have to purchase some. If there was any available wherever she ended up after the Ethereal Sorceress had made use of her.

"You must try the Nimbras caterpillars," said Blasius, holding up a skewer. "The brown sauce is delightful, with just the right amount of black pepper and ginger root."

Arborn eagerly plucked a brown-slime-covered caterpillar from the plate. Raven decided against it and made for the pickled butterflies dusted with crystalized honey that she'd seen earlier. She popped one into her mouth: it just tasted like crunchy, vinegary honey. Something stuck between one of her back teeth, probably a leg.

"Delicious," she said.

While Arborn regaled Blasius with an off-color story about the lead actress in his current play who'd apparently been caught in a flagrant act with the wife of one of the Sansor councilors, Raven excused herself and made for the refreshing rooms. As she slipped through the crowd, many of the other guests tried to catch her eye and engage her in conversation. She avoided those she could, and didn't bother to remember the names or titles of those she couldn't. Everyone here, apart from Blasius and his guards, was insignificant.

Inside the refreshing rooms, Raven drained her glass and patted her face with one of the soft cotton cloths provided. She hadn't done infiltration work like this for a good few years, and her skills were rusty. A light sheen of sweat covered her brow, and she couldn't afford for any sign of nervousness to be noticed. The two glasses of brandy had helped to calm her somewhat, and luckily her transformation had rendered her immune to the strong effects of alcohol, or she'd likely be tipsy and not in full control.

When she exited, she ducked down a corridor that led away from the main function room, into the depths of the building. She and Scorpion had spent some time scouting the place, and there were kitchens and storerooms this way; and beyond them a series of highly expensive apartments for those who wanted to live somewhere unique and could afford to pay for that experience.

She spotted a guard exiting the kitchen and toasted him with her empty glass as she casually turned a corner and disappeared from his sight. She couldn't hear his boots thumping toward her, so she mustn't have aroused his suspicions.

Stairs down appeared exactly where she'd expected—always a good sign. She descended and made her way quickly along a wide corridor to a heavy, locked door. Raven hitched up the hem of her dress and removed a flat leather case tied to her inner thigh with a black silk ribbon. She'd made sure to keep her legs pressed together when the guard had patted her down.

Taking a tension wrench and a standard short hook from the case, she set to work picking the lock. Not long after, it clicked open and she breathed a sigh of relief. It wasn't just her infiltration skills that were rusty, and she'd been worried the lock might prove their downfall.

She tugged the door open and slipped inside, closing it behind her. The walls, floor and ceiling of the room she'd entered were made from the thick wharf timbers. Oilskin coats and hats hung from hooks nailed to one wall, and at the far end was another door, barred closed. Raven yanked the lever across to disengage the bar and left the door slightly ajar.

It led onto more stairs down, which were attached to a floating pontoon underneath the pier—for residents who wanted to arrive inconspicuously by boat. Mostly those who housed mistresses in their apartments, Raven surmised.

She quickly made her way back to the party. When she ascended the stairs to the second floor, she encountered a gray-coated guard who frowned at her, his hand going to a weapon concealed inside his coat.

"You're in a restricted area, my lady."

Raven gave him her best smile. "I'm sorry. I wanted to check out the apartments. It's an excellent layout and I'm considering purchasing one."

"I'm going to have to ask you to return to the party," he said.

"I understand. Please forgive me. My curiosity got the better of me." She held out her empty glass. "Would you be so kind as to get me another? The pearlescent brandy." She turned away, as if confident he would obey her request, and felt his eyes on her as she continued down the corridor toward the party.

Raven ran a hand across Arborn's buttocks before sliding her arm through his. His face was flushed, and there were two empty glasses on a table close by. "I'm sorry I took so long," she said. "There were a few ladies who wanted to chat, and I couldn't get away. Did you miss me?"

"Like the desert misses the rain."

She restrained an eye roll. "Did you try the pickled butterflies? They're quite the delicacy."

"You've been on my mind ever since I saw you at the Card and Coin," Arborn said into her ear. "We should leave as soon as we can."

She pressed against him. "I have to warn you, I can get quite aggressive when I'm aroused."

"Do your worst. I don't scare easily."

"You'd better not. Now, I'll fetch us another drink. The same for you?"

"Perhaps I'd better not—"

"Nonsense. When you're at a party, you drink. It's common courtesy." She caught the eye of a steward. When he returned with their drinks, she clinked her glass against Arborn's. "To not scaring easily."

"To...delight-filled nights," he replied. Raven noted a slight slurring of his words.

"How adventurous are you, Arborn? Do you think we could find some rope, as well as somewhere private? A guard told me the apartments are off-limits tonight. Such a shame. An opportunity wasted."

Arborn's eyes widened, and he took a gulp of his brandy. He glanced toward Blasius, who was standing by a window, looking out over the water, with a group of men and women around him.

"Blasius will tell them to let us through," he said quickly, and weaved unsteadily over to where Blasius held court.

There were a few annoyed looks when the actor barged into

the group, but after a short conversation with Blasius, Raven saw the merchant signal to one of the guards and whisper to him. The man nodded and left.

Arborn returned, drained his glass and licked his lips. "Blasius has an apartment in the building. He's given us permission to use it."

"And where will we find some rope?" Raven asked.

He pressed close to her, his perfume almost causing her to cough. "One of the guards will leave a coil outside the apartment. We'll wait a little bit and then leave."

Raven took his empty glass and raised it high. In moments, a steward appeared and refreshed it. She pointed to another steward moving through the crowd with a tray holding a plate of the pickled butterflies. "Arborn, could you get me a few of those? I'll need my strength for later." She winked at him.

"Anything for you, my lady." Arborn moved off toward the steward, stumbling slightly.

Raven removed the smaller of the perfume vials from her purse, pretended to dab some behind her ears, then discreetly poured a few drops into Arborn's glass. She swirled it to mix the drug into the brandy, which would mask the medicinal taste.

When Arborn returned, she handed him the glass in exchange for the butterflies. "Another toast!" she said. "To ropes and dark apartments!" As soon as he'd drained his glass, she grabbed him by the hand and whispered, "Let's go. I want to see how much you can take before you beg for mercy."

# TWENTY-ONE

ARBORN LURCHED FROM SIDE TO side as he led her to Blasius's apartment. Raven knew it was the effects of the drug she'd administered. The rope was lying outside the door, and she picked it up while he fumbled at the lock with a key Blasius must have slipped him. In the end, Raven had to help him unlock it and support him as he stumbled inside.

Taking hold of both his shoulders, she pushed him toward the biggest four-poster bed she'd ever seen. Burgundy silk drapes hung down the sides, and the posts were carved to resemble thick vines. Arborn tumbled onto the bed and rolled onto his back. His clumsy fingers attempted to unbutton the rest of his shirt.

"Come to me," he slurred. "Give me what I need…"

Raven waited until his eyes closed and he began to snore. Then she pulled his shirt open and tugged his trousers down, leaving his flaccid cock dangling for all to see. Using the rope, she tied his wrists to the headboard.

She dumped the contents of her purse onto the bed, and separated out the foreign coins the guard had thought strange. He'd been right. Scorpion had paid a metalworker to stamp fake coins out of the smaller shreds and coat them with a thin layer of gold. Playing pieces for a game, he'd told the metalworker. Raven placed the shreds in an easily accessible side pocket of her clutch-purse, reclaimed her other coins, vials and scarf, and clipped her purse to her belt. She calculated how much time had elapsed between her unbarring the external door to the docks and now. It should have been enough for Scorpion to enter and make his way to the outside balcony on the west side of the party room. Now that Arbon was out of the way, Raven's next task was to create a diversion.

She opened the door a crack and checked the corridor outside. When she was sure the coast was clear, she exited Blasius's apartment and locked the door. She moved silently along the hallways outside the apartments toward the rear of the kitchen that was supplying Blasius's party with food and drink. The kitchen staff had left the doors open to provide some relief from the heat of the stoves and the large charcoal fire, over which game birds of all different sizes were roasting on iron rods. Raven stayed in the shadows of the hallway, watching as stewards exited bearing more trays of what the wealthy residents of Sansor considered delicacies. She spotted a large copper pot on an iron stand beside the charcoal cooking fire. It seemed to contain oil. One of the men dipped a long-handled brush into the pot and used it to baste the roasting birds. Perfect.

When the man had moved on to another task, Raven sent a pulse of dark-tide power against the pot of oil. The container moved a foot, and teetered on the edge of the stand. Another pulse from her tipped it over into the charcoal fire. There was a muffled whump as the oil ignited, sending flames roaring. A cloud of black smoke billowed into the room, and immediately the cooks began shouting.

"Fire!"

"Get some water!"

"No, fool! Water will—"

Too late. Someone threw a pot of water onto the fire, and it sizzled violently, sending splatters of flaming oil around the room.

A steward came in to see what the fuss was about, and as soon as he opened the door, black smoke poured through the opening. Shouts of alarm came from the main room.

Raven ran along the corridor and through a different doorway into the party room. A number of guards—five—had moved the guests away from the kitchen and formed a cordon between them and the smoke. A couple of other guards were directing their subordinates and the cooks to bring more water from the rain barrels situated outside on the balcony, and soon a bucket line had formed across the room.

Blasius's voice boomed out over the hubbub of exclamations and questions. "Calm down, my friends. There has been a small accident in the kitchen. Rest assured that none of the food was damaged!"

A few chuckles followed his feeble attempt to make light of the disaster.

"Could everyone please make their way out onto the balcony, where the stewards will serve one of my finest vintages of pearlescent alchemical wine. My guards will put out the fire, and we can return to the festivities. Accidents happen occasionally. There is nothing to be concerned about."

His voice projected reasonableness and certainty. The guests made their way across the room, some still clutching their drinks or plates of food. The balcony easily held their number, with space left over for more. Raven joined them, staying as close to the doorway as she could. Guards spread around the railings, eyes wary as they calculated the new danger presented by having everyone outside.

Blasius remained inside, close to the door, with two guards and the sorcerer hovering next to him. He was doing his best to pretend he was calm and the guards were a mere formality for someone in his position, but it was obvious he wouldn't be joining his guests outside. There was too much risk. An expert marksman atop one of the buildings along the shore could possibly make a shot at this range, but the real danger would be a sorcerous assassin. Someone like Scorpion.

Another guard approached Blasius, and they held a short, terse discussion.

"I want to know what in darkness happened!" Blasius said. "I want this mess cleaned up, and the cooks back in there preparing food! Do you hear me? I won't have my night ruined because of some clumsy servant."

"With respect, sir," said the guard, "perhaps it would be best if we moved you somewhere safe until we're sure this isn't a diversion?"

"Yes, yes, of course," Blasius said, sounding calmer. "But if this was an accident, I want all those cooks fired. They won't be able to work in Sansor, or even Kaile, again."

Blasius moved into the corridor that led to the apartments, flanked by his two guards and the sorcerer. His guests milled about on the balcony, laughing and chatting and drinking and eating. The sense of danger and urgency had disappeared. The party resumed and the musicians began to play again.

Raven slowly sipped another glass of brandy and let her gaze roam around both inside and outside the building, attempting to verify where all of Blasius's guards were situated.

One of the gray-coated guards approached her, his eyes narrowed in suspicion. "Excuse me, my lady, where is Arborn? There was speculation that the two of you wouldn't be seen again tonight, but here you are."

A few guests leaned closer to catch the conversation. No doubt it would be a juicy piece of gossip.

Raven affected a smirk. "He drank too much and passed out, so I left him to sleep it off." Arborn would be hard to rouse, but it was unlikely anyone would suspect he'd been drugged.

The guard nodded and left her.

Raven returned to her assessment. There were seven guards on the balcony and just inside the doors. Three, including the sorcerer, had gone upstairs with Blasius, which left at least seven others somewhere in the building. At worst, Blasius would have ten to protect him. At best, there would be just the three for her and Scorpion to take care of.

Raven meandered among the guests on the balcony and glanced up at the floor above. There was no balcony on that level, so she could see right up to the roof of the building. Two guards were situated there, both clutching loaded crossbows and watching the water and the docks for any threat.

Raven smiled politely at the musicians as she edged past them, moved inside the main room, and found a corner to stand in. As soon as she stopped, a guard approached her.

"Excuse me, but could you please move outside, my lady.

We'll inform everyone when it's safe to return."

Raven waved her glass at him, as if to shoo away an annoying fly. "It's too cold out there. Do you think this dress keeps the freezing wind out? Be a good boy and fetch me a warm drink. Something expensive."

"Please, my lady, if you'd just move outside—"

"When I tell Blasius how rude you've been, do you think he'll keep you on?" snapped Raven.

The guard glared at her, gave a curt bow, and left without another word.

Raven knew there was a servants' staircase on the other side of the kitchen. She ducked into the hallway when no one was looking and made her way past the kitchen. Through an open doorway, she could see the cooks and guards had smothered the oil fire and were already tossing shovels of fresh charcoal over blazing kindling. Another pot of marinade stood on the iron stand, ready to be used on the two lines of skewered birds waiting to be roasted.

She moved into the servants' stairwell—a narrow affair made of cheap timbers, barely wide enough to avoid bumping your elbows on the walls if you had to carry something up or down it. She took the steps carefully, making sure the poorly crafted treads didn't make any undue noise that might alert the guards. By now, Scorpion should be on the upper level and would hopefully have taken out a few of them.

Halfway up the stairs, she took the second, larger, perfume vial from her purse and dashed it against the wooden treads. The glass shattered, and with a shrieking hiss the alchemical mixture inside reacted with the air, sending flames crackling across the timber.

Raven took the remaining steps as fast as she could, back into a main corridor, then sensed a burst of dark-tide power that had to be from Scorpion.

Two guards came running along the corridor toward the flames. Raven tossed her small orichalcum sphere toward them and pushed it on with three precise pulses of dark-tide power. The sphere let out its eerie whistling scream, and the closest guard stumbled and fell on his face, blood seeping from a hole in his back. The second man's skull exploded, splashing blood and brain across the wall.

The third pulse returned the sphere to her. She scooped it up with trembling fingers, and a wave of weariness hit her. Ignoring the after-effects of her use of power, Raven took a deep breath and screamed, "Fire! By the goddess, there's another fire!"

Down a hallway to her right, she caught a glimpse of Scorpion as he moved away from the main stairs.

A servant screamed as she exited the refreshing room and saw the two corpses lying in spreading pools of blood. She backed away from the grisly sight. More guards came running, now armed with loaded crossbows. Not knowing who had killed their companions, they had to prevent the guests from leaving the party as all were now suspects. Raven knew that would tie up a good deal of their number.

An older, more seasoned and experienced guard approached the bodies from the servants' stairs. He glanced up at Raven through the flames, a crossbow in his hands.

"Fire!" Raven shouted again, but the guard pointed his crossbow at her.

She used another dark-tide pulse to send her sphere into his chest. His blood splattered the walls. Another guard raced toward her, and she fought off the dark-tide nausea to call her sphere back to her, causing it to puncture his neck from behind.

Raven fumbled a lozenge from her purse and chewed rapidly.

She was operating on the edge now, and would pay for it later, but this was her best chance to take down Blasius.

She backed away from the screaming guests, who were almost berserk now in their attempts to exit the building, and headed toward the safe room where she guessed the guards had taken Blasius.

She sensed another surge of dark-tide ahead of her as Scorpion used his innate powers, then heard shouts emanating from a side corridor. She recognized Scorpion's voice. He was yelling in pain.

Sorcery crackled in the air, and spheres of orange fire sizzled in all directions at the end of the hallway.

There was another dark-tide surge. Then another. Scorpion appeared in the darkness close to her, having shadow-stepped to safety. A crossbow bolt stood out from his chest, and a crimson stain spread across his shirt.

"I'm sorry," he said, the words strained. He held out her sheathed rapier, as if somehow the weapon would save them.

Raven ignored the offered blade, and pressed her hands around the bolt to try to stem the flow of blood.

"A sorcerer. He's dead. Blasius had two," Scorpion managed. Which left only the woman.

"Stop talking," she told him. "We have to get you out of here."

Something hard slammed into her skull. Her head rocked to the side, her vision blurred, and her thoughts scattered. She tried to turn, but her body wouldn't respond and she flailed uselessly before flopping beside Scorpion.

She tried to lever herself up. Failed.

Darkness rushed in to envelop her.

# TWENTY-TWO

THE SMELL OF FRESHLY-BAKED BREAD *wafting through the window makes my stomach grumble.*

*I clutch a stuffed doll with scraggly yellow hair while I watch a woman sweeping out the ashes from the hearth.*

*She glances at me over her shoulder. She has a kindly face— familiar. Her skin is almost as dark as mine, her hair as black as midnight.*

*"Saskia, honey," she says, "go fetch us some bread from next door, and don't forget to pick up some salted butter."*

Acrid smoke tickled Raven's nose. She tried to breathe through her mouth and erupted into harsh coughs as fumes filled her lungs. She opened her eyes a crack. Someone had dragged her to lie beside Scorpion.

He'd managed to raise a hand and press it onto one side of the puncture in his chest. She didn't think it was doing much good.

She could hear blood gurgling in his throat with each labored breath, and see it seeping from the chest wound. Sections of his clothes were charred, and his face was welted with angry red burns. Some of the veins underneath were blackened. Sorcery. Whoever he had run into had been more skilled than him. There was always someone.

Frantic yells drifted up from below, along with a faint, regular squeaking. Probably the firefighters pumping water. She spotted her purse a few feet away, and saw her small orichalcum sphere lying against a wall, apparently undetected. Where was the remaining sorcerer? She couldn't take action until she knew. If Blasius was protected, she'd waste her only chance to kill him.

"Sir, we need to get you away from here, now," a voice said. "The fires are getting worse. And the Watch are inside the building and asking questions. We can't guarantee your safety if you don't leave."

It was Blasius's head of security: Frewer. Raven hadn't seen him since she'd arrived with Arborn. He must have been directing his guards from somewhere else in the building.

"Are you sure it's her?" said Blasius. "She's supposed to be a thousand miles from here. She must have dyed her hair." Raven heard him move closer to her, smelled his sweet breath. "It doesn't really matter how she got here. I'm going to make the bitch pay for what she did to my sister. And then I'm going to strangle her."

"Sir," said Frewer, "we can't delay any longer. There's no time for your revenge—"

"By darkness, I'll not be denied now!" Blasius roared. "Fetch me a sword. I'll cut her head off and take it with me!"

"Time isn't on our side! You need to leave now. Take Jisona— her sorcery will protect you—and go down to the pontoon.

We have a boat waiting for you. The guard will put in a few wharves away, and you can hail a trap or carriage and be back at your estate before anyone is the wiser. I'll tell the Watch you narrowly escaped an assassination attempt—which is essentially true. They'll be satisfied when they see that the only casualties are your own guards. And I'll take care of the woman for you."

More shouting ensued below as the Watch apparently encountered Blasius's men. Raven felt something ripple, and the guards fell silent. The Watch had done something... So, it was true that some of them were blessed by their goddess, Zihanna. Everyone was ordered to lay down their weapons.

Blasius snarled like a wild dog as the Watch's booted footsteps thudded closer. A lancing pain erupted in Raven's side as Blasius stabbed her. As he yanked the blade out, she rolled onto her back and lashed out with a boot. It connected squarely with Blasius, but he merely grunted and smacked her leg away with one hand. He lunged again, sinking his dagger into her stomach. Raven mewled in pain, hands clutching her abdomen. She felt warm blood seeping through her fingers.

Blasius launched a vicious kick into her stomach, and agony exploded all through her. Her vision faded and she had trouble keeping her eyes open.

Frewer grabbed Blasius and dragged him away. "I'll take care of these two. Their bodies won't ever be found. You must go now. You can't be seen among this mess."

Nausea surged from Raven's guts to her throat, but she forced herself to remain motionless.

Blasius spat, and she felt hot sticky spittle land on her cheek. "You bloody bitch! May you rot with the demons in the Abyss!"

"Please, leave while you can," said Frewer again. "She's done for. She'll bleed out, and I'll finish off the big man myself. Get back to your mansion where it's safe."

Frewer hustled Blasius away. Raven opened her eyes a minute crack, enough to see both men disappear along the corridor.

"Now this bitch is taken care of, there's just one last task to complete my revenge," she heard Blasius say. "As soon as all's clear, I'll head to Corvant."

Corvant? A city north of Atya on the western continent. What was there?

Scorpion uttered a low moan, and his fingers twitched. He'd likely heard the entire conversation, too, and was trying to gather what little strength he had left. She could see that his life force was ebbing with each passing moment, though.

The blood had stopped flowing from her own wounds, thanks to her regenerative ability which sped up clotting. She would remain alive for a little while—long enough to deal with Blasius, she hoped—but if she didn't see a healer and get some rest, her chances of long-term survival weren't promising.

Frewer returned, and Raven closed her eyes again, feigning unconsciousness. His powerful hands grasped her wrists, and she felt herself being dragged a short way down the corridor and into a side room. As soon as he released her hands, she let one fall to her waist, where her fingers found her belt buckle.

As Frewer leaned over her, Raven slashed his throat open with the knife she had concealed in the buckle. His hands clutched at the wound in a vain attempt to staunch the hot, sticky blood that splashed over them both. She pushed him, and he slumped, gurgling, to the floor, twitched a few times, then was still.

Raven cut a long strip of cloth from his shirt and wound it around her stomach and side. That done, she retrieved her purse and fished around in it for another lozenge. She ate two, one of each type. They would numb the pain and let her use her dark-tide abilities a few more times. If she survived, the after-effects would be terrible, but it was that or let Blasius escape.

She wiped her knife blade clean and resheathed it in her belt buckle, then quickly made her way to Scorpion and kneeled by his side. His breath was labored, and pink froth surrounded the bolt in his chest—a sign his lung was punctured. His face was ashen, drained of all vitality.

Tears streamed down her cheeks, salty on her lips. "Scorpion…"

But she couldn't do anything. He was dying. She'd known that since she'd come to.

"Saskia… I'm sorry," he murmured.

She had to lean closer to hear him, and felt a stab of pain in her abdomen. "There's no need to be sorry," she said. "I'll get you out of here."

His fingers grabbed her knee, as if he'd found some strength from somewhere deep inside. "I have to tell you something."

"I know. I love you too, Scorpion."

"I'm sorry… I…didn't mean to ruin your happiness."

"You didn't ruin anything. Shhh. I need to get you out of here." She didn't want the Watch to prevent her going after Blasius.

A harsh cough wracked Scorpion's frame, and blood trickled from his mouth. "No. Listen. I'm sorry…about our baby."

Raven froze.

"I found out… I knew," Scorpion continued.

Raven rocked on her knees, unable to think. "She…she's gone." More tears flowed down her cheeks, making dark spots where they splashed onto his shirt. "She died. They couldn't save her."

He shook his head and his grip tightened. "No. She isn't dead."

The words hit her like physical blows. It wasn't possible…

"What do you mean? She died. I saw her. I buried her."

"I had to protect her… She wasn't safe with you… I'm sorry…" Another cough, and more pink foam oozed from his wound. "I wanted to tell you…couldn't… The City States wanted our baby… They thought she would be special… Not safe… I swapped her…"

Raven's mouth gaped open. How did the City States know about their baby? And then what he'd said hit her like a runaway horse.

"You stole my baby?" Her tongue stumbled over the words. "For years you let me believe Amelia was dead?"

His voice became fainter, his eyelids fluttering. "Had to tell them…only option…my daughter too…I did…was best…keep her safe…"

She grabbed his shirt and shook him. "Don't you die on me, you bastard! Where is she? What did you do with her?"

His head lolled, and she slapped his face until his eyes opened. He croaked something she didn't catch.

"What did you say? Where is she?"

Scorpion's lips quivered as he tried to shape the words.

Raven leaned over him, her ear close to his mouth. "Where? Where!"

His eyes squeezed tight with the effort of speaking. "Cor… vant." His breath wheezed and he groaned. "The pain… I'll wait for you…on the other side."

"Don't bother," she said, hate and love for him warring for dominance inside her.

He shuddered and was still, staring sightlessly at her.

"No. Bloody darkness!" She clenched her hands into fists and pounded his chest, trying to bring him back and punish him at the same time.

Scorpion had taken Amelia from her. Her daughter was alive, but he'd taken away the first few precious years of their life together. Years of bonding Raven would never get back.

She scrubbed tears from her face and shook her head to clear it. Scorpion's final confession might have been intended to give her hope, but instead he had condemned himself and her memories of their relationship to eternal damnation. Raven grabbed her purse, her orichalcum sphere, and rapier, and left Scorpion to rot or burn where he lay.

Now Blasius's reference to the city of Corvant made sense. When he'd gotten his hands on Scorpion's journal, he must have learned of Scorpion's plan to kidnap Amelia, and also where he'd hidden her.

But with nothing else to go on, how could Raven find one girl in an entire city?

She made her way to a room that overlooked the harbor, opened the window wide, and backed up half a dozen steps. The pain of her wounds had faded under the effects of her medicine and the rage that flooded through her veins. She shoved her purse down the front of her dress and buckled the rapier's belt tightly around her waist. Then she put on an extra burst of speed and dove out the open window into the cold night air.

# TWENTY-THREE

THE HARBOR WATER'S DARK EMBRACE surrounded her. She kicked hard to propel her away from the building atop the pier. If anyone had seen her, they would be raising a hue and cry, and the Watch might come after her. She stayed under, knowing she was at least safe from crossbows and relatively safe from sorcery.

After what felt like an eternity, her head broke the surface. She gasped for air, glancing around to get her bearings. She could just make out a wooden ladder descending from the nearest wharf to the Rose and swam toward it. Her fingers and palms scraped on barnacles on the ladder's rungs as she dragged herself up onto the wharf. Her silken dress was dripping with salt water, clinging to her body. At least she still had her boots on. The sea had washed most of the blood from her skin and dress, but it had also rinsed off much of her skin tint. The streaks were visible even in the dimness.

Raven peered toward the burning building across the strip of water. The waves rippled orange from the blaze. She hadn't meant to cause that much damage, but it looked like the building wouldn't be saved. Blasius's guests had been herded into a group by at least twenty members of the Watch, and their faces were turned to the fire. She thought she could see Arborn among them, supported on both sides by guards, his head lolling to the side.

She tugged her boots off and emptied them of water, then trudged off in the direction of the main street. As luck would have it, she saw Blasius leaning out the door of a carriage, watching the building burn. He twisted and said something to the driver, then ducked inside. The driver flicked his reins, and the carriage started off along the street.

If Blasius made it to his estate, she might never get to him. He would be informed that Frewer was dead, and perhaps that both Scorpion and Raven had managed to escape, and then he would lock himself in an even tighter web of security. If she let that happen, he would be able to travel to Corvant and do whatever he planned to with Amelia. He probably had details about her location from Scorpion's journal. To Blasius, this was a blood feud. He wouldn't be satisfied until he'd avenged his sister's death and brought his violent wrath down upon Raven and anyone close to her. And the only person that mattered to Raven now was her daughter.

She broke into a sprint along the wharf timbers, past fishing boats secured by lines, and nets spread over crates to dry. As timber turned to paving stone, she searched around for anything she could use to catch up to Blasius.

A group of revelers who'd poured out of a tavern to watch the fire pointed at her, dripping wet in her silk dress, droplets of water spraying and soles leaving a wet mark with each pounding step. Raven snarled at them, and they recoiled as if she were a vengeful spirit emerged from the ocean.

An empty trap turned the corner ahead. Without thinking, she ran for it and leaped into the vehicle while it was still moving. The driver jerked around and opened his mouth to shout at her. Raven snatched coins from her purse and dropped them into his hand. The gold glittered in the pale light, and the driver's eyes opened wide. There was enough coin to keep him in comfort for years. It was probably ten times his annual earnings.

"I need you to follow a carriage that just went up that street," she pointed, "and catch up to it. Think you can do that?"

"Aye. Hold on."

The trap jerked forward as he flicked the reins. Raven clutched the side as they skidded around a corner, narrowly avoiding an oncoming wagon and its surprised driver, who watched them rush past with his mouth open. The trap's iron-banded wheels jolted over cobbles, striking sparks at particularly violent bumps, and the wind buffeted Raven's face and hair as they jerked around slower-moving people and other carriages. Shouts of protest and surprise followed them, quickly fading as they careened away. Raven glanced behind, toward the Rose, and saw a white-masked man of the Watch running after her. He threw his arms up in defeat when the distance between them grew and turned to sprint back toward his colleagues. That was all she needed: the Watch coming after her.

A dozen side streets later, they hurtled onto a wide promenade. Blasius's carriage was only a score of yards ahead of them, its four horses lathered with sweat as they labored up the incline that led to the elevated districts of Sansor. Blasius's estate was located at the city's highest point. Raven's anxiety mounted: those areas were heavily patrolled by the Watch, and there were numerous private security guards who wouldn't hesitate to assist someone as wealthy and powerful as Blasius. She had to intercept him soon.

"Faster!" she implored the driver.

He whipped the reins and yelled at his horse. The beast responded, and they inched closer to Blasius's carriage, but Raven knew a single horse carrying two would tire well before the four horses they were pursuing.

As they drew closer, she clutched a few of the coin shreds in one hand, along with her small orichalcum sphere. She would have to be careful using the dark-tide. It took longer than a day to recover from sustained use, and her surges tonight had already pushed her to the edge of her stamina. Her muscles had begun to spasm and cramp, and the wound in her side felt like it had opened up again. She found the last medicinal lozenge in her purse and choked it down. She couldn't fail now.

She mentally prepared herself as they approached the carriage. Blasius's driver must have heard the clattering of their wheels, because he looked behind then shouted something. An instant later a woman poked her head out of the carriage window. The sorcerer.

"Darkness!" cursed Raven.

The air crackled as the sorcerer drew on her dawn- and dusk-tide repositories. Whatever the woman had planned, it would be swift and deadly, and Raven wasn't able to shield herself.

She wanted to look Blasius in the eye when she killed him, but she had no choice. With a surge of dark-tide power, she sent a shred arrowing across the gap between the two vehicles. The fake coin hammered into the back of the carriage and passed through it, into the interior. She sent another surge into the shred, and a thunderous crack rang out. The windows shattered as hundreds of shadowy spikes burst through the carriage. The back looked like someone had skewered it a hundred times.

The driver fell from his seat onto the cobbles. Raven's driver barely avoided running the man over as he lay lifeless in the street.

Raven grabbed her driver by the shoulder. "When I jump off, you're done. Go home and forget this happened."

Blasius's carriage slowed as the two closest horses struggled against their harness. Raven saw trickles of blood on their hindquarters from the shadowy spikes. They pulled the carriage off-course, and it bowled over a drunk who'd come careening out of an inn's doorway. He spun away and crashed into the wall before flopping to the ground. Heads popped out of windows and doors at the commotion. Raven couldn't do anything about them except hope they weren't hurt in the coming hostility.

The increasing incline and the resistant horses slowed Blasius's carriage to a walking pace. There was no movement from inside, but Raven could sense the sorcerer drawing on her power. She'd survived. Maybe Blasius had as well, if he'd been shielded.

Raven slapped her driver on the back—a thank you, and an instruction to get far away as fast as he could. She jumped out of the trap and watched the vehicle gather speed as it passed the other carriage, then she moved to the side of the street where she could duck into an alley if she needed cover.

The carriage door swung open and the sorcerer emerged. Blasius followed, clutching a loaded crossbow, hunched low to fit inside the spherical shield surrounding the both of them. The sorcerer spoke a cant and another shield extended across the entire street between her and Raven: a shimmering curtain of energy made up of multiple layers. From her training, Raven knew it was at least a tier four shield, and impervious to physical objects as well as heat and cold.

Doors and windows slammed shut along the street as onlookers hid in fear.

As Raven debated her options, another veil sprang up behind her, and a third across the mouth of the alley. The sorcerer had her trapped.

Blasius glared at Raven, but when the sorcerer interrupted her cants to bark a command at him, he obeyed, turning to run away up the street.

Raven cursed as the woman smiled at her. She knew Raven had nowhere to go. This wasn't a middling sorcerer like those she and Scorpion had disposed of in the mountains. Judging from the shield she'd generated, this woman was a master of her craft. If Raven tried to shadow-step inside the shield, it would go badly for her. Badly as in she would be killed.

The sorcerer took a confident step toward Raven.

Raven frowned, a spark of an idea forming. She couldn't use much dark-tide, not if she wanted to kill Blasius, but she also had to survive…

She drew her rapier and charged at the sorcerer.

The woman uttered a cant, and Raven screamed in agony as the virulent power dug into her flesh, penetrating her muscles to the bone. Her entire body burned as if scorched with liquid metal. With an agonized lurch, she threw her rapier toward the sorcerer. It struck the ground with a clang and skidded to a stop a pace from the sorcerous shield.

*Bloody darkness!*

A weight like an anvil pressed Raven to the ground, and her ears rang with a constant chime. She fought against the enchantment and managed to draw out a coin-shred. With another staggering effort, she rolled away from the sorcerer and dragged herself across the cobbles as if she were attempting to escape.

The sorcerer took a step forward. The edge of her shield came into contact with the ensorcelled orichalcum blade of Raven's rapier. Where they touched, lightning threads of disruption erupted, crackling and sizzling across the spherical ward. A heartbeat later, the shield dispersed into motes. The sorcerer's eyes widened in surprise, and she began another cant to regenerate her defenses.

Raven released the shred clutched in her hand. With a surge of dark-tide she sent it skidding across the road and stopped it directly between the woman's feet. A wave of weariness swept through her, but she fought it off and rose to her knees, glaring defiantly at the sorcerer. Smoke rose from Raven's skin now, and it was agony to move, but she didn't have to.

A new shield surrounded the sorcerer, but she frowned, sensing something was wrong. She looked around, as if expecting an attack from someone else close by, but there was no one. As she gave Raven a triumphant smile, Raven sent a surge into the shred. There was a booming crack as hundreds of dark-tide spikes skewered the sorcerer. Blood spattered the inside of the translucent barrier, and then all three of the woman's shields winked out of existence.

Raven tried to rise, but sour spit filled her mouth, and her legs were as limp as a wet washcloth. She forced herself to stand, and stumbled a few steps before straightening. Her fight with the sorcerer had taken twenty heartbeats at most. Blasius wasn't far ahead.

He glanced over his shoulder and saw his dead sorcerer. A look of panic came across his face, and he ran, his booted feet thumping on the cobbles. Raven almost laughed then. Blasius's innate cowardliness had overridden any thought of revenge.

Though she was weak, he also knew who she was and what she was capable of.

With each step, Raven felt like her skin and bones might break from the damaging effects of the sorcerer's cants. She couldn't push herself to more than a slow walk, but she couldn't let Blasius escape. She was so close. Amelia's life depended on it.

Raven gathered the dregs of her dark-tide power and sent her pea-sized orichalcum sphere screaming toward Blasius, not to kill, but to disable. Blood sprayed across the cobbles and she heard the crack of bones shattering. Blasius screamed and fell to the ground, his hands clutching at his ruined shin.

Raven continued to lurch toward him. He struggled to a sitting position and brought up his crossbow in scarlet-covered hands. It slipped in his bloodied grasp, and he cursed, glancing frantically at Raven. She realized her teeth were bared, and her breath hissed between them.

Blasius wrestled the crossbow atop his uninjured knee and sighted the weapon. He loosed the bolt, and Raven sent a surge of dark-tide to deflect it. Blasius gaped as the bolt sped away into the darkness. Her stomach cramped with sharp pains and she fell to the ground, bile rising in her throat and scouring her mouth.

"You bloody bitch!" screamed Blasius, fumbling with the crossbow as he tried to prime it again.

Raven's vision blurred, and she blinked furiously to clear it. She spat stomach acid from her mouth, and the haze surrounding her diminished slightly. But before she could move, Blasius's bolt slammed into her right shoulder, just under her collarbone, jerking her backward. She hit the ground hard, slamming her head on the cobblestones. A scream tore from her throat as the bolt twisted in her flesh, the metal head scraping against bone.

She heard him reloading—the ratcheting of the lever and the

sharp click as the string snapped into place. She forced herself onto her side and looked at him, warm blood pouring from the puncture wound in her shoulder.

His face twisted in hate, Blasius shouted, "I'm going to kill you, and then your daughter—right after I—"

Raven sent another surge. Her orichalcum sphere pierced Blasius's eye and erupted through the back of his skull, spattering brain matter onto the cobbles. He fell backward, the crossbow clattering to the ground from his lifeless fingers.

Raven crawled to the sorcerer's corpse, retching from the effects of too much dark-tide use, and grasped her rapier. Clenching her jaw against the pain, she dragged herself to sit against a wall, her limbs trembling with weakness. Her shoulder throbbed in agony, and sweat dripped from her brow, but she didn't have the strength to wipe it away. If she didn't do something, she would die here. The problem was, she could barely move.

Blasius's grim remains lay in the middle of the street. Blood trickled from underneath his head and ran between the cobbles toward her. Raven rested her head against her knees, hot tears rolling down her cheeks. It was over.

Members of the Watch poured into the far end of the street. She was in no state to fight them. And who knew what powers their goddess had to track her down?

Raven clutched at the minuscule residue of dark-tide energy she had remaining, looked up at the rooftops, and poured her awareness into the darkness around her. Her mind melted and drained away. When she re-formed, the shadows lingered, then crushed her awareness into oblivion.

# AFTERMATH

RAVEN CHEWED THE LAST BITE of her pastry then drained the dregs of her mug of tea.

For the last week the news sheets had been full of the remarkable incident of Blasius's slaying in the streets, and the inferno that destroyed the Rose. Both were attributed to an unknown woman assassin whose eyes glowed like a mythological demon's, and who could disappear into thin air, according to various witnesses.

*People will embellish that story,* thought Raven. *Until the truth is no longer recognizable. It's human nature.*

She stiffened as her mind spun, her heart beating rapidly. When she looked up, the sorcerer Akatta Palek stood beside her table, dressed similarly to before, in a severe black coat. A flush rose to her cheeks, and she self-consciously touched her neck.

"You've been busy," he said, blue eyes regarding her.

Raven shrugged, one hand slipping down to rest on her rapier's

301

hilt. When her skin touched the metal her mind cleared, as if a wind blew away cobwebs. "Sometimes the past doesn't want to let you go." She gripped the hilt tighter. Whatever Akatta desired, she wanted no part of it.

Akatta sat in the chair opposite, his hands clasped before him on the table. Her eyes were drawn to his square-faced ring embellished with Skanuric runes.

"The past makes us who we are. You should know that."

*How much does he know?* Raven decided he was fishing. Sorcerers couldn't be trusted. And whatever Akatta was, he was more than a sorcerer. "I prefer to look forward, to the future. What do you want from me?"

"You are direct. I like that." He reached into a pocket then placed a bulging purse on the table. "Gold. Let's call it an initial payment. My offer of employment stands. Sheelahn is lying to you. She meddles where she has no business. And she's not the only one who can facilitate you traveling to distant lands."

He smiled, and if her ensorcelled rapier hadn't blunted his sorcery she would have acquiesced. Akatta was used to getting his way, by means fair or foul.

The fact that he knew about Sheelahn's traveling trick, and could do something similar, was worrying. "I need time. To think about it."

Akatta frowned, his gaze pinning hers. After a moment, she looked away.

"Join us," said Akatta. "Or it will not end well for you. We have resources. Connections." He let the last linger in the air. "Sheelahn is on the wrong side of history. We can offer power undreamt of for one such as you."

"Who is 'us'?"

"A collection of likeminded individuals. We only want what's best for Wiraya. Come work for me."

*I doubt that.* "I'm just a killer. Nothing more. And I hope to be done with that."

"Everyone has value, in some way. People fear what they don't understand. I hope to persuade you, over time, that my intentions are good."

Gold, threats, and blandishments. *Bloody sorcerers. Always pushing people around.* "I have to find someone first. Then I'll give you my answer." She stood gingerly and shouldered her backpack, then settled her rapier comfortably against her hip.

"I won't wait forever. I'll grant you a day, no longer."

Heart thumping, Raven gave Akatta a nod, then handed a silver talent, one of many she'd scavenged from Scorpion's apartment, to the server on the way out. She could feel the sorcerer's eyes on her back.

Gods, what had she gotten into? What manner of rivalry existed between Akatta and Sheelahn? Connections, he'd mentioned… What connections? None good, that was for certain. But then again, whose were? The Ethereal Sorceress's were probably no better. Then again, Sheelahn professed to be an enemy of the Tainted Cabal and of demons. That had to count for something, didn't it?

Raven slipped outside and hurried along the street, favoring her right leg. It had been a week since she'd dealt with Blasius, and still the sorcerer's attack affected her every movement. Her bones ached, and patches of her skin were raised and bruised. Every morning she had to eat a painkilling lozenge to enable her to haul herself out of bed, and one every night so the pain would recede enough she could sleep.

She'd had the black dye stripped out of her hair, and it had returned to her regular platinum. Even so, she was careful to keep an eye out for anyone acting suspiciously, and when she saw any of the Watch she ducked into the closest shop to wait until they passed by.

Still, it wasn't long until she came into sight of Sheelahn's place of business in Sansor. Another featureless granite building. She paused then, squinting into the morning sun.

She almost couldn't believe this was happening.

If she accepted the Ethereal Sorceress's offer of a job, she might be a few glasses away from arriving in Atya on the western continent. And from there it was a short distance to the city of Corvant, where she would find Amelia. A daughter she'd never met, who had been stolen from her by Scorpion because he thought Raven couldn't protect her.

Maybe he'd been right about that. Maybe she could never escape her past. But he'd taken the choice from her. His betrayal still felt devastating whenever she dwelled upon it. But she remembered telling him time and again that she wouldn't make a good mother. There was always a chance she'd be killed, or an enemy would come seeking her when she least expected it—as Blasius had.

But still... Scorpion had always felt like he needed to be in control. That was who he was, who he had been.

Raven couldn't escape the feeling that a part of her had died when he'd confessed his unforgivable crime to her. Just as a part had been lost when she'd believed Amelia had died. And the thought of the last few days she'd spent with Scorpion, when a bright new future had seemed possible, crushed her so completely she thought she'd never recover. Even to hide again and try to regain a semblance of a normal life seemed impossible.

Did she hate Scorpion or love him? He'd hurt her, but you couldn't die from deception. Some things would never make sense to her. Her life, as with most others, was always messy like that. You lifted your chin and you soldiered on, nursing your wounds both physical and emotional. The only thing Raven knew for certain was that in this life, no one, not even the favored of the gods, got out of it alive.

She took one last look behind her at the city of Sansor, back at a world she didn't understand, and probably never would. She didn't belong.

Raven hitched her backpack and, exhausted, hand still gripping the hilt of her rapier, trudged forward to meet Sheelahn.


END OF BOOK ONE

# TO MY READERS

As always, if you enjoyed the read, leaving a review supports the books and helps keep me writing! You can return to where you purchased the novel to review it or simply visit my website and follow the links: WWW.MITCHELLHOGAN.COM

There are also websites such as Goodreads where members discuss the books they've read or want to read or suggest books others might read: WWW.GOODREADS.COM/AUTHOR/SHOW/7189594.MITCHELL_HOGAN

If you never want to miss the latest book sign up here for my newsletter. I send one every few months, so I won't clutter your inbox. MITCHELLHOGAN.COM/NEW-RELEASE-ALERTS/

Having readers eager for the next installment of a series, or anticipating a new series, is the best motivation for a writer to create new stories. Thank you for your support and be sure to check out my other novels!